D1647067

'Nork-Grabbing Quimboid' is the **BRAND NEW SINGLE** from Camel Toe – AKA Blossom Uxley-Michaels and Petrina-Ola Olsen, inventors of the genre 'punch-the-air-helicopter-your-hair-electro-rock'.

LISTEN TO IT HERE:

PRAISE FOR 'NORK-GRABBING QUIMBOID':

Get ready to tap those (camel) toes to this beauty. They are the most important thing to happen to music since Hard-Fi.

GREG JAMES, BBC RADIO 1

The most poignant song about nork grabbing that I've ever heard. I was moved to my manly core.

SHAUN KEAVENY, BBC 6 MUSIC

Camel Toe's 'Nork Grabbing Quimboid' latches on and won't let go.

NEMONE METAXAS BBC 6 MUSIC

LISTEN TO CAMEL TOE'S DEBUT TRACK, 'PONCERAMA', HERE:

PRAISE FOR WEIRDOS VS. BUMSKULLS:

'One of the funniest books I've read this year. Loved it!' Sister Spooky

'If you love Georgia Nicholson you'll adore Blossom and this wonderful series of books.' The Overflowing Library

'Just as hilariously rude as the brilliant first book!' YA Yeah Yeah

'This second instalment is more hilarious, more shocking and more near the knuckle than the last book, making it a laugh-a-minute read from start to finish.' Wondrous Reads

'This book is as good as all the others I haven't read.' Karl Pilkington

PRAISE FOR WEIRDOS VS. QUIMBOIDS:

'Thank you, Tash Desborough, for writing a book which has seen both of my teenagers disappear into their rooms for two days, only emerging every few hours to attempt to read me a line or two, but failing due to their fits of giggles . . . Please write another, immediately.' Liz Fraser, best-selling author and broadcaster

'I haven't put this book down since the I read the back cover and choked on my own spit, I laughed so much.' Emily (15), Liz Fraser's daughter

'It's so good, it made me envious; I wish I'd written it!' Andy Robb, author of Geekhood: Close Encounters of the Girl Kind and Geekhood: Mission Improbable

'...brilliantly funny moments...a cringeworthy account of life for a teenage geek.' School Library Association

WEIRDOS VS. BUMSKULLS

NATASHA DESBOROUGH

Catnip

CATNIP BOOKS
Published by Catnip Publishing Ltd
Quality Court
off Chancery Lane
London WC2A 1HR

First published 2014
1 3 5 7 9 10 8 6 4 2

Text © 2014 Natasha Desborough
Illustrations by Vicky Barker

A CIP catalogue record for this book is available from the British Library

ISBN 978-1-84647-182-7

Printed and bound by CPI Group (UK) Ltd, Croydon, CR0 4YY

www.catnippublishing.co.uk

For Lisa

To: rachel.ferloine@poptasticmanagement.com
Sent: May 29th 04:01:08
From: Blossom Uxley-Michaels
Subj: SCHOOL DISCO

Dear Rachel,

OH. MY. GOD. I literally cannot sleep. The combination of the full moon last night, meeting Josh Raven and the seven drops of Rescue Remedy that I then took to calm myself down have left me on a LEGAL HIGH. It's just gone 4AM and I am off my face with adrenaline-fuelled JOY.

I know it's a strange time to be emailing, but I thought I'd take this opportunity to thank you for getting Josh to perform at Bridge Mount Secondary School. I don't know if you've heard, but right before Josh came on stage, Wazzock (legendary guitarist from rock band Steel Dragon) performed with my band Camel Toe AND sang a song that helped my two best friends Walter and Petrina finally get it on. Having not just one but two such enormous megastars in our humble school blew everyone's minds. It's a shame we're not talking literally, because stupid, dumb slangers Fiona Tittledown and Lucy Perkins were there and if their heads had ACTUALLY been blown up into tiny,

7

gunky fragments it would have been the most perfect day EVER.

Please pass on my personal thanks to Josh. He really is one of the kindest, most thoughtful men I have ever met and if he wasn't gay then I would definitely view him as husband material. (I'm assuming that he is 100% gay? If he is anything under 99% certain, then please let me know as I think I might be able to turn him. I am very flat-chested, so he wouldn't get intimidated by my norks.)

Many thanks,
Blossom Uxley-Michaels

P.S. I will be looking for a part-time job over the summer, so if you need anyone to tune up guitars or taste-test Josh's packed lunches or lips for poison then please consider me.

To: rachel.ferloine@poptasticmanagement.com
Sent: June 9th 17:19:27
From: Blossom Uxley-Michaels
Subj: Exams

Dear Rachel,

I thought you would like to know that Josh Raven has literally been a lifeline to me in my first full week of GCSE exams. Just before I went into my maths exam I was mucking about with the 'Reverse Music' app on my phone and began listening to Moonlight Stalker (my favourite song in the world) played backwards. Suddenly my ears were filled with the inspiring words 'You can do it. You can do it. I love your baked potato' as clear as day. Wowzoids!!! Slipping a secret message into a song when it's played in reverse is nothing short of pure GENIUS. In terms of sheer braininess Josh is right up there with Albert Einstein, Charles Darwin and a four-year-old boy I once saw on TV who could sing Jingle Bells in fifty-four languages. It really got me through my essay on 'The effects of the Great Depression on the people of the USA'. BUT I have to ask – is 'baked potato':

a) A lady-parts euphemism OR

b) Does Josh simply adore baked potatoes? (In which case he's in luck! I may not be a very good cook, but baked potatoes are my speciality. If he wants to pop round for tea one day then I'd be happy to serve up baked potatoes with cheese and beans. Yum!)

Many thanks,

Blossom Uxley-Michaels

P.S. If 'baked potato' IS a vagina euphemism then

I'm totally cool with that. I might be a feminist, but don't forget I'm in a band called Camel Toe!!! I'm TOTALLY liberal-minded with an awesome sense of humour. 'Baked potato' – hahahahahaha! Brilliant!!!

To: rachel.ferloine@poptasticmanagement.com
Sent: June 15th 10:21:34
From: Blossom Uxley-Michaels
Subj: Dark Times

Dear Rachel,

I'm midway through my last week of exams and feel that I'm on the verge of an anxiety-induced breakdown. Why do I need to know if ions are 'more concentrated in plasma or in urine' anyway? It's not going to help win me the Mercury Music Prize or an Ivor Novello is it? Thank God I've got Josh Raven's two-album back catalogue to help get me through the dark times. And, believe me, those dark times can get very, VERY dark indeed. I'm not saying I would ever want to end it all, but a free preview copy of Josh's new album would really make sure that I didn't do something stupid. Not that I ever would of course. But if I were to feel that the heavy pressure of exams was crushing the life out of me, then a free album would really help me to not kill myself.

Many thanks,
Blossom Uxley-Michaels

P.S. Is it true that Josh's new album was recorded so that it syncs up exactly with the film Bite Me – Dusky Dark Part 1? Because that would be AMAZING.

To: Blossom Uxley-Michaels
Sent: June 17th 12:09:22
From: rachel.ferloine@poptasticmanagement.com
RE: Dark Times

Dear Blossom,

I hope you have survived your exams without injury. I put a copy of Josh's new album, *Dark Lover of the Night*, in the post a couple of days ago so hopefully you'll have received it by now.

We were also hoping that you, your family and a few friends would be free to attend Glastonbury Festival next weekend (25th June) as Josh Raven's V.I.P. guests. Josh is headlining on the Saturday night and would like to offer this as a personal thank you for the fabulous

welcome that he received at the Bridge Mount school disco.

The tickets are for one night's stay and you'll need to provide your own tent. We'd also suggest bringing wellies in case of wet, muddy weather.

Please let me know if you are able to attend A.S.A.P.

Best wishes,
Rachel Ferloine

Management Assistant
Poptastic Management

P.S. I'm afraid the new album doesn't sync up with the Bite Me film. And there is no secret backward message on 'Moonlight Stalker'. But Josh does like baked potatoes so if he did come to your house one day, I'm sure he would be thrilled to receive your generous hospitality.

To: rachel.ferloine@poptasticmanagement.com
Sent: June 18th 06:01:08
From: Blossom Uxley-Michaels
RE: re: Dark Times

Dear Rachel,

YES PLEASE!!

I would LOVE to come to the festival. I have asked my parents, who are both seasoned Glastonbury festival-goers, and they're good to go. Mum says it'll be a relief to put the memory of her last Glastonbury experience, when she had 'an unsavoury encounter with a man who claimed to be a Goblin king from The Land of Calliwampus', behind her.

Alongside my parents, I will also bring my two best friends Petrina and Walter. Because they are boyfriend and girlfriend now, I will be sleeping in between the two of them to ensure that no sexual activity takes place. Not that this is likely – it would take a highly experienced and talented escapologist to break through the hundreds of poppers and fasteners on the onesie that Petrina wears in bed.

The new album is BRILLIANT by the way. I've listened to it nonstop since it arrived and it's made me love Josh even more than I did already (in a non psycho-obsessive-stalker-type way).

Many thanks,
Blossom Uxley-Michaels

P.S. If there is a spare Gibson ES-335 guitar lying around the office (preferably cherry-red although I'm not really that fussy) then I'd be extremely grateful if you could send it to me, especially if Josh has touched it with his unusually long fingers. (I know for a fact that his fingers are exceptionally long as I measured them on my life-sized Josh Raven cardboard cut-out and they exceed the national average length by half a centimetre.)

We stand on the Pyramid Stage, soaking up the adulation that comes in roars from the enormous crowd. Everyone knows that festival audiences are the best and this is no exception.

'Poncerama, Poncerama, Poncerama,' they chant.

We've saved the best till last. The final encore. The pièce de Camel Toe résistance.

As we strike the first familiar chords, the crowd goes CRAZY. Camel Toe is the Saturday night headliner. Josh Raven was merely our warm-up act. I look at the side of the stage, where he stands in the VIP area giving us the thumbs up.

'You are AWESOME,' he mouths at us. 'You've made me five per cent less gay. Best band ever.'

'I know,' I mouth back. I'm not being cocky. It's a plain and simple truth.

Every person in the field knows the words to Poncerama. We are a single voice enriched by a backdrop of magic, history, spirituality and vaginal euphemisms.

'Poncerama oooh, Poncerama ooooh,

It's no wonder that nobody really likes you.'

And, as I strum my mega expensive, cherry-red Gibson ES-335 guitar that glints under the bright stage spotlights, I know that this is my destiny. Petrina knows it too. She is floating with her keyboard above my head on the MASSIVE hydraulic arm that we had custom made and imported from an Indian sweatshop. It is not gimmicky in any way at all. The arm carries her directly over the audience. Petrina throws mini chocolate eggs and Jelly Babies (which are totally FREE) directly into their mouths (she has a brilliant aim) in an act of kindness and generosity. We are literally feeding the one hundred thousand.

And then, as we play the final chord, there is an eruption of applause. Camel Toe are right now the BIGGEST band in the world.

'GOODNIGHT GLASTONBURY. I LOVE YOU,' I shouted at the top of my voice. I awoke from my dream to find myself in mid-air, star-jumping off of my bed with Cassiopeia, my beloved guitar, slung across my shoulders. I have no idea how it got there, so I must have put it on in my sleep. Suddenly the bright light of my bedside lamp blinded my sleepy eyes.

'Blossom, are you OK?' asked my bleary-looking best friend, who was staying over while her parents were in Norway.

'Is it morning?' I was still half asleep.

Petrina felt around blindly on the floor next to her fold-out bed until she found her glasses. 'It's half past three,' she mumbled, squinting at her phone.

'What were you doing anyway?' she continued. 'Your face is all flushed.'

I sat back down on the bed and felt my burning cheeks.

That was a pretty active dream.

'Oh, you know,' I explained. 'I was just strumming my cherry-red –'

'Well a girl's gotta do what a girl's gotta do,' said Petrina, taking off her glasses again. 'But can't you do it a bit more quietly?'

What?

ARRRGGGHH! She thinks I was gusset typing!

'No . . . noooo,' I continued, now in a bit of a panic. 'I mean I was fantasising about playing myself on The Pyramid Stage in front of a hundred thousand people.'

That sounds even worse.

'I don't care *what* floats your boat,' said Petrina, slumping back on to the fold-out bed. 'But can you please just hurry up so we can go back to sleep? We've both got our last exams in the morning and I want to be firing on all cylinders even if you don't.'

Brilliant. My best friend now thinks I've got a public fuzzbox-flashing fetish. Well that's just GREAT.

I inhaled the scent of the freshly cut grass on the playing field as I stepped out of the stagnant school hall with Walter. It smelt like FREEDOM! Our last exam (History), during which Paulette Dempsey's stomach was rumbling SO loudly that I was tempted to ask if I could re-sit the exam due to digestive distraction, had just finished and the prospect of a long hot summer was the only thing on our minds.

'HEY BLOSSOM,' called an all-too-familiar voice. I turned to see Matthew Ludlow leaning against the brick wall of the hall and trying to look casual, until he realised that one side of his T-shirt was caught on a nail. Had he been waiting for me for all that time?

'Wait up!' Matthew began jogging over, his freshly torn T-shirt billowing out beside him like a lopsided superhero cape. I noticed straight away that his face was relatively free of spots and I wondered if he'd managed to somehow curb his drinking.

'I loved this T-shirt,' he groaned, looking down at the massive rip.

I couldn't help but notice that the side of his torso was quite fit. But I absolutely wasn't perving. I mean, this is Matthew Ludlow we're talking about! He caught me staring and I quickly averted my eyes, not wanting to give the wrong impression. 'Blossom . . . I just wanted to ask –' he began.

Oh God. He's going to ask me out again like he did that time by the school vending machine. Quick, think of an excuse. Fast.

'I can't,' I interrupted. 'I . . . I'm having my tyres changed.'

Matthew looked surprised. 'You have a car? Cool.'

I'm having my tyres changed? I am SO rubbish when I'm put on the spot.

'No . . . erm,' I stammered. 'It's more of a bike.'

'You have a bike?' asked Walter, sounding puzzled. 'Since when?'

Shut UP Walter. Shut up.

'Yeah,' I lied. 'I've been riding bikes since I could support

18

my own head. And sit up. And pedal. Without stabilisers.'

'I love cycling,' said Matthew. 'We should go out mountain-biking sometime.'

NO WE SHOULD NOT!

'Mine's a BMX.' I was digging myself a hole. A big deep hole, heading directly down into The Cavern Of Lies And DOOM. 'I can do some amazing stunts and . . . flips.'

'Cool, I can't wait to see them.' Matthew was looking at me as if I was standing on top of a golden, glittering pedestal. Through his fringe, Walter was staring at me as if I was utterly bonkers.

'Anyway, I wanted to ask you something,' Matthew continued, running his hand through his short (strawberry-blonde) hair. 'I'd like to become Camel Toe's manager.'

Well I wasn't expecting that.

'I can get you gigs and a bit of publicity. And my dad's company has agreed to sponsor the band. He'll pay for transport and equipment and stuff.'

He bit his lip and began to rock back and forth on his heels with his hands in his pockets.

Matthew's dad is Roy Ludlow, business bigwig and boss of Ludlow's Luxury Loos, a company that specialises in making lavish leather toilets. He is *loaded!* But . . .

'No,' I panicked. 'Walter's going to be our manager.'

Matthew's head dropped. 'Oh, OK,' he said as he backed away. 'I'll see you around.'

'*Will* you be our manager?' I asked Walter hopefully, once Matthew was out of earshot.

19

'Nope,' he replied in his typically blunt way.

And that was the end of that conversation.

Matthew Ludlow's unlikely popularity is almost certainly down to the fact that he holds the best parties in the entire school. And, once again, the Ludlow house is where the action is taking place, because this Thursday Matthew is hosting an end-of-exams party for everyone in Year 11. So with tickets to Glastonbury already in the bag, Matthew's party makes it TWO invitations in just one week!! I've already made a vow to myself that there will not be a repeat performance of what happened at the last Ludlow party. I will absolutely NOT get drunk, snog Matthew on a beanbag OR ride around the house on a motorbike with two pieces of processed ham Sellotaped to my norks.

Things have been awkward between me and Matthew ever since. And between me and the rest of the school, some of whom STILL call me 'Ham Hooters'. I suppose I didn't really improve the situation when I fobbed off his offer of an ice-skating date by inventing an ice allergy. He still gives me worried looks when it's a bit chilly out. It's not that I don't like Matthew – it's just that he's not really what I have in mind as a boyfriend. I'm thinking more along the lines of a charismatic, chiselled rock star like Josh Raven (except not as gay) or a downright proper real-time sexy hot love GOD, like Felix Winters (for a brief moment I thought our time had come, when Fiona cheated on Felix right before our exams, but annoyingly they've been joined at the lips ever since the school disco).

20

PROS AND CONS OF GOING OUT WITH MATTHEW LUDLOW

CONS

1. He is an alcoholic
2. He is embarrassing
3. Everyone thinks he's a quimboid
4. He says 'haitch' instead of 'aitch'
5. He's always late
6. He chews gum loudly
7. He knocks his cutlery against his teeth when he eats (I HATE THAT)
8. He doesn't really care much about music
9. He smokes when he's drunk
10. He throws up all over himself when he's drunk
11. He's been suspended from school three times already
12. He likes to show off his disgusting bad toe fungus
13. He can burp the entire alphabet in one breath (utterly revolting . . . yet secretly quite impressive)

PROS

1. He is funny
2. He is kind
3. He is quite nice-looking
4. He is a great kisser
5. He smells lovely (a bit like a baby covered in spicy hot chocolate)

6. He has good dress sense
7. He has nice strawberry-blonde hair
8. He has good legs
9. He likes me
10. He can burp the entire alphabet in one breath (quite impressive)

So the 'cons' outweigh the 'pros' thirteen to ten, meaning that I definitely won't be going out with Matthew Ludlow in the near or distant future.

JUNE 21ST: SUMMER SOLSTICE

It took Neolithic builders an estimated 1,500 years to erect the Stonehenge circle but it only took Mum and a couple of men from *www.buildyourownstonecircle.com* just under an hour to recreate the half-scale, original-state replica in our back garden. (Mum's had her eye on it for months and snapped it up when she saw it in a 70% off mid-summer discount sale.) Today is the summer solstice, the longest day of the year, which my parents usually celebrate with their Pagan Druid order friends at Stonehenge. This year, however, because we'll be trekking down to Glastonbury in a few days, they've decided to hold a belated summer solstice party at the music festival and celebrate the actual occasion privately in our back garden. When I looked out of my bedroom window as the sun rose at 4.33AM, Mum was skipping around the grey polystyrene stones as happily as a drug-dealing fairy in a ring of magic mushrooms. She was naked, of course. As was my father, with his buttock resting on the central Altar Stone and his acoustic guitar concealing his modesty (THANK GOD). As the horizon broke into an ethereal orange glow, the two of them began to perform their old band Flying Rapunzel's crowd-pleasing favourite 'Greenpeace Makes Me Horny' three times in a row. I'm not really a religious person, but right then I closed my eyes and prayed to the Sun God for a set of normal parents.

Later that morning, feeling excited and carefree (and a bit bleary-eyed having watched the sun rise), I set off into town with Petrina to buy new outfits for Matthew's party. I was thinking of getting a new black T-shirt and Petrina had her heart set on a pair of 'skull-and-roses' black woolly tights. For the Winners (like Lucy Perkins and Fiona Tittledown) every day not spent at school is yet another fashion show – a chance to show off their newest designer labels and nork-enhancing underwear. For a Weirdo like me it's the realisation that one pair of cut-off jeans and a black hoodie really isn't enough to get me through the whole summer (even if I turn it inside out and remove the label).

We were sitting on a bench in Westbury Shopping Centre enjoying our Big Macs, fries and chocolate milkshakes, when the urine-blonde Fiona Tittledown and Lucy Perkins Show came strutting down the walkway. Fiona was wearing a frou-frou, white tulle, dip-hem skirt and matching bodice that emphasised her perfect hourglass figure and Lucy had squeezed herself into a bright pink feathered dress that barely had enough material to contain her gigantic norks.

Their imaginary runway stopped directly in front of us, where the slangers paused to strike a pose.

'We're going to Ladies Day at Royal Ascot,' sneered Fiona. 'Lucy's dad got us tickets. What are you doing – apart from demonstrating your amazing ability to mimic a corpse?'

'Eating a Big Mac,' I replied with my mouth crammed full of meat.

'Ugh – that's so many calories,' winced Fiona.

'I never eat calories,' said Lucy proudly.

Petrina was frowning. 'What's that on your hair?' she asked Lucy, who appeared to have something soft, brown and sparkling stuck on the side of her head.

'It's a fascinator,' she said proudly. 'A Stephen Jones.'

'That's not a fascinator,' said Petrina, squinting at Lucy's headwear. 'It's a tiny, glittery poo.'

'What would you two gothbags know about fashion?' snapped Fiona, her white tulle skirt flapping about at her knees. (Her headwear wasn't much better than Lucy's – a kind of paper doily decorated with Dairylea Triangles).

'Yeah,' agreed Lucy. 'You wouldn't know a Steve McQueen from a Primark end-of-line.' (She's right. The only brands that I care about are Dr Martens, Gibson Guitars and Lil-Lets Tampons.)

'We're not bothered about fashion,' said Petrina. 'Music is our energy.'

'Interesting . . .' smirked Fiona, linking arms with her friend and giving a significant look, which I couldn't work out.

'Fascinating,' shot back Petrina (she is SO highly intelligent).

'Interesting,' said Lucy, because she didn't know any other words.

'Fascinating,' I said (I blame the exams for draining my usually average brain).

And, with that, Bridezilla and the poo-headed Las Vegas Showgirl threw each other a knowing glance and headed off to hang out with the posh people at Ladies Day.

'They're up to something,' I said with certainty.

But Petrina was still scowling.

'Look at them,' she growled. 'Off to give Cerberus a bowl of cream I expect.'

'Oh, do you treat it in the same way that you treat thrush then?' I wondered.

Petrina frowned. 'What?'

'I always sit in a bowl of live yoghurt.' I said. 'Mum says it's the best natural healing method, though I would've thought you'd treat something as nasty as Cerberus with antibiotics.'

'Cerberus is the three-headed beast who guards the entrance to Hades' Underworld,' explained Petrina kindly. 'It's not a yeast infection.'

'I knew that,' I mumbled into my Big Mac. *I SO DIDN'T KNOW THAT.*

Manor Park is a great place to 'eye-cruise' the cute boys. Sitting on a rug in the shade of a silver birch later that day, Petrina

25

and I watched the beautiful people go by as we slurped on our ice creams. By my scientifically accurate calculations, I've concluded that a bit of sunlight and pair of cool shades can make an otherwise average person look around 10% more attractive. But even the flattering rays of summer couldn't help me bag a HOT sex god. Petrina, however, is obviously having much better luck in the boy department, seeing as she has an actual, real-life, breathing boyfriend. Thankfully, since she and Walter got together at the school disco, nothing seems to have changed in the dynamics of our friendship. They're not prone to big public displays of affection, so there's no snogging behind the bike sheds or love letters passed across the classroom. But, nevertheless, their new found love caught the attention of the slangers. Fiona and Lucy's taunts of 'Watch out, it's Goth Boy and his corpse bride' and 'Here comes the zombie couple' could be heard echoing down the corridors throughout our exams. Not that my best friends are bothered, of course. When you've been teased and jeered as much as we have, you learn to ignore.

REASONS WHY PETRINA AND WALTER ARE THE PERFECT COUPLE

1. They have the initials W.E.E. (Walter Edward Ecclestone) and P.O.O. (Petrina-Ola Olsen). 'Wee and poo' go together like 'cookies and cream', 'champagne and caviar' and 'sugar and diabetes'. And that is an actual scientific FACT.

2. They are 'primal scream buddies'. When I told Petrina that we were going to Glastonbury, she screamed in my face for a good forty seconds. It's her standard reaction for anything that really, really excites her. When I told Walter he roared at me. He does that when his emotions are too overwhelming. I try hard NOT to imagine what might happen when things get 'intimate' between them in the future, but I might suggest they invest in soundproofing systems in both of their bedrooms.

3. Neither of them like celebrating their birthdays. Walter's birthday happened sometime in May without any fanfare (although Petrina did buy him a new record bag) and Petrina insisted on a no-fuss sixteenth birthday last week. But, of course, Walter bought her the most thoughtful present EVER: an actual star!!! With the purchase of the star he'd been sent a certificate of registration, a fancy red wax seal, and a silver-plated paperweight engraved with the star's name (which is a secret between them), the constellation and the star's coordinates. Knowing how Petrina felt about her birthday and her dislike of materialistic gifts, he threw them all away. If I ever manage to find someone as kind and thoughtful as Walter, I'll be a very, very happy girl.

4. Even though it's been around twenty-seven degrees

for the past few days, Petrina still insists on wearing thick woolly tights (knickers over and under of course) with her cardigan zipped right up to the neck. Her stockinged feet emit the disgusting stench of a field of corpse plants in full bloom, yet Walter claims not to notice (supporting what is no doubt a scientific fact that love can stunt your sense of smell).

5. According to the online 'Dempsey Love Calculator'* (the formula of which Paulette refuses to disclose) Walter + Petrina = 92.5%, which is pretty AMAZING. (Out of interest, Blossom + Josh = 2%. Given that he is gay, I'm thinking 2% sounds pretty good . . . after all, nothing in love is certain.)

*Paulette Dempsey is Bridge Mount Secondary School's very own budding Richard Branson (and I reckon it won't be long before she's also grown a beard and bought her own luxury island somewhere exotic like the Outer Hebrides). 'Dempsey Love' is her fast-growing, money-spinning dating service and she's expanding it online.

To: rachel.ferloine@poptasticmanagement.com
Sent: June 22nd 14:47:12
From: Blossom Uxley-Michaels
Subj: ADVICE

Dear Rachel,

First of all, I would like to say how much I am looking forward to seeing Josh Raven at the Glastonbury festival this weekend. My parents will be sleeping in their ancient camper van and Walter is bringing along his four-man tent that he'll be sharing with me and Petrina. Having heard some terrible stories about the portaloos, I am borrowing my sister's Shewee for convenience and hygiene. I tried it out in various public places (the park, McDonald's and at the checkout in the supermarket) and I can confirm that it is not only discreet, but also very comfortable to use. I'm also trying not to eat too much fibre in the run up to the festival. I therefore hope I will be able to hold on to my number twos until we get back home. (Dad told me that he used to eat ten raw eggs to 'bind him up' before going to a music festival, but I think that if I were to do the same, it would probably have an opposite effect and that would be just gross. An eggsplosion. Hahahahaha!)

Anyway, I am emailing to ask for a bit of advice. A boy in my class at school called Matthew Ludlow (who is NOT my boyfriend) has asked my band Camel Toe to perform at his party tomorrow night. Do you know of any way I could hire a massive hydraulic arm that we could use on stage to lift my friend Petrina and her Roland keyboard up into the air? Also how much would it cost roughly? And do you think you could get me a discount?

Many thanks,
Blossom Uxley-Michaels

P.S. It's my birthday on August 3rd. I will be sixteen. This is not a hint for presents. I just thought you might require this information for your files.

To: Blossom Uxley-Michaels
Sent: June 22nd 16:34:41
From: rachel.ferloine@poptasticmanagement.com
RE: ADVICE

Dear Blossom,

Thank you for your email.

The portaloos at Glastonbury are not the most pleasant of places, but they are cleaned regularly and will provide a much safer bowel experience than eating ten raw eggs.

I'm afraid I cannot help you in your search for a 'massive hydraulic arm'. They are very expensive pieces of machinery and only used on stage by well-

established acts as part of huge stadium/arena tours.

Best wishes,
Rachel Ferloine

Management Assistant
Poptastic Management

P.S. Happy birthday for next month.

So with everyone's exams officially over, it was finally time to really celebrate our freedom, kicking off with Matthew's party. His dad, Roy Ludlow (who was away on a business trip to Amsterdam, where he will surely not be partaking in any recreational drug taking in cafés, no matter how legal it might be), had hired a party planner to ensure his youngest son's event was as spectacular as possible. A large marquee was erected (ha ha ha!) on the back lawn of Matthew's enormous house. Inside, was our very own exclusive nightclub, complete with stage, dance floor and an uber cool mocktail bar. A giant mirror ball sparkled under the bright coloured lights that hung from the ceiling and a 'chill-out area' had been roped off where couples could relax on the huge, soft, squishy sofas (although most people rejected the comfort of communal snogging for the dark privacy at the end of the garden).

Up on the decks Matthew's older brother DJ Loopy Luke was rinsing some massive tunes. It's Luke I blame for the ham hooters incident at the last Ludlow party, because it was his motorbike I was riding in my ham-chested state.

But this time I had promised to behave myself. After all, I was here not only as a guest, but also in a professional capacity as a member of Camel Toe.

Elsewhere, Paulette Dempsey (wearing her Dempsey Love Ltd promotional outfit, which consisted of a small pair of angel wings over a far-too-tight T-shirt bearing the slogan *I'M CUPID'S BOSS*) was milling about taking photos of guests with her digital SLR camera. Fiona was making absolutely sure that EVERYONE knew that she and Felix were an item once more. Having split up last term due to Fiona's brazen infidelity, they were now publicly declaring their 'togetherness' by wearing matching his 'n' hers T-shirts, brandishing the 'ironic, comedy' slogans *Property of Fiona* and *Property of Felix*. Lucky old Toby Richmond was being treated to his own public sex dance by Lucy. She was rapidly thrusting her bottom back and forth in a way that might have seemed sexy to her deluded boyfriend, but to me just looked like she was furiously trying to dislodge an uncomfortable wedgie.

'Do you like what you see?' she rasped, her huge norks heaving like the poor fox who raided our bin after Mum attempted to bake a Tofu, sea kelp and peanut butter pie.

'S'alright,' replied Toby with a grin, as he casually moonwalked across the dance floor. He's one of those boys who can wow people with his eye-popping, but perfectly effortless dance moves. His dad is a former Jamaican Olympic athlete and Toby has inherited his sporty genes, not to mention his FIT body. But whilst Fiona and Felix's public displays of affection are obviously a grotesque spectacle to prove a point, Lucy and Toby seem like they might really be in love. According to the 'Dempsey Love Calculator', Lucy + Toby = 95%. (Fiona + Felix = 8.5% hahahahahahaha!!!)

As if illustrating my point, Fiona had draped herself territorially around Felix at the mocktail bar. As always, he was looking hotter than Satan's sweaty armpit (aside from his bad taste T-shirt) in tight cut-off jeans that shamelessly flaunted his two peachy denim doughnuts.

Stop staring, Blossom. You'll make yourself go blind.

I could sense from the constant glances she threw in my direction that Fiona was feeling insecure, knowing that when I got up to perform with Camel Toe, her boyfriend would be utterly captivated by my onstage presence. When Felix saw me on stage with Wazzock from international rock band Steel Dragon at the school disco, he was staring like a greedy fly catching a whiff of a freshly laid dog turd.

'Watch out – Ham Hooters on the horizon!' jeered Fiona.

Lucy clutched her stomach as her raucous laughter bellowed around the room. I turned away, trying to ignore them.

'Hey Blossom,' Fiona continued. 'What did the ghost-goth say to the hornet? Boo, Bee!'

Listen to the stupid slanger. She's about as funny as a love bite (not that I know from experience BUT ruptured blood vessels under the skin are not amusing in any way).

Lucy paused for a moment as she waited for the punchline to make sense then clapped her hands joyfully.

'Aren't you going to write that one down?' I retorted. 'Use it in your stand-up routine?'

Lucy Perkins had a spiritual calling last term when Ricky Gervais appeared to her in a dream, saying that stand-up comedy was her vocation.

'Nope,' she smirked. 'Change of career plan.'

She nudged Fiona and the two of them giggled at their own private joke. Fiona opened her mouth to speak, but Lucy stopped her.

'Later,' she hissed. 'It's ammo of the highest amazeballs.'

Before I could work out what she was on about, I found my gaze all of a sudden being drawn away from the slangers. It was as if someone had cast a fish hook into my eyeballs and was reeling me in the opposite direction. I found myself face to face with the most EYE-GOGGLING, LOIN-RUMBLING, NORK-AWAKENING boy I have ever seen in the entire history of my life. Felix and Josh Raven paled into insignificance compared to the proper, real-time hot MANCAKE in front of me. He had messy blonde hair, bright blue eyes, and wore a fitted checked shirt and jeans that had a big rip at the top of his left thigh.

GOD I'd LOVE to tear a slash at the top of the other thigh with my bare (braced) teeth.

He smiled at me.

Arrrrgggghhh. What do I do? What do I say? How do I be? Be do I who? Who do I bub?

34

'Your hole is so cool,' I spluttered.

Oh God NOOOOOOO. That was absolutely NOT a psychologically-inappropriate Freudian slip.

The hot boy looked a bit startled, raising one quizzical eyebrow. Then he pushed past me and wandered off into the crowd of party revellers.

Well I think I handled that well.

An hour later, I was sitting alone on the patio sofa, blowing into a pitch pipe as I attempted to tune up the strings of Cassiopeia, my faithful blue guitar. Behind the dancing party-goers, I could see Petrina's small silhouetted figure emerging from the darkness at bottom of the garden.

'You've got a bit of eye-liner there,' I said pointing at the corner of her mouth. Petrina wiped her lips roughly with the back of her sleeve. 'How did it get down there?' she asked. 'Has it gone?'

'Yeah, but it's on your cheek too,' I laughed. 'And on your nose. And on your forehead'.

Perina ran off towards the mobile ladies toilet block with her hands covering her face.

I wondered what kind of snogging technique Walter had been using to cause such a facial catastrophe.

'You look great,' said Matthew, suddenly flinging his arm around my shoulders. He was drinking a lurid blue mocktail through a long straw.

'There's a guy here with a checked shirt and ripped jeans who I've never seen before.' *Does that sound desperate? DO I*

CARE?' Do you know who he is?'

Matthew burped quietly in my face. His breath smelt of alcoholic bubblegum. He had obviously been mixing booze into his mocktail.

'Could be anyone,' he said shrugging his shoulders. 'The party's been gatecrashed by just about everyone who's on the internet. So, are you ready then?'

I struck a G chord on Cassiopeia. She sounded perfect thanks to Dad's tuning pitch pipe.

'Petrina's just gone to sort out her vandalised face, then we're all set,' I replied.

'Would you like a sip of my Smurf Wee?' he asked, holding his long straw towards me.

I wonder if I look more attractive to Matthew when he is wearing his Smurf Wee goggles?

'I never drink before a show,' I said quickly. 'Or after'.

Knowing that there was a proper real-time hot boy somewhere in the audience really spurred me on to give an AWESOME Camel Toe performance. Matthew had hired a sophisticated lighting system and during the chorus of 'Poncerama' he faded up some uber cool neon lights that made Cassiopeia glow like a guitar from some futuristic post-apocalyptic cyber-rock band (it's amazing he managed this given how inebriated he was). When I turned to Petrina her teeth had gone purple under the lights, which didn't look at all attractive, so I made a point of keeping my lips as tightly pursed as was humanly possible whilst singing. The space-age lighting had also clearly affected Petrina's senses as she was making some weird 'thumbs up' gestures at me, wildly poking at her chest like a Norwegian King Kong. In the audience, Paulette Dempsey had assumed the role of the paparazzi, the rapid flashes of her camera dazzling my eyes as I glanced in her direction.

My heart was suddenly catapulted into my loins as, just behind Paulette, I spotted the sexy Mancake in the audience. Now I know this sounds unlikely, and I was as unconvinced as anyone else would be, but I swear he was winking at me. Nobody ever winks at me. I'm just not winking material. I pouted my lips (to conceal my potentially purple teeth) and repeatedly looked around to make sure that one of the slangers hadn't snuck up on stage behind me.

'He was even hotter than Felix Winters and Josh Raven if you mixed them together in a food blender,' I explained to Petrina when we came off stage and peered into the audience through a gap in the curtain wing.

'Look, there he is!'

Petrina studied the SEX GOD (who had now made his way up to the bar) through her thick glasses, just as his eye flashed in my direction again.

'He's beautiful,' she gasped in awe. 'Love what he's done with his Mofro.'

WHAT? He doesn't have afro hair.

Following Petrina's eye line, I realised that Petrina wasn't looking at the Mancake, but at the tall black boy he was now

37

chatting to. He had razor-sharp cheekbones and wouldn't have looked out of place in a boy band. I gave Petrina a playful nudge in the ribs, knowing that she'd never really be interested in another boy while she was with Walter.

'Stop window shopping!' I teased.

Petrina frowned at me. 'I wasn't,' she protested.

'So do you think the hot guy could have actually been winking at me?' I asked hopefully.

Petrina shook her head. 'It was probably just a twitch,' she said as kindly as she could. 'Or he's got conjunctivitis.'

I knew she was probably right. Why would a boy *that* perfect give a Weirdo like me a second glance?

'I really liked your bold feminist statement of not wearing a bra on stage,' said Petrina.

WHAT? Has she got a secret pervert camera rigged up in my room?

'How do you know?'

'Oh everyone could see when Matthew put those neon lights on you. Your norks were proud and visible through your T-shirt throughout the whole of Poncerama.' Petrina put her hands firmly on her hips. 'Emmeline Pankhurst would have been proud.'

Because that was TOTALLY my intention and nothing to do with the fact that every single bra I own was in the wash when I was getting ready. Let's hope the Mancake was too busy winking to notice my horrendous wardrobe malfunction.

'OK guys,' came DJ Loopy Ludlow's voice over the speakers. 'Time for a little more live music.'

What?

Who?

I had a dreadful moment of panic that Matthew was forcing us to perform an encore just so he could show everyone my norks again.

'Please welcome to the stage the biggest sensation to come out of Bridge Mount Secondary School since Josh Raven,' said Luke enthusiastically.

I grabbed Petrina by the arm. 'Give me your bra – QUICKLY!'

'What?' she replied. 'Blossom you are not throwing my underwear on stage.'

The audience giggled as Luke continued. 'You've seen Camel Toe – not to mention the camel humps . . .'

I covered my chest with my hands. 'OH MY GOD,' I yelped. 'It's an encore.'

'No it's not,' said Petrina calmly. 'We don't have any more songs.'

'Now put your hands together for something completely new,' Luke shouted.

Eh?

'Ladies and gentlemen, please welcome to the stage – Perkitits!'

The room descended into a sudden darkness that caused an instant frenzy of excitement. A single note from a pre-recorded electric guitar rang out through the speakers. It was a chord I could not play. A bar chord. It sounded sarcastic, as if it was mocking me with its impossible complexity. F#m, I think. Gradually the lights lifted to reveal two perfect hourglass silhouettes posing motionless on stage; the provocative glossy sheen of skin-tight, black PVC catsuits and six-inch stiletto heels igniting the hormones of the captivated teenage onlookers. The F#m chord gave way to a G#, then a KILLER electro pop intro kicked in. I turned to Petrina, but no words came out of my mouth. She responded with an equally silent gasp. There before us like two spicy she-devils with huge nork cleavages, stood Fiona Tittledown and Lucy Perkins. The slangers. And although it makes me feel like barfing to say it, they looked sexy as hell. My stomach churned. Watching them strut about the stage with their luscious hair flowing behind them, freaking out to a sickeningly catchy and vaguely familiar track (which I know they didn't write as, even combined, they have the creative talent of a blobfish), was almost unbearable. Petrina and I don't care that we're not sexy because our music does the talking. But it seems that, to most people, music means NOTHING compared to the sight of a pair of foxy pop nymphets. We had to face the fact that Fiona and Lucy had well and truly stolen our spotlight. Now everyone at school would remember Perkitits' dazzling display of pop-guff and totally forget the awesome moral/social/political genius of Camel Toe.

The Year 11 party-goers were lapping it up. It was as if Fiona and Lucy had cast a wicked spell over the marquee as every single audience member was struck gormless. Even Mei Miyagi and Kirsty Mackerby (who had only just got back together after splitting up last term because of Mei's non-lesbian fling with fat-necked rugby prop Max Burcott) had been duped by the affected, soulless rot that the slangers were churning out. They were holding hands, foolishly rocking back and forth like a couple of lust-struck lunatics.

Shame on you, Mei. I thought you had more class.

Felix and Toby looked on from the side of the stage, their tongues lolling out of their mouths like a couple of dehydrated German Shepherds (the sexiest of all dog breeds).

'What do you think?' asked Matthew who had sidled up beside us with Walter. Matthew was holding a bright pink concoction (a Flaming Fuzzy Navel laced with vodka apparently).

'Pretty good,' Walter nodded, until Petrina nudged him hard in the ribs.

'Yeah, but Fiona's bass face is lacking conviction,' she said.

'Her what?' Matthew and I replied in unison.

'Her bass face. You know, when the bass line is so good that you have to pull an expression like a monkey trying to kiss a banana? Hers just isn't authentic.'

The slangers were pouting shamelessly on stage. They didn't look like monkeys – more like collagen-enhanced llamas.

'Still, you've got some competition now,' said Matthew taking a sip of his fluorescent drink. 'Perhaps you need to think about getting a manager?' The straw flicked out of the glass, spraying flecks of vodka into his face.

'No offence, Matthew, but I don't really think it's us who need help.'

Matthew rubbed his reddening eye. 'I know of a way that

Camel Toe could play at the Kaleidoscope Festival,' he said.

Wait! Hold everything . . . Kaleidoscope? The second biggest music festival in the UK?

'How?' I asked.

'It might help if I'm your manager.'

Is this blackmail?

Petrina's hostility was obvious. 'We don't need a man's input,' she said sternly. 'Remember Emmeline Pankhurst, Blossom.'

I paused and thought about the leader of the Women's Social and Political Union. We'd recently appointed her as the official Camel Toe band mascot and I'd even gone so far as to transform my old Barbie doll into a Suffragette using an old pirate flag and a black marker pen.

I turned to Walter, who was now gazing down at his manky Converse boots. 'Are you sure you don't want to be our manager?' (Walter doesn't count as a real man. He sometimes plucks his eyebrows, even though they are permanently obscured by his fringe. I can't be bothered to do mine even though they are in full view.)

'Nope,' he said firmly. Petrina nodded in admiration.

But the Kaleidoscope Festival? Steel Dragon are playing this year. So is Josh Raven. And we have an opportunity to play alongside them? It's a no brainer.

'OK!' I blurted at Matthew. 'You can be our manager.'

Petrina was horrified. 'What?'

Matthew raised his hand in a high-five gesture which neither Petrina or I chose to return. 'Cool,' he said, high-fiving the air. 'You won't be disappointed.'

Petrina was not amused. She took Walter by the arm and began to walk down towards the bar. Walter looked over his shoulder at me and shrugged.

And that was how Bridge Mount Secondary School's drunken joker became Camel Toe's manager. The fate of our career lies solely in his hands. What could possibly go wrong?

To: Blossom Uxley-Michaels
Sent: June 24th 02:06:44
From: pervertedchicken666@noogler.com
Subj: Kaleidoscope Battle of the Bands

Yo!

Awesome party right? I'm just finishing off the last of the cocktails at the bar. Waahooooooo!

I've attached a flyer for 'School Rocks' Battle of the Bands. My dad's company is one of the main sponsors. I emailed him in Vietnam and he says he'll provide new outfits and transport you and your equipment to and from the venue.

I really think you guys could win this.

Sent from Matty's iPhone
Kinky is using a feather. Perverted is using the whole chicken.

KALEIDOSCOPE PRESENTS

'SCHOOL ROCKS'
BATTLE OF THE BANDS

THE PRIZE:

- *THE OPPORTUNITY TO PERFORM A FULL SET, LIVE ON THE MAIN STAGE AT THE KALEIDOSCOPE FESTIVAL*
- *ACCESS-ALL-AREAS VIP FESTIVAL PASSES*
- *LUXURY ACCOMMODATION IN A GLAMPING YURT.*
- *RECORDING TIME AND MASTERING OF A SINGLE AT PETE HARTLEY'S RECORDING STUDIO WITH AN ACTUAL RELEASE DATE AND PROMOTIONAL SCHEDULE.*

THE PROGRAMME:

ALL HEATS WILL TAKE PLACE AT BRAMBLEDOWN GOLF CLUB.
THE FINAL WILL BE HELD AT THE LEGENDARY HONEY DOME.

HEAT 1 (DANCE / URBAN) 12 JULY, 7PM
HEAT 2 (INDIE / ROCK) 13 JULY, 7PM
HEAT 3 (SOLO SINGER/SONGWRITER) 14 JULY, 7PM
HEAT 4 (POP) 15 JULY, 7PM
QUARTER-FINALS 21 & 22 JULY, 7PM
SEMI-FINALS 10 & 11 AUGUST, 7PM
FINAL WEDS 24 AUGUST, 8PM

IMPORTANT INFORMATION

ALL PARTICIPANTS MUST BE 18 OR UNDER AND ATTENDING SCHOOL OR COLLEGE TO TAKE PART.

Sponsored by   **Ludlow's Luxury Loos**   **CAK ENERGY DRINKS**   **DUNGLEBERT'S BURGERS**

END OF WEEK 25. MY TABLE OF ACHIEVEMENT

SHAME LEVEL PEAK*	*7 (neon nork flashing)*
GUITAR PRACTICE	*Enough to ensure that I played well on stage. Playing guitar has become as natural to me as trumping in my sleep.*
PARTY INVITATIONS	*Matthew's party, plus an invite to the Glastonbury Festival, which is essentially the party of ALL parties!*
SNOGS	*0* *But there is a hot MANCAKE on the horizon . . .*

* Peek at the back of the book for the Scale of Shame!

45

GLASTONBURY WEEKEND
TENT OF EVIL

It was still dark when we left the house at the crack of a blue tit's fart. Naturally the conversation revolved mainly around music war – our perky new rivals and the impending Battle of the Bands competition, although we'd decided not to plan our set until after the Glastonbury weekend. Astonishingly our multi-coloured VW camper van only broke down once – when we got stuck in a massive traffic jam on the A303, causing the knackered old piece of metal to overheat. While Mum and Dad faffed around under the bonnet, Petrina, Walter and I sat by the roadside, trying to make sense of what had happened the night before. The slangers had formed a pop band. And while they might not play their own instruments, their pre-recorded backing tracks were brilliantly produced. I'm not saying I would actually buy their cheesy records myself, because quite frankly I would rather set my teeth on fire, but there was no denying that they sounded good.

'They've got a rubbish name, though,' I said.

Walter stood up and stretched his lanky legs.

'It's a portmanteau,' said Petrina.

'A poor man's toe?' I literally had no idea what she was on about.

'It's originally a French word for a type of bag,' she explained. 'One holdall that opens into two compartments.'

Petrina thought for a moment. 'A word mash-up,' she stated.

'Oh right! Perkins plus Tittledown equals Perkitits! How very clever.' I inserted a HEAVY sarcastic insinuation at this point.

OUR TOP 10 PORTMANTEAUS

1. CRAPTACULAR (something that is spectacularly crap. Rather like the band name Perkitits)

2. SHART (an unfortunate 'follow through')

3. GUITARSOLE (arrogant guitarist in a rock band)

4. WALTINA (Walter and Petrina – ahhhh!)

5. FLOSSOM/BLOSH (me and Felix/me and Josh)

6. MORKS (massive norks)

7. KISSUE (an important snogging matter)

8. LESBROMANTIC (a romantic lesbian like Kirsty Mackerby, who cleaned out Mei's manky old pencil case last week without her even asking. How sweet is that?)

9. TURPER (tea slurper)

10. FRUNK (a friendly drunk – like Matthew Ludlow)

By midday we had pitched our sky-blue tent (in the pouring rain) next to the camper van and wandered off in our pac-a-macs and wellies to explore the site. We were quite happy to leave my parents to prepare for their postponed summer solstice party, which was taking place tomorrow at dawn in a small, ancient stone circle. They'd already invited a group of crazy seasoned festival-goers who they'd known since the days when the festival was 'a place of free love, free spirits and free from the corporate beast' (which is basically code for the times they used to illegally jump the fence and get in without paying).

Josh Raven wasn't arriving until the evening, so we spent the afternoon checking out bands, getting freaked out by the spooky woman in the Shangri-La field who had pointed razor blades instead of teeth, running away from a MASSIVE robot made entirely from landfill junk and avoiding the dodgy drug dealers who were easy to spot by their unfortunate physical similarities to hobgoblins.

At around 6PM we headed back to the tent to get changed and freshen up before we met Josh Raven in the VIP area. I had itchy, muddy, dreadlocky hair, but that was nothing compared to Petrina's stinky hand. Walter had laughed when I told him I'd packed fifteen packs of wet wipes, but he wasn't laughing now.

'You really honk,' I said holding my nose. Earlier Petrina had spectacularly scissor kicked herself into the air after slipping on a discarded falafel kebab. Then she landed in a giant soggy cowpat.

Walter dry-retched into his hand as Petrina added yet another brown stained wipe to the huge steaming pile.

'Can't you do that outside?' he begged, tears now streaming down his face. I had no idea he was so squeamish.

'Thanks for being supportive, guys,' Petrina grumbled. I know she was upset, but I could sympathise with Walter. Showing concern and compassion when he was so close to blowing chunks would be an impossible act of love.

'There are flakes of cattle poo on my sleeping bag,' I shrieked as she scraped out more rancid bits from under her fingernails.

Walter burped loudly (one of those thunderous uncontrollable belches that comes just before the spew) causing Petrina's bottom lip to tremble. I felt honoured to be present in this intimate moment – their first lovers' tiff. Walter turned a pale shade of green and darted out of the tent with his hand over his mouth.

Half an hour later Walter and Petrina had kissed (not literally as Walter's breath was foul) and made up (although I noticed that Walter remained downwind of his girlfriend's left hand). With our VIP passes hung proudly round our necks, we crawled excitedly out of the tent. The rain had stopped and the air was charged with anticipation. To be honest, I don't think it had quite sunk in yet. We were the personal guests of INTERNATIONAL MEGASTAR Josh Raven!!! My parents had also been given Access-All-Areas passes, but in typical fashion they'd shunned the special treatment to hang out with their crusty, cider-drinking friends in the boggy stone circle.

As the last one out of the tent, I crouched down to zip up the entrance securely.

'Come on!' said Petrina impatiently.

But as I pulled on the zipper cord, the end of my hair became caught. I gave it a tug.

Uh-oh!

'I can't,' I said. 'It's jammed.'

'What?' Petrina was getting annoyed.

I yanked the zipper cord as hard as I could but only succeeded in catching more of my hair in the plastic teeth. It was stuck almost right up to my scalp.

'My hair is trapped in the zip.'

I was beginning to feel quite panicked.

'Let me have a go,' said Petrina, kneeling down next to me. She tugged and wiggled and prised and jiggled, but it was no good. My dark barnet would not budge.

Walter's solution to the problem was: 'Cut it?'

Both Petrina and I were horrified.

'NO!' we screamed in unison.

I AM NOT A FAN OF THE ASYMMETRICAL HAIR-DO.

A swell of trepidation rose up through my body. We were due to meet Josh backstage in half an hour and I was ensnared by this merciless, vampire fanged, Tent. Of. Evil.

'What am I going to do?' I wailed.

Walter shrugged and thrust his hands deep into the pockets of his jeans. He pulled out an old, corroded penknife.

'I always knew this would come in handy one day,' he said as he attempted to cut me free with the rusty piece of metal.

And so it came to be that fifteen minutes later I set off to meet a proper real-time HOT sex god, sporting a lopjob haircut. EVEN WORSE Walter had left a bit of zip and a small flap of Vango tent material hanging from a chunk of my hair because it had been too close to my scalp to cut. Petrina tried to console me by saying that it was 'uber post-ironic', but I knew the truth: I looked like a GIANT QUIMBOID.

The VIP hospitality area is basically an extravagant caravan park with a few massive luxury wigwams scattered about, where celebrities (and other Very Important People) can pretend to live the authentic hippie dream without actually giving up any luxuries. Petrina, Walter and I couldn't have felt more conspicuous – three awkward, black-clad Weirdos gawping at a backstage runway of Winners flaunting their designer shades, Hunter wellie boots and ridiculously expensive festival outfits. Within two minutes of our arrival we'd spotted two supermodels, nineteen reality TV hangers on, five television presenters, loads of band members from the festival line-up, an A-List Hollywood film star, a soap star, seven radio presenters and Matthew Ludlow. WAIT! Rewind . . .

MATTHEW LUDLOW?

Standing before us, with a bottle of Coke in his hand and looking a little bit pink and sunburnt, was Bridge Mount's answer to the loud-mouthed lush on the street corner.

'Hey guys,' he grinned. 'Free drinks!' I don't think he could have been any more thrilled to see us if he tried.

Is he STALKING me?

'What are *you* doing here?' asked Petrina sounding as surprised as I felt.

'Dad knows the C.E.O. of one of the big festival sponsors,' he said taking a big swig of Coke. 'He's in Singapore . . . no, Japan, now, but he gave me and my brother VIP tickets.'

'Is your mum here with you?' I asked.

'She's um . . . not well,' he said, before quickly changing the subject. 'Hey have you had your hair done?'

'Yeah,' I snapped, anticipating an inevitable insult. 'It's uber post-ironic. Got a problem with that?'

'No,' said Matthew carefully. 'It looks . . . pretty.'

In his shabby, mud-caked flip-flops and faded surfer shorts, Matthew looked as unfashionably out of place as the rest of us. We were nothing but four teenage scruffbags, shuffling indiscernibly amongst the cool people.

A deafening sound and a sudden gale-force wind caused us (and everyone else) to blink up at the sky. Petrina protectively shielded Walter's eyes with her stinky hand as the gust blew his fringe from his face. A helicopter was dramatically lowering itself down on to the grassy area next to the VIP enclosure. It was a noisy and impressively rock 'n' roll entrance for Josh Raven, who emerged from the silver whirlybird in a typical bent-down-so-that-you-don't-get-your-head-chopped-off-even-though-the-rotor-blades-are-about-twenty-feet-above-you manner.

He was wearing his trademark heavy charcoal guy-liner, skinny, blue Levis and a tight, dark grey T-shirt that showed off his RIPPED body. I am not exaggerating when I say that he looked hotter than the devil's metal nipple ring. Much air kissing and *mwah-mwahing* followed as he made his way through the sea of beautiful people, which parted before him like a hippie hairdo.

He noticed the four of us watching on the sideline and waggled his fingers excitedly. 'YOO HOO! Blossom!' he trilled.

I waved back sheepishly and watched as the international sex symbol skipped gleefully towards us.

He really is the campest man I have EVER seen in my life.

I wasn't sure of the pop star etiquette.

Should I lean in for a peck on the cheek or do I just curtsey?

In my star-struck fluster I ended up leaning in and curtseying at the same time, meaning that my face was now exactly level with Josh's crotch.

OH GOD. Act as if it was intentional.

'Do you know you've got toothpaste on your . . . groin?' I said, casually licking my thumb and wiping away an imaginary mark.

There was a sudden snort from Matthew and a jet of Coca-Cola came cascading out of his nostrils. Petrina and Walter both had their mouths open.

'Thanks darling,' said Josh appreciatively. 'It's totes amaze to see you all again. I'm so glad you could be my guests.'

'Thanks for inviting us,' said Petrina, blushing ever so slightly. I glanced over at Walter to see if he'd noticed, but he was busy helping Matthew wipe down his Coke-covered T-shirt.

Josh turned to me. He cocked his head and smiled, then he HUGGED me. He smelt like I'd imagine an angel of heaven would – like sunshine, sea salt and Mr Sheen furniture polish.

Oh God. He's noticed the piece of blue tent in my hair.

'That is an interesting fascinator darling,' he said. 'Stephen Jones?'

'No, Argos,' I replied shamefully.

'Well the colour looks great against your skin tone.'

And with a flick of his jet black curly hair and the promise of a personal wave on stage, Josh Raven dived back into the sea of beautiful people, where he demonstrated a masterclass in the art of showbiz mingling.

Ten minutes passed before Walter suggested that we should release ourselves back into the wild. I was glad because I think that standing in the same, stunned, Josh-Raven-hugged-me pose for any longer might have left me with permanent damage.

Josh's headlining performance was naturally awesome and at one point during the Moonlight Stalker encore a shaven-headed woman with mad eyes came up and complimented me on my 'non-conformist, radical look'. For a short while I enjoyed feeling like a bit of a rebel, but then later in the evening I spotted no less than NINE festival-goers walking around with tent flaps in their hair. It was blatant plagiarism and totally ruined my unintentional non-conformity.

It took Mum and Dad two hours and an Aboriginal musical

clapstick to prise my hair free from The Tent of Evil without resorting to any more hackage with a blunt rusty knife. It's amazing how quickly you can become accustomed to a physical deformity – even now I keep reaching out to touch the tent, expecting to find it still attached. I'd imagine this is what it feels like to have a phantom limb after an amputation.

'MORNING! Does anyone need a wee before we greet the Sun God?' are not the words anyone wants to hear at 4.01AM. Mum's face was poking through the torn front flap of our tent. Her eyes looked a bit wild and, even though I knew she'd been up all night and had been forced to give up A-class drugs when she started her yoga teacher training seven years ago, I still hoped she hadn't had a relapse.

Petrina sat up, blinking rapidly as she felt about for her glasses. Walter grunted from somewhere within his sleeping bag.

I pressed my face into my pillow. 'We'll be out in a minute,' I replied blearily.

The sight before us as we emerged from our tent five minutes later was like an old English wonderland. The trees twinkled in the darkness with white fairy lights that had been strung casually across the branches. Hundreds of candles flickered around the ancient stone circle, at the centre of which a topless, dreadlocked man was breathing out jets of fire. The smell of vegan food wafted out of the yurt, where a group of

Druids and hippies were dancing, giddy with the midsummer energy. I had a bit of a fright when I noticed a group of people with blacked-up faces, wearing dark rags and black bells on their knees and leaping around a large bonfire to the sound of a melodeon and a jolly fiddle. At first glance it looked like some kind of archaic, racist political rally. Petrina was so appalled that she immediately got out her phone ready to call the police, but I stopped her when, to my utter horror I noticed that one of the dancers was wind-milling his arm about in an unmistakably freakish, double-jointed way. How could I not recognise the hypermobility trait that I had inherited from MY FATHER. This was potentially even worse than when I discovered Mum was having an extra-marital relationship with a medieval wizard a few months ago. Thankfully Dad was quick to explain that he'd simply joined a Border Morris Dancing group, who dress up in the traditional black rag costume and prance about banging sticks and waving handkerchiefs in the air. Why was I not surprised?

The carnivalesque air was infectious and, before we knew what we were doing, Petrina and I found ourselves dancing amongst the throng. There must have been over a hundred festival-goers mingling with my parent's friends, their curiosity getting the better of them.

'Happy solstice,' said Dad, his eyes glistening brightly against his black face paint.

'Excellent timing, Blossom,' said Mum, dancing on tippy-toes. She was dressed as a Druid hippie in a long, flowing white robe with a sharp, pointed hood pulled up over her head.

56

I looked at my parents for a moment. My father, the blacked-up dancer, and my mother, member of the Ku Klux Klan.

'We need a sacrificial virgin,' she continued. 'Could you hop up on to the Altar Stone for a few minutes?'

Pardon?

'Duncan,' yelled Mum to a Pagan High Priest, who was chatting animatedly to a woman on stilts wearing a set of plastic deer antlers. 'Come and meet our virgin.'

'Can't someone else do it?' I asked in a panic.

'Don't look at me,' said Petrina firmly.

Mum frowned. 'Don't be so silly Blossom. Let's celebrate your virginity.'

The bearded Pagan High Priest came over with a serene smile on his face.

'Come my child,' he said, taking hold of my arm. All at once I found myself surrounded by wild-eyed, robed strangers.

I am not comfortable with this situation in ANY WAY.

Dad instantly recognised my fear. 'Don't worry,' he smiled. 'They don't actually harm anyone these days. You won't die.'

Was that meant to be reassuring?

'I'll only die of embarrassment,' I sobbed.

And so at 4.32AM the High Priest ceremoniously led me into a stone circle while chanting an ancient (and slightly creepy) prayer. An expectant silence fell as I climbed on to the cold stone and lay down on my back. All eyes were fixed on me and I suddenly felt like a magician's assistant ready to be cut in half (except I was wearing a Steel Dragon hoodie and pyjama

57

bottoms instead of a spangly, high-leg leotard). The High Priest theatrically raised his arms towards the sky and everyone held their breath in anticipation of the first glimpse of the sun rising up over the Heel Stone. I waited . . .

And waited . . .

And waited . . .

And waited. I checked my watch. It was 4.36am. The sun was due to rise in approximately thirty seconds. This was getting boring. Still I waited . . .

Until . . .

'YOO HOO! Blossom!'

OH PLEASE NO! This can't be happening.

Everyone turned 180° to where Josh Raven was standing with a group of about fifteen stupidly beautiful people, most of whom I recognised as being from the uber cool North London set of actor, model and rock star friends, labelled by the media as the Camden Collective. How did Josh manage to look so proper real-time HOT at that time in the morning?

'Everyone says *this* is the place to be,' he trilled as one of his pretty friends passed him a bottle of wine.

'Ooh look, it's John Craven,' squealed my mum excitedly, pointing at Josh. 'Blossom has the biggest crush on you! She fantasises about you every night.'

ARRRGGGGHHHHH! SHUT UP.

'Most people do darling,' laughed Josh, taking a big swig from the bottle.

This has surely got to be the peak of all embarrassing situations. I'm about to be sacrificed on a cold slab of rock, by a

bunch of Druids, in front of Josh Raven and some A-list celebrities.
I mean there is no way on earth it could get any worse. Could it?

'Enter me, Mother Nature,' cried my mother, casting aside her white robes to reveal her NAKED body. She threw her head back and held her arms aloft to the rising sun.

KILL ME NOW!

Walter and Petrina quickly turned away. And who could blame them – it was a sight that might well have struck them both blind.

'PAAAAARTY!' A familiar voice rang through the air.

Everyone turned round again to where an ethereal figure now stood, arms outstretched, with the rising sun creating a golden halo-like aura as it glowed majestically from behind.

'All hail the great and powerful sun,' declared the High Priest. 'We welcome you and celebrate your eternal light.'

'All hail the great and powerful sun,' repeated the mesmerised crowd of celebrities, hippies, Druids, witches, fire-eaters and all manner of other festival-goers.

'All right, Blossom?' said Matthew Ludlow, stepping out of the sun's rays, a four pack of lager dangling by his side. 'Heard your folks were having a party. Thought this might be a good way to have a bit of one-to-one quality time together. Fancy a beer?'

Right then, I died a small shameful death on that ancient stone plinth. Petrina and Walter smiled encouragingly as the High Priest pretended to rip out my guts with a plastic dagger, Josh and his cronies cheered as my mum began a round of naked yoga sun salutations and Matthew gave me a double thumbs up as the Border Morris Dancers (including Dad) began to dance in a circle around me to the sound of an accordion. For the second time in a week I said a little prayer, this time asking for the appearance of a time tunnel to another dimension or a futuristic electronic device that would beam me up to a spaceship full of conventional people from the planet Normal.

END OF GLASTONBURY WEEKEND.
MY TABLE OF ACHIEVEMENT

SHAME LEVEL PEAK	Tent in hair + public sacrificing + naked mother + Josh Raven = EXPLODED Shameometer.
GUITAR PRACTICE	0 – although watching some of the AMAZING guitarists on stage at Glastonbury was essentially a masterclass in how to play.
SCHOOL WORK	Finished!
PARTY INVITATIONS	0
SNOGS	0

DYAN MOON

ALSO KNOWN AS: PLANTING MOON,
MOON WHEN JUNEBERRIES ARE RIPE,
MOON OF HORSES, STRAWBERRY MOON.

WEEK 26
SELF-DEFENCE

Paulette Dempsey is a gigantic, fat-faced quimboid (and that is an actual scientific FACT). I'd noticed her at Matthew's party taking pictures of the guests, but I'd assumed she'd just been trying out a new fancy camera. I did NOT suspect in any way, that she'd taken up PORNOGRAPHIC photography and had been using ME as her sex muse. I received a text from Petrina first thing this morning telling me to log on immediately to the new Dempsey Love website, which had just gone live and you can imagine my surprise/horror/embarrassment when I saw my own gurning expression and lit-up, bare, neon norks on the homepage.

Feeling naturally outraged and violated, I marched round to her house (with Petrina and Walter as back-up) to confront her. Paulette answered the door wearing an outfit that completely wiped the speech I'd rehearsed from my memory. She had squeezed herself into shocking-pink-tight-cropped-T-shirt-and-leggings get-up that made Walter actually gasp for breath.

'What?' she snapped.

'You know what,' I replied. 'You've made me a laughing stock.'

Paulette raised her eyebrows. 'You should be grateful.'

Erm?

'Oh, don't get me wrong,' she smirked. 'You weren't my first-choice cover girl, but Fiona and Lucy both wanted a ridiculously high fee. You're no supermodel, but you're not as ugly as a hatful of bumholes either so I figured you'd do.'

Is that a compliment?

'It was underhand, Paulette,' said Petrina. 'You can't just exploit people like that.'

Paulette ignored her. 'Oh come on, Blossom,' she reasoned. 'Your face all over my website. Think of all the cute guys who will see you.'

Hmmm. She might actually have a point.

Petrina grabbed me by the shoulders and looked me in the eyes. 'What would Emmeline Pankhurst do?' she asked with a knowing nod.

That's a good question to ponder. How would our band mascot react if a ruthless teenage business tycoon tried to use her small, naked breasts to promote a dating website without permission?

'OK,' I said. 'I'll do it for the sisterhood.'

I turned to high-five Petrina, but she was already walking back down the garden path with Walter. Norwegians are very sensitive and I think the confrontation must have been a little too much for her so early in the morning.

Mum's response to the Dempsey Love website was one of pure joy.

'I couldn't be more proud,' she beamed as she viewed the laptop on the kitchen table. 'Like mother, like daughter. Using your body to make a bold, political statement about the media sexualisation of teenage girls. God, I love you.'

'Er, thanks Mum,' I mumbled, hoping this wouldn't inspire her to make me watch the now infamous YouTube clip, where she is sitting naked astride a white horse, riding through the town centre (her Lady Godiva protest demonstration).

'Great sex face,' she said, studying my open-mouthed expression on the screen.

'Wha . . . ? Gah . . . Noooooo!' I stammered. 'That's not my . . . yuck . . . God . . . No . . . I was singing the "Oooh" bit of the Poncerama chorus when Paulette took the photo.'

Mum patted my arm and smiled.

Oh God. That is the absolute WORST. CRINGE.

Dad's boss has agreed to let me work in his music shop Blue Nile over the summer holidays. It's pretty much my dream job (apart from having to be with my father all day) as I'll be in a shop full of guitars.

Petrina has got herself a part time job in Skadi the frozen food supermarket. I'm not going to lie, the canary yellow uniform she has to wear is utterly hideous, but it includes a fleece that can be zipped up to the neck so Petrina's happy enough. Meanwhile, I can just hang out with the customers (not that we get many) amongst a sea of musical instruments, which more than makes up for the fact that Petrina is getting paid twice as much as me (and gets free gone-off burgers).

The only other thing that would make my life better (apart from a HOT rock star boyfriend, Fiona and Lucy both developing faces full of sexually-transmitted cold sores, the removal of my teeth braces, winning the Battle of the Bands competition, slightly bigger norks, a smaller nose, better hair, a cherry-red Gibson ES-335 guitar, normal parents and a lifetime supply of Ferrero Rochers) is moving into Breeze's bedroom. I've longed to live in my sister's much larger room for as long as I can remember and finally I'm about to stake my claim. Although she says she has absolutely no intention of ever getting married, Breeze has agreed to move in with her night club manager boyfriend Andreas. So the two of them (along with the help of my parents) spent the day moving my sister's belongings into his flat. I kept well out of it, staying in my bedroom to watch music videos, but, no matter what my 'noise-cancelling' headphones claimed, I could still hear the yelling, arguments, crashing and bashing.

'Of course I need my Retro Hanging Bubble Pod Chair,' screamed my sister as my dad and Andreas lifted the transparent sphere into the hired van. 'It's the only place I can really relax and get comfy.'

For an eco-friendly environmentalist, Breeze owns a remarkable amount of plastic, non-biodegradable tat.

'But it's huge,' raged Andreas. 'And there's nowhere to put it.'

Breeze's oscillating nostrils had gone into overdrive. 'Well MAKE ROOM,' she shouted. 'You're not living in a bachelor pad any more. Get rid of your home entertainment system.'

A few neighbours had come outside to enjoy the spectacle,

including Mr Parkin at number 34, who was sitting in his camping chair and snacking on a tube of Pringles.

Dad knows better than to interfere when Breeze and her boyfriend clash swords, so he quietly continued loading the van. My sister might look like a 1960s flower child hippie, but her fearsome temper is legendary – like the time Dad gave her a driving lesson in the camper van. She accused him of being an 'aggressive dictator' and threw such a massive wobbly behind the wheel that the gear stick broke off in her hand and they ended up stranded on a roundabout in the middle of the A22. That combined with Andreas' fiery disposition means their relationship is not only volatile, but intensely passionate as well.

'Are you insane?' yelled Andreas. 'It cost thousands.'

'It's excessive. Nobody needs an amp and five speakers when they've only got two ears.'

'It enhances my listening pleasure.'

'It's a waste of space. I could put Ursula in the corner where your amp is.'

'You are NOT putting that bloody umbrella plant in my flat.'

'She gives me clean oxygen.'

'It's over six feet tall.'

'Don't make me choose between you and Ursula. You won't like my decision.'

Andreas put his hands on his hips. 'You'd dare to choose a plant over me?' he said firmly.

'Yep,' replied my sister. 'What ya gonna do about it?'

Andreas laughed defiantly. 'Ha! Look at me. I'm a man. A

pure-bred, perfect, five-foot seven specimen of beef.'

'You're a revolting, hairy-armed wombat,' screeched Breeze.

From across the road, Mr Parker applauded loudly. 'Hairy-armed wombat!' he chirped. 'That's a goodie. Haven't heard that one before. I must put it on my blog.'

Breeze scowled at our bald-headed neighbour. 'Mind your own business,' she snapped. Mr Parker continued stuffing Pringles into his mouth, clearly enjoying the outdoor show.

Mum stepped outside clutching a bin bag. 'I've never known anyone have this much underwear,' she said, holding out a tiny green thong. On seeing this, Andreas wiped his brow, swallowed hard, then traipsed back into the house, grumbling filthy obscenities under his breath. He re-emerged a few moments later struggling under the weight of Ursula the oxygen-replenishing umbrella plant. I never knew a simple pair of organic hemp pants could be such a powerful weapon.

Amazingly, Matthew hadn't mentioned my humiliating sacrificial experience to anyone (loyalty is a trait that I will add to the Matthew Ludlow PROS list), but Petrina and I couldn't help but notice that the slangers were glaring at us more than usual. When I passed Fiona Tittledown in the street on my way home from Blue Nile this afternoon she actually hissed at me like a feral cat. She already hates my guts, but now that Perkitits are treading on our musical territory, Fiona and Lucy have pretty much declared rock 'n' roll war. It is mainly for this reason that Petrina and I have signed up for self-defence classes. The other reasons are a) violent street crime in suburban areas has increased by 2.3% and, other than a few basic wrestling moves that I learned from watching men in leotards on WWF, I have no clue how to defend myself, b) Petrina thinks it's essential for all feminists to learn how to crush a man with their bare hands and c) it seems that my dad has befriended a rapist who may be invited into our house at some point.

When I walked into the kitchen first thing this morning, I immediately noticed the Post-it note stuck on the bottom of the moon-phase clock. In my dad's handwriting, it said:

Monday 4th July 11AM
See the rapist.

First I find out that my liberal-minded parents are in a consensual three-way relationship, now I learn that my father is befriending dangerous sex offenders? I confronted my mother at the first available opportunity. At first I thought she was trying to ease her constipation, then I realised she was practising the one-legged eagle pose in the kitchen while she waited for the kettle to boil.

'Mum, do you and Dad believe that rapists should be given a second chance?' I wanted to approach the subject in an indirect way. It's a sensitive subject. She looked thoughtful for a moment as she put her raised foot back down on solid ground, but remained in the twisted squatting position.

'Justice doesn't mean an eye for an eye Blossom,' she began. 'We need suitable punishment for the crime and a rehabilitation regime to minimise reoffending. If I'd been around in the seventeenth century do you honestly think I'd be here now?'

Erm.

'Of course I wouldn't.' She was in full rhetorical flow. 'I'd be drowned in a trial by ordeal to the cries of "witch, witch, witch!"'

'Actually, Mum, you'd only be considered a witch if you ended up floating. In which case you'd have been burned alive at the stake'.

We'd covered all this years ago in history. I liked all the bloody, gory torture stuff. Much more interesting than all the boring Cold War guff we've been doing for our exams.

But Mum wasn't listening. 'And after I'd been persecuted and murdered for witchcraft,' she continued. 'What do you think would happen to you?'

I'd be adopted by a buxom wench?

'Your father would die of a broken heart, leaving you orphaned and left out on the street, where you'd succumb to a life of petty crime and prostitution. And, when you were locked up in your prison cell with the lowlifes and scurvy-ridden rats, would you deserve a second chance?'

Can rats get scurvy?

Mum put her hands on her hips to emphasise the seriousness of her statement. Then she turned and walked out of the kitchen. I took that answer as a 'yes' and pondered the prospect of a life on the dangerous seventeenth-century streets of England, thankful that my self-defence classes were starting tonight.

That evening I dressed myself in a pair of comfortable black leggings and a T-shirt, ready for my new self-defence class. Petrina was wearing her standard woolly tights, black shorts and black-cardigan-zipped-up-to-the-neck combo.

The class was supposed to give me confidence and reassurance. Instead it brought me nothing but SHAME (Level 9, to be precise). When we arrived at St James' church hall I was desperate for the toilet, but, as we were already ten minutes late (Petrina wouldn't get off the phone to Walter), I thought I'd hang on until after the class.

Our instructor was a triangular-shaped (the upside-down kind), shaven-headed man in an Adidas tracksuit called Kenny, who spoke to us as if he were an army sergeant major. I don't think I've ever met a person with such a huge face. It was massive and fleshy like Mr Potato Head with his mouth on the wrong way round (no hat though).

'Right then,' he boomed with his hands on his hips. 'This course will cover the basic essentials of women's self-protection. All the methods have been rigorously tested on grubby oiks who've been stupid enough to attack me.'

I tried to imagine what kind of idiot quimboid would consider trying to mug a man as intimidating as Kenny. His biceps were bigger than my thighs and his thighs were bigger than my head (I do actually have quite a large head for a girl).

'But let me tell you,' he growled. 'By the time I'd finished with them they were nothing more than guts and offal.'

Kenny licked his lips in way that conjured up an image of a lion tearing into a piece of raw meat.

'So this class is personally designed by me so that when you go about your daily life, you *own* the street. Ladies, repeat after me: I'm a warrior not a worrier.'

We all glanced at each other before whispering in uncoordinated unison, 'I'm a warrior not a worrier'. The sound barely filled the hall.

Kenny was not happy. His face had begun to turn purple and the veins in his neck were bulging like overcooked spaghetti strands.

'If you spoke like that to your attacker, he'd not only kill you, he'd *rip* out your intestines and feed them to his pitbull terrier for elevenses.'

Funny. I would never have put Kenny down as an elevenses kind of guy.

'Say it again,' he snarled, punching his own hand like a proper mental case. 'Like your life depends on it.'

'I'M A WARRIOR NOT A WORRIER,' we all yelled at the top of our voices. Only we *were* worried about Kenny shouting at us. The man was absolutely terrifying.

Half an hour later and we were standing in pairs on gym mats practising our 'escape from strangulation techniques'. Petrina was with a chubby, friendly woman and I was paired up with a short-haired, middle-aged lady called Wendy.

'He's quite sexy isn't he?' she said of our instructor with her hands firmly around my throat.

Yuck. I'd rather kiss the bum of a naked mole rat.

I went to strike Wendy firmly in the windpipe. 'He's not really my type,' I replied.

'I like them rough and ready,' she grinned as I palmed her on the chin.

'Remember – your attacker's a lowlife, filthy scumbag,' snarled Kenny, appearing out of nowhere and taking us both by surprise. 'If it's a man, kick him in the balls. If it's a woman, punch her in the tits.'

I was LITERALLY stunned for a few moments.

'Well?' thundered Kenny.

'What?' I trembled.

'Visualise your attacker. Is she a man or a woman?'

Wendy smiled sweetly at me. 'A woman?' I replied timidly.

'Tits then,' yelled Kenny. 'TITS!'

I fumbled about for a few moments before gingerly striking Wendy on the left nork with my fist.

'You think that'd stop her?' snorted the PSYCHO. 'She'd snap your scrawny throat and rip out your tongue. Swap over.'

We duly obeyed, with Wendy becoming the victim as I placed my hands around her neck.

'Man or woman?' he asked.

'She's a nasty male youth, with a hoodie,' said Wendy, with an alarming look in her eye.

'An oik,' sneered Kenny, pacing slowly and eyeing me up suspiciously. 'A wretched slimeball.'

They were both glaring at me in a way that made feel proper vulnerable, like a soft, cuddly wombat about to be mauled by two bloodthirsty dingoes.

'Whatcha gonna do, Wendy?' he teased. 'You gonna let him hurt ya?'

Wendy's eyes hadn't left mine. 'I'm gonna kick him hard in the knackers.'

And with that she raised her foot and slammed it right into my overfull bladder. The sounds around me became muffled, but the rush of blood pulsing through my skull was louder than a kick drum. My vision became blurry. I saw Petrina running towards me, but before I could speak everything went yellow.

Right before I passed out, it dawned on me that I'd just wet myself.

Well that's just BRILLIANT.

Afterwards, Petrina tried to reassure me that it could have happened to anyone, but I know for a fact that the only other person you'd ever find lying on the floor of a church hall in a puddle of their own wee is Matthew Ludlow.

I met Petrina for lunch in Manor Park today. We both take our lunch breaks at half-past twelve so we can catch up to find out what's been going on at work. To be honest, working at Blue Nile is fairly dull. Nile is visiting family in Jamaica at the moment, so it's just Dad and me running the shop. For the most part it's pretty dead, with only the odd customer drifting in every hour or so. Nevertheless I've managed to get in a fair bit of guitar practice this week and test out different makes of guitar, which has been brilliant. But it doesn't make for interesting gossip, unlike Skadi, where it's all going on! This week not only has Petrina prevented a potential shoplifter from walking out with seven packets of frozen fish fingers crammed down his trousers, BUT the tall black boy with razor-sharp cheekbones (who had been chatting to the Mancake at Matthew's party) has started working there. His name is Leon and Petrina says that, if she wasn't going out with Walter, she would have been mortified to have met such a proper real-time HOT boy in such an uncool location.

TOP 5 WORST PLACES TO BE WHEN MEETING A HOT BOY.

1. In the supermarket frozen meat aisle with three twelve-pound turkeys balanced in your arms (poor Petrina).

2. In an underwear department holding a bra, thus revealing your size and instantly stripping away any enticing nork mystery that there might have been.

3. In a chemist. Buying anything in a pharmacy is awkward. But you definitely don't want to meet a

74

hot boy when you are holding: spot cream, tampons, sanitary towels, facial hair cream, deodorant or any treatment for itchy lady parts. This would be akin to Level 6 on the Scale of Shame.

4. At a funeral. Last year at Great Aunt Edna's funeral one of the mourners was a teenage boy who looked a little bit like Josh Raven. But there was no way I would have been able to approach him as a) if we had got it together we'd always have death as our common link and b) he might have been a distant relative which means that we could have had inbred children (although a baby with two heads and a tail would be quite cool, especially if it could breathe fire).

5. Having a healthy snack in public. It's impossible to eat a banana without it looking hideously suggestive. I can't even eat one in front of Petrina and the memory of walking in on my mum eating a huge one in the bath will haunt my thoughts FOREVER. To be eating one in front of a hot boy is just too awful to even think about.

Felix Winters came into the shop this morning. He was looking for a new guitar amp to replace the one that he'd put his foot through after a row with Fiona, so I showed him the best in our range. Felix was wearing a T-shirt and tight jeans that made his bum cheeks look like two GIANT fruity gumballs. Yet for some reason, I didn't feel myself getting all tongue tied and stupid.

'Camel Toe sounded really cool at Matthew's party last week,' he said casually as he fiddled with the dials on a Fender Combo amp.

'Thanks,' I replied calmly.

What's going on? He's twiddling knobs in a suggestive way with his beautiful long fingers and I'm not even blushing or talking rubbish. Oh no. What if I've lost my mojo?

'Perkitits were . . . um . . . good,' I added.

Fiona and Lucy's stupid Perkitits have been on my mind almost constantly for the past week. I couldn't believe that they'd written such great, catchy pop songs. But then it had it dawned on me that they weren't actually original songs at all, but in fact covers of lesser-known songs by girl-fronted bands from decades ago. My parents have an entire section of their record collection dedicated to female-led bands and, being a music geek, I've listened to them all. So I was genuinely impressed that Fiona and Lucy had even heard of ancient but cool bands such as The Bangles, Hole, Sleeper and Echobelly.

Felix smiled proudly. He leaned in close. Normally I would have had an overwhelming urge to lick his face, but right then I felt . . . nothing.

Have my ovaries died?

'Me and Toby chose the songs and recorded the backing tracks,' he whispered. 'We've turned indie classics into pure synth-pop. Of course most people thought it was all original material.'

'Not me,' I said confidently. 'That L7 track is one of Mum's favourites.'

'I knew we couldn't fool you!' Felix flashed his perfectly straight teeth.

Nope. Not even a tummy lurch. Am I asexual like Paulette Dempsey? What has happened to me?

'You've got excellent taste,' he smiled and gave me a wink.

And there it was. That cheeky one-eyed gesture was all it took to remind me of the Mancake and my stomach flipped an acrobatic somersault.

That's it! The reason I'm totally over Felix is because I can't stop thinking about the Mancake. I need to see him again.

When I arrived home from work this afternoon, the only greeting I got was two messages on the answer phone:

Message 1. 'Hello. This is just a message to let you know that we are currently out of stock of our Vaginal Energy Crystal in Rose Quartz. We do however have it in Amethyst, Aventurine, Citrine, and Red Tiger Eye, which is super for aligning your root chakra and stimulating your sex drive. If you'd like to wait for the Rose Quartz, we should be getting more in about three to four weeks. Thank you.

OH MY GOD! I'm going to puke.

Message 2. 'Hi, this is John. I'm going to have to move

our next meeting a little later. So midday on Monday, instead of eleven. Hope that works for you. Let me know if that's inconvenient and we can reschedule. OK? Bye now.'

So the rapist my dad is meeting next week is called John. I have spent the afternoon Googling convicted 'rapists' with that first name and there are literally THOUSANDS. If in the future, I ever give birth to a little boy, I wouldn't dream of calling him John. The odds would be so unfairly stacked against him. The poor boy would be doomed from the moment he poked out his head and cried. If I have a boy I will call him something hopeful and strong like Mancake Junior or Josh Adonis.

Mei Miyagi has started a gay and lesbian holiday club called Mei's Gay Soirée. They meet every Sunday afternoon in McDonald's to 'hang out, make friends and enjoy gay life'. At first she and Kirsty Mackerby (who has a holiday job there for the summer thanks to her manager cousin putting in a good word for her) were the only members, but Mei was confident it would only be a matter of time before loads of other Bridge Mount pupils 'revealed their inner gayness' and signed up. Sure enough, the event gets busier every week. Mei strongly believes that every straight person has a would-be homosexual hiding inside. And she might have a point as I've often wondered if I've got lesbian potential. Looking around at the large turnout of curious Year 11 girls,

I could totally appreciate their beauty. I still wasn't sure I wanted to ever touch their lady parts, not that I would totally rule it out in the future of course.

There were just as many boys present at the soirée, but judging by the way they were gawping at any of the girls standing in pairs, I suspected they had come to check out any possible hot lesbian action (which quite frankly is never going to happen in a McDonald's restaurant. Unless of course you find greasy gerkins covered in cheesy mayonnaise sexually arousing, in which case you'll be in pervert heaven). Mei was proudly wearing the shirt that Matthew had defaced with a marker pen on the last day of term (it's traditional to write farewell notes all over each other's school shirt). But Matthew's 'special message' to his fellow Year 11s had been so explicit that the entire class were ordered to spend the day shrouded in dust sheets provided by the art department. Of course Mei had found the whole thing hilarious and was delighted to have what she called 'an empowering and beautiful word' scrawled across her chest. However, it clearly wasn't appropriate attire to wear in a fast food restaurant and in the end, having been threatened with ejection, Mei had no option other than to remove her shirt. And YES, she happily paraded round for the rest of the afternoon wearing just her bra, much to everyone's delight.

Josh Raven looks proper real time HOT as he links his arm through mine.

'Will you be my beard?' he asks.

'OK,' I reply.

I don't mind pretending to be Josh's girlfriend, especially as it will annoy all his fans who dream of being with him. Shielding our eyes from the dazzling flashlights of the paparazzi, Josh gallantly steers me towards the entrance of the Pink Cowboy night club. The plan has worked. Nobody suspects a thing. As far as they're concerned, Josh Raven is as straight as a Roman dual carriageway.

The gay and lesbian club is full of beautiful, confident people. I immediately spot a sexy looking strawberry-blonde lesbian, wearing a long, silky red dress. Wowzoids! SHE'S HOT!!!

Josh has wandered off to dance with some greasy, topless men, leaving me alone at the bar.

All at once, an alluring scent drifts under my nose – the unmistakable expensive spicy chocolate-covered baby elixir of seduction. The sexy strawberry-blonde is standing next to me. Her lips are plump and squashy. Her eyes are blue and sparkling. She is wearing loads of mascara, but has no black eye bogies. How can this be?

'Hey!' she says in a deep voice that I instantly recognize.

'MATTHEW LUDLOW?!!'

I'm all confused.

'I want you,' he murmurs.

I am surprised. 'I didn't know you were a gay lesbian,' I say.

'Yeah, I love ladies.' Matthew smiles. His teeth are like

glistening white Tic Tacs. 'I will lead you through the garden of joy,' he says.

His long eyelashes are beckoning me to join the lesbian sisterhood.

'Will I have to touch your lady parts?' I enquire.

'Yes of course,' he says.

I think about figs and melons for a few moments and in my heart I know that we can never be together.

'You are the most beautiful gay lesbian I have ever known, but I like my love interest to have bigger hands,' I want to let him know that it's not his fault. Matthew is distraught.

'I will always love you,' he sobs as I turn and walk out of his life forever.

A girl's lady parts are a massive hurdle that I'm not sure I can straddle. I'd never say never, but for now I'm on the hunt for a hot boy (but NOT Matthew Ludlow who I can't help but think of as a hot girl after that dream).

To cheer myself up after a pretty stressful week, I spent a couple of hours this evening looking at the profiles on the Dempsey Love website (I skipped the homepage of course). Members can now post and view profiles online and be matched purely on compatibility. Paulette's not one for beating around the bush and has made the 'criteria search' really concise. I typed in my basic details and hoped for the best.

I'M A... *girl looking for a guy (although I wouldn't rule out a lesbian match as long as I don't have to partake in any sexual touching).*

LOOKS:
Not fussy – although I don't want hot guys to think I am discriminating against them. I TOTALLY love hot guys. I just want it noted that I will lower my standards if need be.

HEIGHT:
Over 5ft 7, not that I'm racially prejudiced against short people of course.

HAIR:
Not fussy – as long as it's not on your back.

BUILD:
Not fussy although I'm not too keen on guys who spend so much time at the gym bulking up that their testicles shrivel up and go infertile. I intend to have children one day so I need to ensure that your testicles are more important to you than your biceps.

As soon as my profile went live, I checked that my information was correct.

Note to self: when putting up a dating profile, always check that the website displays your entire tagline in search results and doesn't cut them short.

User Name	Tagline
RAVENGIRLOO7	*I'm a hot-looking girl with a nice fig . . .*

THE BASICS

AGE: *15*
SEX: *Female*
HEIGHT: *5ft 10*
BUILD: *Marilyn Monroe hourglass figure*
HAIR: *blonde*
LOOKS: *attractive*

PROFILE

I'm a hot-looking girl with a nice figure and magnificent norks. When I leave school I will go to university to study linguistics or I will become a professional dancer.

IDEAL MATCH

Josh Raven lookalike or has at least five similar features

I might have bent the truth a little bit (I'm not actually sure what 'linguistics' is, though I think you have to be quite intelligent to study it), but that's what everyone does on the internet. There were five instant 'perfect' matches, which raised my hopes, but none of the avatars were actual mug-shot photographs (they were all cartoons or photos of everyday random objects. Mine was a picture of a black camel, which I think is pretty clever). I couldn't help but hope that one of them might have been the Mancake's profile, although I suppose someone as good-looking as him wouldn't need to be on a dating website in the first place.

User Name	Tagline
NINJABOY1	*I'll smack you in the face . . .*

THE BASICS

AGE: 15
SEX: Male
HEIGHT: 5ft 7
BUILD: athletic
HAIR: brown with blonde highlights
LOOKS: pretty awesome

PROFILE

I'll smack you in the face with my awesome love. I have a black belt in Karate, Ju-Jitsu, Taekwondo, No Kando, Sushigami and Ikea. I can do 500 press-ups on one finger and 1000 sit-ups with my legs crossed. AND I Karate-chopped my first concrete breeze block at the age of just two. Now aged fifteen I can Karate-chop through thirty-nine IN ONE GO. Hajime.

IDEAL MATCH

Fit, sexy, big tits, nice firm bum, long legs, silky hair. Not fussy about hair colour. Appearance isn't everything

User Name	Tagline
NATURIST4000	*I'm looking for a total dog . . .*

THE BASICS

AGE: 16
SEX: Male
HEIGHT: 5ft 10
BUILD: slim
HAIR: dark brown
LOOKS: average

PROFILE

I'm looking for a total dog-lover to share long country walks with. I love jumping in muddy puddles and sniffing the scents of nature. One of my top five smells in the whole world is the aroma of horse manure. It makes me feel alive and aroused. My other favourite smells are cow pats, bat faeces, pig dung and cock droppings.

IDEAL MATCH

Big teeth, ample bosom, sturdy thighs and a long face.

User Name	Tagline
LONELYLAD	Please help me get off . . .

THE BASICS

AGE: 16
SEX: Male
HEIGHT: 5ft 10
BUILD: average
HAIR: black
LOOKS: my mother says I'm distinguished-looking

PROFILE

Please help me get off this site by being my perfect match. I love dancing and, although I've never had an actual girlfriend before, I practise doing the tango every night with Veronica, my life-size clothes mannequin.

IDEAL MATCH

Petite, kind, loves dancing and preferably has clean fingernails.

User Name	Tagline
CUDDLY_LOVERLOVER	Come and see my crack . . .

THE BASICS
AGE: 16
SEX: Male
HEIGHT: 6ft 1
BUILD: cuddly
HAIR: blonde
LOOKS: baby blue eyes and chubby cute cheeks

PROFILE
Come and see my cracking profile. I'm fun, but considerate.
I'm a loveable cutie-pie with a big heart and a big cuddle
for the right girl.

IDEAL MATCH
I'm looking for a roly poly play mate. Ideal girl would look
like Velma from Scooby Doo. But with thicker legs and
blonde hair. Oh and glasses are a no no.
They remind me of my dead grandmother.

User Name	Tagline
I_AM_NOT_A_MURDERER	I hope to become a famous psycho . . .

THE BASICS
AGE: 16
SEX: Male
HEIGHT: 5ft 7'
BUILD: fit
HAIR: brown
LOOKS: chiselled and angular

PROFILE

I hope to become a famous psychotherapist when I leave school. Sigmund Freud is my hero. I strive to be just like him.

IDEAL MATCH

Someone who comes from an unstable, possibly violent, background and is looking for emotional help. I hope the right girl will join me in offering the fruits of their pain (i.e. tears caught in an egg cup) to my Sigmund Freud shrine in the corner of my bedroom . . .

User Name	Tagline
NOODLEBRAIN12	I've got a sexy six-pack . . .

THE BASICS

AGE: 16
SEX: Male
HEIGHT: 5ft 8'
BUILD: average
HAIR: strawberry blonde
LOOKS: average

PROFILE

I've got a sexy six-pack of Stella Artois that I'd like to share with someone special. I'm a fun guy who likes to party BIG TIME. WAAHOOOOOOOOOOOOOO!!!!!!!!!!!!!!!!!

IDEAL MATCH

Someone who strays from the flock.

I'll admit, it wasn't quite the result I'd been hoping for. Nevertheless, I decided to message Noodlebrain12 as I like the fact he's searching for 'someone who strays from the flock'.

From: RavenGirl007
To: Noodlebrain12
Sent: July 3rd 20:03:54

Hi!

Just thought I'd drop you a message seeing as I liked the look of your profile. You obviously like to have fun. Well, so do I! I'll do anything for an adrenaline kick. Apart from violence and cruelty to animals. I might be a crazy party girl, but I'm a pacifist and wouldn't knowingly harm even an ant. But otherwise I am TOTALLY up for all mad things. Apart from drugs and joy-riding. Oh and playing knock down ginger, which can be quite frightening for house owners (especially elderly ladies who live alone).

Anyway, get in touch if you want to find out more.
YAYBALLS!
RavenGirl007

I'm not actually exaggerating my wild side that much. I am after all the same girl who rode a motorbike in a house with two pieces of processed ham strapped to her hooters.

END OF WEEK 26. MY TABLE OF ACHIEVEMENT

SHAME LEVEL PEAK	9 (I am almost 16 years old and I wet myself in public. Thank goodness Petrina always 'does the double' as she was able to lend me a dry pair of knickers to walk home in) + 10 ('Great sex face' ARRRGGGGHHH). *Shame Level Total = 19*
GUITAR PRACTICE	4hrs 23 minutes. (We spent all of Saturday rehearsing for the Battle of the Bands competition. I was strumming so furiously that I made my finger bleed. Now THAT'S dedication.)
SNOGS	0
PARTY INVITATIONS	0

WEEK 27
PHALLIC BANANA

Dad and I left the house extra early this morning to receive delivery of a batch of Musicman Stingray bass guitars (his favourite) at the shop. We also put out the beautiful cherry-red Gibson ES-335 (my ABSOLUTE dream guitar) that had arrived over the weekend. It's a vintage 1960 model, supposedly once played by the rock 'n' roll legend Chuck Berry, and has to be locked up at night as it's so valuable. In terms of sexiness, it's right up there with Josh Raven, the Mancake and beatboxing. (SERIOUSLY, beatboxing's a natural aphrodisiac to me. Forget oysters, powdered rhino horns and liquidised deer testicles, it's the sound of a beatboxing boy that tickles my pickle).

Knowing that dad was set to meet a rapist in just a couple of hours, I decided to use this quality father/daughter time to get to the bottom of things.

'Dad, do you know a criminal called John?'

He slowly lowered the bass guitar that he'd been thumb-slapping for the past twenty minutes.

'Well . . .' he said thoughtfully. 'There's John Baker, who was arrested for possession of class A drugs, Jon Collins, who was done for having a cannabis farm, John Clinton, who did three months for criminal damage on an anti-capitalist march. Jonathan Braithwaite got done for being drunk and disorderly, oh and John Hawthorne, who was caught for indecent exposure . . . or was that Johnny Walker? No, Johnny Walker was a part-time rent boy. Why are you asking?'

'Because I know you are meeting a rapist called John,' I blurted out. 'That's why.'

Dad looked puzzled.

'I saw the note. "Monday 4th July. 11am. See the rapist."'

My father paused thoughtfully for a moment, then frowned.

'THERAPIST, Blossom,' he explained. 'John's my counsellor. He's helping me deal with my open relationship with your mum. She's become very sexually demanding and it's put a real on strain me. John thinks it might have something to do with her impending menopause, even though it's a good ten years away. But don't worry – we can talk it through tonight if you like over a nice cup of soya milk cocoa.'

The rapist. Therapist. Oh . . .

'No, you're all right,' I said, feeling a bit queasy at the thought of Dad discussing his 'sex strain'. 'But you need to work on your handwriting. It's appalling.'

Dad grinned and started furiously thumbing the bass strings again.

I wonder if John helps teenagers cope with parents who share WAY TOO MUCH private information?

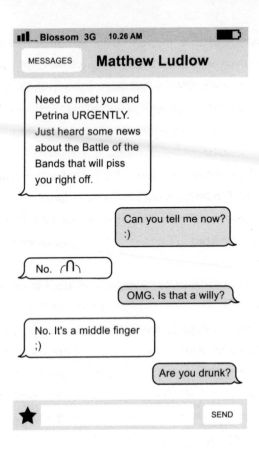

Fast forward an hour and a half and I was sitting anxiously in Joe's Café with Petrina on our lunch break, waiting for Matthew to tell us the news.

'Maybe the competition has been cancelled,' said Petrina, draining the dregs of chocolate milkshake through her straw.

'No, I checked the website before leaving,' I spluttered with a gobful of hamburger.

'Maybe the judging panel has been announced?'

'But why would that piss us off?' I wondered. 'Unless of course it's a panel of jazz musicians.' (It's a well-known scientific fact that jazz music is AWFUL and bad for your mental health.)

Petrina suddenly looked deadly serious. 'What if we've been moved into the "dance" category?' she whispered.

'Over my dead body,' I exclaimed.

Camel Toe's music is 'punch-the-air-helicopter-your-hair-electro-rock' NOT 'bum-shaking-arm-waving-dance'.

I nodded my head and pulled the intense 'bass face' that I had recently perfected in front of the mirror, to emphasise just how serious I was.

'Have you farted?' asked Petrina, edging away as she looked at my expression.

I was about to explain when Matthew came barging in, smiling broadly as soon as he saw us. His strawberry-blonde hair was styled differently – much shorter round the sides and back. It suited him, but didn't distract from his freshly spotty chin. He was fast developing the face of a functioning alcoholic (a term I learned off daytime TV). I made a mental note to forward him a link to the Alcoholics Anonymous website as soon as I got home.

'All right?' he asked. 'Can I get you both something to eat?'

Petrina and I had almost finished our tasty burgers.

'We're OK, thanks,' I replied. 'So what's the big news then?'

Matthew sat down on the chair opposite and clasped his hands on the table. He looked as if he was about to tell us something really awful. My mind quickly raced through the worst possible scenarios:

1. Matthew has been diagnosed with a terminal illness and wants me to be a pallbearer at his funeral (I do not ever want to be that close to a gross dead body).

2. Matthew DID have oral herpes that time we kissed at his party last term and as a result I have contracted a (dormant, but potentially explosive) sexually transmitted cold sore.

3. Or . . . *OH. MY. GOD. Is Josh Raven dead? Please don't tell me he's dead.*

'Perkitits are competing in Battle of the Bands,' said Matthew gravely.

THANK GOODNESS. Wait . . . WHAT?

'I know it's not ideal,' he continued. 'But at least they fall into the "pop" category so you won't be competing directly against them, unless . . .'

I laughed LOUDLY. 'They might be quite good but they'll never get to the final.' *Will they?*

But Matthew wasn't smiling. 'They're *really* good, Blossom. And Felix and Toby are pretty talented producers.'

'You can't polish a turd though, can you?' quipped Petrina.

'No, but you can sprinkle it with glitter and sequins,' said Matthew. 'And squeeze it into a tight, foxy catsuit.'

Suddenly my burger didn't taste quite as delicious anymore. What if it came down to a Camel Toe vs. Perkitits final? I couldn't help thinking the unthinkable: what if we lost?

From: <u>Noodlebrain12</u>
To: RavenGirl007
Sent: July 4th 21:14:01

Hey!

It was a nice surprise to get a message from you. I wasn't really expecting any replies as I'm not usually that popular with the girls. You are a girl aren't you? Ha ha ha! ;) So many people use the internet as a mask to hide their true identity. For all I know you could be the total opposite of your profile description!!! Ha ha ha!!! Yes – I love to have a good time, though I'd prefer not to have to do it alone. It would be cool to find someone to have fun with. Want to have some fun?

Cheers,
Noodlebrain12

From: <u>RavenGirl007</u>
To: Noodlebrain12
Sent: July 4th 21:33:23

Hi,

I'm always up for fun –as I said on my Dempsey Love profile – I'm an attractive blonde and we all know – blondes have more fun!! Which reminds me – I REALLY have to get my hair cut before I meet you for the first time. I might even go dark for a change. I've got an appointment with my hairdresser next Monday so maybe we could arrange a date (!!!) sometime after that? Whadda ya think?

RavenGirl007

I took out my frustrations on Wendy, the short-haired, slightly scary lady at my self-defence class that evening. Petrina really had to (literally) twist my arm to get me to go again after last week's mortifying incident. Kenny kindly only made one reference to it at the beginning of the class when he shouted, 'RIGHT ladies. We're not here to pee our pants like cowards. We're Trojans and TROJANS DON'T PEE THEIR PANTS. Let me hear you say it.'

The nervous women in the hall all quietly replied, 'Trojans don't pee their pants.'

Kenny placed his hands on hips, 'What's that? I CAN'T HEAR YOU.'

'TROJANS DON'T PEE THEIR PANTS.'

But after that Kenny didn't mention it again, so I was able to spend the evening elbowing Wendy violently in the norks (which was a brilliantly cathartic experience).

OH MY GOD. OH MY GOD. OH MY GOD.

I was alone in the shop, sitting cross-legged on the floor,

eating a casual banana and admiring the cherry-red Gibson ES-335, when the shop door opened and in walked THE MANCAKE. He was wearing a white T-shirt and those mesmerising ripped jeans with the thigh hole. His scruffy, blonde hair made his eyes look even more fabulously blue than I'd remembered,

Arrrgghhhh. I've got a phallic banana in my mouth. Nooooooo. This is THE ABSOLUTE WORST SITUATION.

'Wow, what a beauty,' he said looking the Gibson up and down.

I didn't dare move a muscle. Perhaps if I stayed very still he wouldn't notice the banana was there. If I tried to remove it, it would look as if I was trying to be sexually seductive, but if I bit off a chunk that would also seem flirtatious. It was a no win situation. He smiled at me and winked.

I bet someone super cool, like Josh Raven, would know what to do in a situation like this.

'I've seen you before,' he grinned. 'At that party the other week. You were pretty hot on stage.' He winked again. I was dying slowly inside. The sexiest guy I had ever encountered had just called me 'hot' and I couldn't reply because I had a banana wedged in my mouth. I was in a dilemma.

'You got a couple of plectrums?' he asked, his eyes fixed on my full mouth.

What would Josh Raven do?

'Blover blere,' I spluttered, accidentally chomping off a piece of the soft fruit.

Now what? Spit or swallow?

97

'Eh?' said the hot boy.

What would Josh Raven do?

I quickly swallowed the lump of banana.

'Over there,' I repeated, tossing the rest of the perverted fruit behind the rack of sheet music. I walked over to the counter where there was a whole shelf full of different-sized guitar picks. He chose a packet of standard Jim Dunlop Gator Grips and also bought a packet of nickel-plated steel guitar strings. Then he winked goodbye and walked out of the shop.

I ACTUALLY LOVE HIM (even if he does wink a bit too often).

Breeze turned up at home in a strop this afternoon, convinced that Andreas is having an affair with a woman at one of his Movie Nights London club nights. She is basing her accusations on the fact that he has been receiving flirtatious calls.

'His phone rings, he goes all glassy-eyed and says, "Hello, *moro mou*",' Breeze spat as I stood guard by MY bedroom. 'It's Greek for "my baby". He doesn't even call *me* "my baby".'

'That's because you hate terms of endearment. You think they're degrading.'

And it was true. Once when a landscaper remarked 'Cheer up, darling' as she passed him by in the park Breeze chased him out of the gates with his own gardening shears.

'That's not the point,' she fumed.

Subsequently, she wants to move back home again, but when Breeze attempted to reclaim her old bedroom from me, I firmly stood my ground by barricading myself across the doorway. It doesn't take much to ignite my sister's rage and within seconds she'd gone completely ballistic – eyes blazing, massive nostrils fanning. It's a good job I've been going to self-defence classes as I was able to swiftly elbow her in the nork before she'd even managed to grab hold of my hair. Self-defence is becoming as instinctive to me as breathing and song-writing. So strong was my resistance that my melodramatic sister is sleeping in the spare room.

Mum and Dad have welcomed their eldest daughter back into the fold with open arms, especially as she's agreed to join them when they take part in an organised protest against 'hydraulic fracking' at the nearby company head office. This is my parents' first protest for over nineteen years and to say they are excited is something of an understatement. They've been behaving like a couple of teenagers, singing their own protest songs and making crude banners ('Frack Off, You Motherfrackers') with marker pens and Sellotape.

'It's bloody outrageous,' screamed Mum as she watched a fracking item on the BBC news. 'Radioactive wastewater, chemical contamination. It should be classed as criminal behaviour, endangering public safety like this.'

If either of my parents dresses up as a superhero and climbs on top of Buckingham Palace then I'm hiring a solicitor and divorcing them.

While they were downstairs plotting their radical cheerleading chants, Petrina and I were playing a makeshift gig in my bedroom for Walter, whose opinion we always value. Camel Toe have been rehearsing like crazy for Battle of the Bands. Not only are we polishing our already tight set, we are also introducing a heart-wrenching ballad about sexuality that we've been working on (Petrina composed the music and I've written the lyrics). We're still restricted by the number of chords that we use as I haven't yet mastered bar chords on Cassiopeia, BUT it's amazing how many songs you can write based on just a handful of simple notes.

You're So Gay
By Blossom Uxley-Michaels and Petrina-Ola Olsen

(verse 1)
The way you act, no one would know,
The homosexual secrets you hide.
But I can see it, though. Come on and let it go,
Release the homosexual that's inside.

(bridge)
I'll be your beard, your goatie, your silky, side-burn sash,
I'll be your chin strap, your walrus, your pencil moustache.

(chorus)
You're so gay,
But that's really OK
I don't want to hurt ya,
Won't ever try to convert ya.

100

You're so gay, gay, gay.

(verse 2)
I really don't care whose hand you want to hold,
So let me be your gay protector,
It's not big news, so forget your silly ruse,
I've got a built-in gay detector.

(bridge)
I'll be your beard, your goatie, your silky side-burn sash,
I'll be your chin strap, your walrus, your pencil moustache.

(chorus)
You're so gay,
But that's really OK
I don't want to hurt ya,
Won't ever try to convert ya.
You're so gay, gay, gay.

(middle eight)
But if you ever spurn, the homo way, I'll be with ya, I'll flee with ya.
And if you ever turn, stop being gay, I'll weep with ya, oooh, I'll sleep with ya,

Repeat chorus.
Repeat verse 1
Repeat chorus to fade.

All participating acts have to perform three of their own tracks and one cover version of Steel Dragon's huge worldwide hit single 'Harassing Hot Women (They Love It)'. I can't help but wonder if Perkitits have an unfair advantage as ALL of their songs are covers.

OUR SET LIST IS AS FOLLOWS:

1. 'PONCERAMA' (we thought we'd open with a big crowd pleaser)

2. 'LUTRAPHOBIA' (we've never played our song about Petrina's crippling fear of otters live before)

3. 'YOU'RE SO GAY' (to show we are versatile and can be sensitive when required)

4. 'HARASSING HOT WOMEN (THEY LOVE IT)' (Petrina says that our feminist arrangement is 'an excellent example of how pervasive sexism can be'. I don't yet fully understand what that means, but Petrina has assured me that Emmeline Pankhurst would give our version the thumbs up if she were alive today.)

Out of courtesy, we invited Matthew to listen to the Camel Toe run-through, but he said he was too busy making our transport arrangements. Petrina's initial objection to our new manager has lifted now that Matthew's made it clear that he won't interfere with the creative side of the band. It seems his main goal is to get Camel Toe the maximum exposure that we deserve. So it was down to Walter to give us some constructive criticism.

'S'good,' he said in his typically succinct manner, after we'd poured our hearts into those five songs. Walter was stretched out on my bed with his arm draped casually across Boris, my pink fluffy bunny.

'Would you care to elaborate?' asked Petrina, sounding rather annoyed.

Walter shrugged. 'I like the one about Josh Raven,' he said.

Petrina and I looked at each other, slightly alarmed. How did he know that 'You're So Gay' was about Josh? I'd been so careful to keep the subject anonymous.

'What gave it away?' I asked.

Walter smiled. 'Oh, I dunno. Maybe it's just my amazing intuition.'

He might be right. Walter does have a remarkably astute sixth sense (like the time he knew his cat Picasso had been injured even before it turned up in the back garden with its head stuck in an empty frankfurter jar). It's almost as if Walter's fringe-induced visual impairment has forced his spiritual third eye to develop into something powerful and all-seeing.

The sign reads The World of Wonders: Strangest Show on Earth. *I walk amongst the freaks and oddities, past The Boy With An Ear On His Forehead, around The Girl In Year 12 Who Is Rumoured To Have Three Nipples and through The Tunnel Of Merkins. Then I notice a tall, striped tent that says* Monsieur

Walter Ecclestone: Les Fortune Teller Très Spooky. *Against my will, I find myself being drawn towards it. It's as if I am a pigeon in flight, trying to resist the coos and calls of the dirty old tramp tossing stale Twiglets on to the pavement below in Trafalgar Square.*

I step inside the tent. It smells of destiny. Sitting cross-legged on the floor behind a low table is a teenage boy. His eyes are obscured by his long fringe, which pokes out from underneath the enormous shiny turquoise turban that sits on his head. He holds out his hand.

'Cross my palm,' he says.

'I've only got a tenner,' I reply. 'Do you have any change?'

'You get what you pay for,' he mumbles.

I hand him the ten-pound note and silently vow to myself that I'll contact the Trading Standards Agency the moment I get home if he doesn't give me a 100% accurate reading.

He shuffles the deck of cards that sit face down in front of him. He lays them out in a heart shape. I am anxious. My future is about to be revealed. Monsieur Ecclestone turns over the first card. It's Mr Bacon the Butcher.

'Romance is around the corner,' he says as he turns over the next card. It's Miss Streetwalker the Prostitute's daughter.

Monsieur Ecclestone nods wisely. 'I see a pale boy who lacks the love and attention he deserves at home.'

I quickly run through a list of the boys that I know – it can't be Felix, because he isn't pale. I rule out Matthew Ludlow (phew), whose wealthy parents give him everything he could ever want. Then who could it be . . . the Mancake? OH YES PLEASE.

'What is his hair like?' I NEED TO KNOW.

'Shortish.'

'What colour?'

'I don't know. I only see in black and white. Lightish.'

The Mancake has lightish hair. That'll do nicely.

The Fortune Teller has a grave expression on his face as his hand hovers over the final card. I gulp a little too hard, forcing a small burp to rise in my throat. I don't think he heard it. I watch as he slowly turns it over. WOWZOIDS. It's Master Snuffet the Undertaker's son. This is THE WORST CARD IN THE DECK. Monsieur Ecclestone throws his head back and laughs one of those evil 'mwahaha' laughs. He sweeps his fringe to one side. OH MY GOD. He has no eyes. Only deep, dark cavernous holes filled with wriggling worms. I scream my head off and run out of the tent as fast as I possibly can.

✳ ✳ ✳

Petrina, Walter and I decided to show Mei a bit of support and solidarity at her Gay Soirée in McDonald's. The weather was glorious as we walked through Manor Park – the kind of day that makes all your worries just evaporate into the sunshine. That is until we came to the slangers, who were basking in the sun like a couple of cold-blooded komodo dragons trying to feel human.

'Look Lucy,' sneered Fiona as she rubbed sun cream into her already tanned legs. 'Bumface's mum has been at her hair with the organic gardening shears.'

I have GOT to get my Glastonbury lopjob hair sorted out. Roll on Monday.

'Just ignore them.' Petrina was sweating buckets. Her cardigan was zipped up to the neck and she was wearing her thickest winter tights. She looked like she might faint at any moment.

'You won't be able to ignore us soon,' giggled Lucy. 'Not when you find out who's on the competition judging panel.'

But the judges haven't been announced yet. How did they get inside information?

Walter firmly ushered us on before we could rise to Lucy's bait. But Petrina had been visibly aggravated to such a degree that she overheated and had to be carried by her boyfriend to Mei's Gay Soirée, where a large group of Bridge Mount pupils had gathered in McDonald's.

Just as Mei predicted, the event was continuing to prove incredibly popular. Although, rather than being the coming together of like-minded people that Mei had intended, most members had signed up because of the ten percent discount and free McDonald's Happy Meal toy that Kirsty had promised. In fact the lure of a pair of multi-coloured flashing Snow White sunglasses was so successful that within half an hour Walter, Petrina (who had by then recovered) and I had all signed up as members too. Who says bribery doesn't pay?

END OF WEEK 27. MY TABLE OF ACHIEVEMENT

SHAME LEVEL PEAK	9 – having a huge phallic banana in my mouth in front of a HOT guy was akin to being caught naked in public.
GUITAR PRACTICE	5hrs 1 minute (Camel Toe are sounding AWESOME right now.)
PARTY INVITATIONS	0
SNOGS	0

WEEK 28
BUMSKULLS

My hairdresser is a woman called Gayle with an asymmetrical, bright red bob.

'Hmmm. This is a right mess, Blossom. You could probably get away with a really short crop, y'know,' she said.

'No thanks. My hair is my shield.'

Gayle stepped back to get a proper look at me. She nodded and smiled. 'Yeah, short hair would suit you cos you've got a face like a pygmy marmoset.'

'A what?' I literally had no idea.

Gayle wandered off to the magazine rack and pulled out a copy of *National Geographic*. She flicked through the pages.

'I was looking at this in my fag break,' she said, holding the scissors between her teeth. Her low-cut black top revealed a tattoo of what I initially thought was a sperm swimming towards her gigantic nork, but that she later explained was a tadpole returning to the horny toad, which was (thankfully) hidden next to her left nipple. 'It's much more interesting than those celeb magazines,' she continued. 'Who wants to see an A-list wedding when you can learn all about the mating rituals of a sea hare. It's well interesting. They're actually hermaphrodites. Do you know what that is?'

'Yes, I do thanks.' I was pretty sure I'd come in for a haircut, not a biology lesson.

'Ah, here it is,' said Gayle thrusting the magazine in front of my face. 'A pygmy marmoset. Imagine it wearing goth clothes. That's you, that is.' She smiled as if she'd just paid me the kindest compliment ever.

In front of me was a picture of a tiny, short-haired monkey from the upper Amazon basin. I'm not going to lie – it was an ugly little fella. Suddenly I was distracted from the awkwardness of being compared to a miniature New World primate when my phone pinged with a text message.

As I'd taken a couple of days off work to sort out my hair and get in a bit of band practice (Petrina had taken the day off too), I suggested Petrina and I met Matthew at his place. But he said it wasn't a good time, so instead he came round to my house an hour later. It was a lovely afternoon and the three of us sat on a picnic blanket in the centre of Polystyrene Stonehenge (which Mum and Dad love so much that they're keeping it until the end of summer).

'Your parents are really cool,' said Matthew, biting into the floppy ham sandwich that I'd rustled up.

'You are kidding?' I snorted, enjoying the fact that my hair was now level on all sides. 'They dance around naked at every full moon, they're swingers AND they're going on an anti-fracking protest tomorrow where they intend to chain themselves to the railings.'

'What at Goldmill Resources HQ?' he asked, looking slightly panicked.

'Yeah,' I said shaking my head. 'The shame.'

'My dad's on the board of directors,' he mumbled, looking down.

'But I thought he was the boss of Ludlow's Luxury Loos,' enquired Petrina.

Matthew was urgently pulling out blades of grass. 'Yeah, he is . . . but he's got loads of other business interests. Singapore . . . Germany . . . all around the world. Making money is the only thing he knows how to do.' His eyes had become pink and watery. Another sure sign of his ever-worsening alcoholism. Matthew then seemed to suddenly remember that he'd brought a plastic bag with him and he opened it roughly.

'Here,' he said tossing two pieces of dark fabric to each of us. 'Your new Camel Toe T-shirts.'

WOWZOIDS!!!! They were brand new, black, uber cool T-shirts (Petrina's was long sleeved of course) with a funked-up Camel Toe logo on the front and *Ludlow's Luxury Loos: drop your anchor in comfort* embroidered on the back.

'They're fantastic, Matthew,' said Petrina, holding it up proudly.

'Yeah, thank you,' I said. 'And thank your dad, too. It's good to know he has enough confidence to invest in us.'

'So come on then.' Petrina nudged Matthew with her elbow. 'You've kept us waiting long enough. Who are the judges?'

'They were only confirmed this morning,' Matthew explained. 'The heat judges are Pete Hartley and Margo Tittledown.'

Silence . . .

Pete Hartley is the legendary producer who has worked with some of the world's biggest artists including Josh Raven and Camel Toe!! Margo Tittledown is the chairperson of Brambledown Sports and Leisure Group (including Brambledown Golf Club, where the four heats, the quarter-finals and semi-finals will be taking place) and mother of the number one slanger in town, Fiona Tittledown.

'But the judges are supposed to be impartial,' said

111

Petrina. 'This surely gives Perkitits an unfair advantage.'

'Wouldn't the slangers argue that *we've* worked with Pete Hartley?' I asked.

'He's an experienced professional,' Petrina said firmly. 'He's had physical fights with world-famous musicians who couldn't handle his criticism. Pete's not going to feel obliged to do us a favour.'

I knew she was right. Pete's rock 'n' roll punch ups are as legendary as his musical genius (like the time he told Nik Nutter from Steel Dragon that they needed to do another take because Nik had played a bum note. Nik lived up to his name, smashing his bass guitar over Pete's shoulder before the producer retaliated by breaking a kick drum over the bass player's head). Not only that, Pete's taken so many drugs in the past that I'd be surprised if he can actually remember who we are anyway.

'I don't really see it as being a problem,' said Matthew, who had gone back to yanking out individual blades of grass. 'Camel Toe are a class act. Nothing and no one can take that away.'

After finishing our floppy sandwiches we went inside to rehearse for our Wednesday evening heat. We asked Matthew to stay and watch, but he said he had to pop to the supermarket to pick up some 'essentials' for his mum. She sounds like a right slacker to me – rich husband keeping her in a fancy home and two crazy, alcoholic sons running all over the place for her, tending to her every need. Nice life eh?

From: Noodlebrain12
To: RavenGirl007
Sent: July 11th 22:54:21

Hey!
How's your hair?
**So do you still fancy going out sometime then?
Maybe we could do something really crazy like go to
Disneyland Paris on Eurostar? We could probably have
Champagne in First Class. Don't worry about the cost
– it's my shout.**

Cheers,
Noodlebrain12

Mum, Dad and Breeze (who is still sleeping in the spare room) left the house early to join the peaceful protest at the Goldmill Resources head office. The camper van had been rigged up with banners and loud speakers so that they could really get their message heard. All went to according to plan, with around forty-one protesters staging the demonstration (where Flying Rapunzel's song 'Fracking is a Dirty Word' became the theme tune for the day). Then, just after lunch, Dad got a bit carried away and decided to jump up and down on Roy Ludlow's silver Bentley. The board members were greatly offended at this affront to their CEO and Roy (who was back in town) took it upon himself to remove the 'vandal'

from the car roof, causing a scuffle between the activists and the Goldmill security guards. The police were called and as a result thirty-four of the forty-one protesters were arrested and thrown into police cells – including Breeze and my parents.

They were eventually released a few hours later without charge (Breeze was so relieved to see Andreas when he came to pick them all up that she has forgotten their argument and gone back to the flat), but the excitement of the day's events appears to have given Mum and Dad some kind of legal high. Mum was literally off her face on the adrenaline, giggling and shrieking like a frenzied raver. Dad's reaction was more subdued, with a melancholy expression and heavy eyelids as if he were stoned.

'Are you in a mood because I was flirting with the security guard?' asked Mum as she practised her downward-facing dog yoga pose.

'No,' slurred Dad, who was observing Mum as he lay resting on the sofa next to me. 'John has helped me understand that I need to believe in my own sexual supremacy. I can fulfil you. I WILL fulfil you.'

I AM TOTALLY GOING TO BE SICK.

'Let's do this again,' whooped Mum. 'I fancy saving some sea birds. Let's find a massive offshore oil slick to get cross about. We could chain ourselves to the rigging. Naked.'

Sometimes having a politically opinionated, liberal-minded family is just simply the most awful thing EVER. As a teenager, rebellion against my parents is a rite of passage and a stepping stone into finding my true adult identity, so that I can ceremoniously cut the invisible umbilical cord that emotionally binds us together. But it's going to be tricky rebelling against people who have generally pushed the boundaries of all that is socially acceptable and legal to the very limit. So it's taken me a lot of time and consideration to work out my own effective teenage rebellion plan that would get up the noses of my stupid, leftie, hippie parents.

TOP 5 INSTANT WAYS TO REBEL AGAINST MY WOOLLY LIBERAL PARENTS

1. Join the Young Conservatives (this would be a really effective act of rebellion, but I think you have to come from a posh family of drunken tax avoiders to actually qualify which rules me out).

2. Join the Territorial Army (after the Glastonbury Festival 'tent in my hair' ordeal, I'm not sure I could put myself into any situation where I have to camp again. Plus their uniforms look really itchy).

3. Take up a violent competitive sport like cage-fighting or bare-knuckle boxing (self-defence classes are all very well, but, as pacifists, Mum and Dad would HATE me to partake in anything combative. Thing is I really don't like the idea of grappling with other sweaty women whilst wearing a leotard).

4. Become a fame-seeking reality TV star (Mum and Dad hate 'celebrity culture', believing that people should be recognised for their outstanding achievements and merits rather than just because they've sprayed themselves orange and had sex with seven Premier League footballers).

5. Become a Daily Mail reader (ha ha ha ha ha!)

Number five seems the easiest. I've set a reminder on my phone to pick up a copy of the *Daily Mail* on my next lunch break.

So it turns out that not only is the Mancake just as mancakey as I remember, he's also a *musical* Mancake. Quite frankly he couldn't be any more perfect.

Brambledown Golf Club wasn't the ideal place for a cool, edgy Battle of the Bands music venue, but it had easy access to public transport, a stage, professional lighting and a brilliant sound system (courtesy of Pete Hartley). The walls had been decorated with huge posters of some of the biggest names in music (from about forty or fifty years ago) and sawdust had been scattered all over the floor to create an authentic, last-century feel.

The tickets had all sold out for Heat 1 and the venue was packed – a heaving mass of young music lovers full of expectation and excitement. Petrina, Walter, Matthew and I stood at the back of the room drinking Coke and soaking up the atmosphere. In front of the stage was a table, behind which sat the two judges. Pete Hartley, who had greeted Petrina and I warmly when we arrived (thank God he remembered us), was as brightly dressed as ever in his Hawaiian shirt and leather waistcoat. And then there was Fiona's mum, Margo. She wore an expensive-looking, electric-blue, tailored trouser-suit, was sporting rock-solid, back-combed blonde hair, and her obviously Botoxed forehead and drawn-on eyebrows gave her an expression of constant anger. She looked like an evil humanoid from a futuristic Conservative party political broadcast. Fiona and Lucy were noticeable in their absence. Walter thought they might be rehearsing, but Petrina and I figured they were more likely to be at home picking each other's fleas and watching reality TV.

HEAT 1. URBAN/DANCE –
The Judges' Comments

BAND	PETE'S COMMENTS	MARGO'S COMMENTS
GLAD 'E' 8ERS	'uninspired'	'I was clicking my fingers to your hipperty hopperty beat'
JUICY JANES	'surprisingly good'	'I thought you were really groovy'
SOVEREIGN NRG	'interesting'	'You made my tush shake'
BUMSKULLS	'a breath of fresh air'	'It's very loud'

The first band on stage was an all-male hip-hop group called Glad 'E' 8er, who were cool and uber slick. Juicy Jane were a funky mixed four-piece who got everybody dancing. Sovereign NRG were an all-girl electronic dance trio with street cred. And then there was Bumskulls. Four guys with attitude playing old skool Breakbeat hardcore, fronted by the boy I had been lusting over ever since Matthew's party three weeks ago. I was transfixed. He was emitting the same kind of sexy, rock god aura that radiated from Josh Raven when he performed on stage at Glastonbury. My eyes were immediately drawn to the rip in his jeans at the top of his left thigh.

GOD, that thigh hole is so hot it ought to be ILLEGAL!

Petrina stood next to me, looking equally gobsmacked, as her TOPLESS, chisel-faced colleague Leon slammed on his bass guitar.

'He mentioned he was in a band,' she gawped. 'But I never guessed . . . I mean he's so quiet and polite at work, but up there he's . . . he's wearing LEATHER trousers!'

Her voice trailed off as Leon snarled and aggressively thrust his groin towards the audience. I couldn't help but notice Walter shifting uncomfortably while Petrina quickly wiped away the giveaway dribble that had appeared in the corners of her mouth (Petrina produces excessive saliva whenever she finds someone attractive). But he needn't have worried as his girlfriend is as loyal as a Focker Spaniel (the Cocker Spaniel and Fox Terrier crossbreed that wouldn't leave my great aunt Edna's side).

Beside Leon, the Mancake strutted about like he owned the stage. He was a natural front man, his rock 'n' roll charisma radiating from his presence like a sexually attractive hot-water bottle. He spotted me in the audience and flashed a grin in my direction. Petrina nudged me with her elbow, just in case I'd missed it. AS IF! But I couldn't help wondering why a boy as perfect as the one on stage would give a Weirdo like me a second glance. I'm as forgettable as my Mum's car keys. He rounded off a perfect, testosterone-fuelled set by stage diving into the adoring audience who passed him around above their heads as if they were servants carrying their Roman Emperor on his luxurious lectica (which was a kind of portable bed. I remember this fact because in the same lesson we were also told that Queen Cleopatra was reclining on one when a poisonous snake bit her on the nork and killed her. What a way to go).

Of course, Bumskulls were one of the two acts sent through to the quarter finals along with Sovereign NRG.

'Hi,' said the blonde GORGEOUS Mancake, when I 'accidentally' knocked his arm as he stood at the bar. 'So do you think the best bands got through?'

Play it cool Blossom. Play it cool.

'I'm not sure,' I said, EVER so casually. 'I always like to sit on the face.'

ARRRRRGGGGHHHHHHHHHHH!

'FENCE . . . Sit on the FENCE.'

The proper real time HOT Mancake SEX GOD smiled and

moved even closer. I could smell his breath. If I could have inhaled that sweet scent then I would have filled my lungs until they exploded.

'I'll come and watch your band tomorrow night if you like?' he whispered. 'I *really* liked your onstage outfit.'

His eyes wandered slowly down towards my chest and I suddenly remembered the long string of toothpaste that I'd gobbed all down my black top just before I left the house.

No! Don't look at my dribble. Look at my eyes. I'm fluttering my eyelashes. Look! Look!

But before I could explain that I wasn't the human equivalent of a drooling St Bernard dog, there was an enormous crash. Matthew had apparently been breakdancing. He'd somehow managed to split his forehead and lip open when he attempted a one-armed handstand and toppled into the audio mixing desk. Yet, despite the gallons of blood that were gushing from his face, any pain he might have felt was secondary to the astonishing fact that he hadn't spilt any of the rum and Coke he was holding in his free hand. Looking at him lying flat on his back, in the middle of the venue, while the students around him laughed and jeered, I wondered if we'd done the right thing inviting Matthew to steer the career of Camel Toe. Tomorrow is the biggest night of our lives so far. What if he lets us down?

I couldn't sleep. Too many horrendous scenarios whizzing through my mind at a hundred miles an hour.

The crowd go wild chanting our name excitedly.

'Camel Toe, Camel Toe, Camel Toe!'

They are all in floods of tears. Our rendition of 'You're So Gay' was so moving that we have had to provide a counselling service at the back of the venue. God we are GOOD.

The tempo changes as we begin the rousing intro to 'Harassing Hot Women (They Love It)'. Right at the front of the stage is the Mancake. He is drenched in sweat and wearing only a vest and tiny sports shorts (this is NOT a pervy sex image. He has actually just come straight from the gym, where he worked primarily on his inner thigh muscles). He flashes a dazzling smile at me. He wants me. And I want him. But not yet. Right now I only have eyes for ELECTRO ROCK.

The raw energy of the audience is astounding. It's as if everyone knows that this is a significant moment in pop culture and we are all making musical history. Fists pounding the air, mouths sounding the lyrics. I am so proud. This is me. This is my destiny.

And then, from nowhere, something comes whizzing through the air and strikes me hard on the forehead. A bottle of rum. I am a true professional. I ignore the pain and blood, ploughing my thoughts back into my music. I strum my mega expensive, cherry-red Gibson ES-335 guitar more furiously than ever before. It's as if my right hand was possessed by the spindly (non-arthritic) fingers of a speed knitting world champion.

And then, from the back of the room, I see something being flung towards me. My eyes are fast and I spot the culprits. The slangers, laughing and pointing as a tampon soaked in Coca Cola comes hurtling towards me. This time I am poised, I think, but the tampon speeds through the air like a menstrual missile and hits me hard in the eye. As it drops down, the cord catches on the end of the fret board where it comes to rest, dangling down like a soggy, feminist talisman. I can hear a few sniggers arising from the audience. The Mancake is watching me. He is not smiling any more. I swallow my pride and continue playing as if nothing has happened. And then, before I can prepare myself, I am struck by a HUGE sexually phallic banana, right on my bladder. And that's when I knew I should have gone to the toilet before the show. It happened at self-defence and it was happening again. I felt a warm rush cascading down my legs. Oh brilliant. I am three weeks away from turning sixteen and I am incontinent. The crowd is laughing . . . laughing . . . pointing . . .

I turn to explain to the Mancake, but he has gone. Our fiery passion has been extinguished by a shower of yellow rain before it even began.

And I am alone on the stage . . .

Alone . . .

Alone . . . forever . . .

When I woke the next day I not only felt nervous about our impending heat that night, but I was literally sick to the stomach with desire. Butterflies are one thing, but being on the verge of puking my guts up at the mere thought of a boy is surely not normal. Am I suffering from actual lovesickness or was that late-night corned-beef, pork luncheon meat and bacon sarnie not such a great idea after all? And how can it be that my physical health has been so affected by a boy whose name I don't even know? I was very rudely shaken from my pit of self-doubt and nausea when Mum's voice rang out loudly from downstairs.

'Stay still! The health benefits are endless.'

'Well please be a bit more gentle,' said Dad.

'Don't be stupid,' yelled Mum. 'Open your backward little mind and embrace the scrotum-biting.'

My ears are melting.

'Come back! It's good for you.'

Petrina and I were both still off work to relax so that we would be fresh and full of energy for our performance in Heat 2 tonight. We didn't have the budget for a five-star spa hotel facial treatment and massage, but Matthew treated us (and Walter) to a slap up dinner at Pizza Express instead.

'So did your dad mention anything about the protest?' I enquired.

'Didn't get the chance to ask,' Matthew shrugged. 'He was on a plane to New York by the end of the day.'

'Your mum must be so easy going,' said Petrina. 'Mine would have a FIT if my dad was away that much. She always says, "If you give a man too much freedom, he'll knock up the nearest Elkhound."'

'Is that a Norwegian saying?' I asked.

'No, it's a quote from her favourite book, *Why Men Are Like Dogs*.'

I quickly tried to think of some other similarities between men and dogs.

1. ~~They cock their legs on lamp posts~~
2. ~~They try to dry hump sofa legs~~
3. ~~They poo in the flowerbeds~~
4. ~~They bark at the postman~~
5. They are too big to get in the house through a cat flap

I have absolutely no idea how the author managed to find enough comparisons to write a whole book.

Matthew was visibly uncomfortably with the topic of conversation. He fumbled anxiously around in his pockets as if he were searching for something (probably his hip flask). 'Our gardener will pick us all up in the van,' he said, changing the subject. 'He'll be round at six thirty. His name is Bob Ollox.'

A gush of Coke came cascading out of Walter's nostrils. 'Let me guess – he's an ex-punk with a stutter."

'Yep', confirmed Matthew. 'He's been our gardener for as long as I can remember. He's like a member of the family'

I thought about my parents and found myself longing for my own ridiculously named family gardener who ate meat, didn't openly discuss sex at breakfast and wasn't planning a massive Hot Flush party to welcome 'the menopausal phase of life'. God, how I wish Bob Ollox was my mum.

Once again, the golf club venue was packed full of excited teenagers ready for the competing bands. Camel Toe were fourth on the bill, which would give us the chance to check out all the other acts in the Indie/Rock category. We'd arrived with all our equipment in a proper van (driven erratically by Bob Ollox, who had a shaved head and a tattoo of a raised middle finger in the centre of his forehead) which made us feel a bit like real rock stars. It put me in the right frame of mind and helped me to feel prepared for our performance. I knew we looked great in our new Ludlow's Luxury Loos-sponsored Camel Toe T-shirts, and my Tena Lady pad gave me reassurance in case of any accidental onstage leakage (I pulled my hood right over my face when I bought them from Boots just in case there were any hot boys lurking about. Mum doesn't use Tena Lady pads. She says that, despite having pushed out two kids, her 'vaginal muscles are as tight as a gnat's bumhole' due to constant yoga and clenching. Bleurrrggh!)

The first two acts on stage, Blowtorch Child and The Humphreys, were both solid indie acts, but it was the hard-rock band Liquid Maggot who really worried us. They looked good, sounded great and had the excitement factor that so many bands lack. Even if rock isn't your bag, Liquid Maggot made you sit up and listen. When it was our time to go on stage, we went out and gave as good as we possibly could. No bad notes, no fluffed lyrics and not a single drop of wee in my pants.

HEAT 2. INDIE/ROCK –
The Judges' Comments

BAND	PETE'S COMMENTS	MARGO'S COMMENTS
BLOWTORCH CHILD	'adequate'	'Lovely, pretty girls'
THE HUMPHREYS	'dull'	'I think you are brilliant. Really with it'
LIQUID MAGGOT	'electrifying'	'I think I've gone deaf'
CAMEL TOE	'effervescent'	'Boring'

My parents watched on proudly with Matthew, while Fiona Tittledown and Lucy Perkins stood with their arms folded, glaring at us during our five song set to try and distract us and make us slip up. Then, when the judges gave their thoughts, the slangers booed at the glowing, positive comments Pete showered upon us. It was obvious that Fiona had told her mum Margo to call us 'boring' – she was dancing and singing along to Poncerama as enthusiastically as everyone else. But Petrina and I were immune to the ill will sent in our direction, thanks to the protection of a SHIELD OF TESTOSTERONE-FLAVOURED HOTNESS. Yes, that's right, at the very front of the stage, pounding the air with their fists, were Walter, the Mancake AND Leon – the mega sexy

Bumskulls bassist and Petrina's Skadi workmate. However, rather than putting us off, the sight of these beautiful male creatures (I am speaking for Petrina as well – I do NOT fancy Walter) spurred Camel Toe on to be utterly AWESOME.

After it had been announced that Liquid Maggot and Camel Toe had gone through to the quarter-final (YAAAAAAY!!!!), Leon came up to congratulate his colleague. Petrina was standing with me and Walter at the bar when he came over in his white vest top, which showed off his dark, toned biceps.

Wow! He's even more beautiful up close.

'You were brilliant, Petrina,' he said, flashing an affectionate smile.

'Thanks,' she replied casually, although I could see that a small blob of saliva had formed in the corner of her mouth. Perhaps Walter had noticed too as he shuffled a little closer to her.

'This is my boyfriend, Walter,' Petrina said.

Leon held out his hand. 'I'm Leon,' he smiled warmly.

Walter dug his hands into his pockets and rudely stared down at his scruffy Converse boots until Petrina nudged him hard in the ribs with her elbow.

'Hi,' he mumbled reluctantly under his breath.

Leon retracted his unshaken hand. Petrina had gone a bright shade of pink. This was not a good sign. The obvious blushing and the increased production of saliva was a sure sign that my best friend found this boy attractive. Not that

127

she would ever actually *do* anything about it as she is totally and utterly in love with her boyfriend.

'And I'm Blossom,' I added. 'Petrina's best friend. And Walter's best friend.'

I gave the lovely Leon a warning look, but he just smiled back and watched as Petrina shuffled off after her boyfriend who had begun to walk away.

'There's something stuck on your foot,' said a familiar, SEXY voice.

THE MANCAKE!

I reached down and, sure enough, there was what looked like a piece of paper attached to the bottom of my right DM boot. The last time someone told me I had 'something stuck on my foot' I was mortified to find a pair of brown Scooby Doo knickers hanging out the end of my trouser leg. Whatever was down there at that moment, it couldn't have been any more embarrassing than cartoon dog pants. OR COULD IT. I reached down to my shoe.

'Oh God,' I trembled, holding out the Tena Lady pad in my hand.

This is the absolute WORST.

'It's OK,' said the hot singer understandingly. 'I've got sisters. It's cool.'

'What? Oh! No.' I had to set him straight. 'I don't have my period.'

Stop it, Blossom.

'I use tampons.'

Shut up for God's sake.

'This is an incontinence pad in case I wet myself.'

Somebody kill me NOW.

Amazingly, the two boys didn't turn and run for the fire exit. Instead they laughed loudly, as if I'd just told the funniest joke ever. Then the Mancake reached out and gently PUNCHED MY SHOULDER.

'My name's Vince,' he said.

'Vince is a really cool name,' I spat.

Why can't I speak normally?

Vince shook his head. 'Not when your surname is Aston-Granger.'

I paused.

The cogs in my brain whirled round . . .

Tick, tock, tick, tock . . .

And then . . .

'OH MY GOD!'

It's fate. Not only does he fit the 'shortish, lightish hair' description that Monsieur Ecclestone foretold, he's also been burdened with the initials V.A.G. This has GOT to be love. VAG and BUM. Separated only by a tiny sensitive skin of destiny.

'So would you like to maybe hang out with me tomorrow?' he asked.

At that moment (aside from holding a Tena Lady pad in my hand) I LITERALLY couldn't have been any happier.

'Does the Pope poo in the woods?' I exclaimed.

'You're quite uninhibited aren't you?' he breathed in a sexy voice.

I wasn't entirely sure what he meant – I'm not a fan of

nakedness like my crazy parents. Before I could correct him, I spotted Matthew Ludlow out of the corner of my eye. He waved and then began busting some serious dance moves even though there was no music playing. I assumed he must have been drunk again.

From: Noodlebrain12
To: RavenGirl007
Sent: July 13th 22:56:33

Hey!

You didn't reply to my last message so I'm guessing the date is off. Was it the mention of Champagne that made you change your mind? I probably sounded like a right flash idiot. Never mind. Still, I was hoping you can help me out – I'm locked out of my house and I seem to have lost my clothes. Have you got any idea where they might be?

Cheers
Noodlebrain12

From: RavenGirl007
To: Noodlebrain12
Sent: July 13th 23:00:10

Hi!

It wasn't the mention of Champagne (which would have been nice!). I just got distracted by my personal life. It's mad how things can be so boring and then suddenly get so exciting and complicated!

I have no idea where your clothes are, but I might still be able to help you. Why don't you make a racket in the garden (a fox mating cry would be quite easy to imitate or a dying owl might be effective). Then, when your parents come down to see what the noise is, you can make a quick dash into the house without them seeing you naked. That's what I would do.

RavenGirl007
P.S. Are you drunk?

From: Noodlebrain12
To: RavenGirl007
Sent: July 13th 23:10:12

Hey!

My parents aren't home – it's only me and my brother tonight and he's got a girl in his room. I know he'd go crazy if I disturbed him. But I just tried the dying owl impersonation and he came outside, just like you said. While he was attacking the bush with a snooker cue, I managed to slip inside unseen. Now he won't shove

my head into the tropical fish tank like the last time I locked myself out.

That was a great idea . Thank you.

Cheers

Noodlebrain12

P.S. I'm not drunk. I'm just a bit merry.

YES – I am now a sexy, womanly lady who reeks of oestrogen and arousing, childbearing hormones. I have a date with a genuine, proper real time hot SEX GOD. When I told Mum that I would be meeting the singer of Bumskulls she gave me a stern warning.

'Remember, the good-looking pedigrees are extremely high maintenance. If you don't pamper them constantly, they'll be off with the nearest bitch.'

'Is that what Grandma told you?' I asked.

'No,' said Mum. 'Chapter four of *Why Men Are Like Dogs*.'

I must read this book.

I couldn't concentrate at work – the only thing on my mind was VAG. He was everywhere – in my head, on every guitar fret board, in my cup of tea and in my own father's face (which was the MOST disturbing thing EVER).

Following on from the 'Tena Lady incident', I was pretty sure Vince had seen me at my worst, but, just in case, I made a list to prepare myself for any other further embarrassment.

TOP 5 WORST THINGS THAT COULD HAPPEN ON A FIRST DATE WITH VINCE

1. I forget how to speak (it has happened before).

2. I find out that he loves jazz music.

3. He moves in to kiss me and I panic and lick his eyeball. (I've only ever had a slightly drunken snog with Matthew Ludlow, which I can barely remember).

4. We have such a successful kiss that he decides to touch my nork. WHAT DO I DO? WHAT DO I DO?

5. He touches my nork and, as I gently go to move his hand away, I somehow brush my fingers against his groin. IT WAS AN ACCIDENT. WHAT DO I DO? WHAT DO I DO?

I vowed to keep my hands in my pockets and to save any kissing until date number two. Meanwhile, there was no kissing action going on between Walter and Petrina. The bad vibes between them last night had escalated into their first proper argument, which had kicked off in the van on the way back home.

'You're behaving like a jealous teenager,' snapped Petrina.

'Erm, that's because I AM a teenager,' he mumbled.

'I was only *talking* to Leon,' Petrina continued defensively. 'I wasn't chatting him up.'

'You were all dribbly,' Walter said sadly. And it was true. Other than have her salivary glands removed, there is no way for Petrina to hide her tell-tale sign of sexual attraction.

'Yeah well, I'm allowed to window shop, aren't I?'

Petrina was in danger of sounding like a middle-aged man perving at school girls. Except Leon was not a school girl. He was a HOT, steaming, slab of young man.

Throughout the terrifying journey home, Matthew was unusually quiet. He didn't even scream like the rest of us, when Bob Ollox almost ran over a pedestrian crossing the road.

'D-d-d-d-daft cow,' he yelled as the poor woman ran to the safety of the pavement.

As the three of us in the back of the van clung on to whatever we could, Matthew sat calmly in the front next to his furious home helper without saying a word. Although I hadn't actually seen him drinking alcohol, there was no doubt in my mind that Matthew was in a drunken state. His eyes were red and his face was all droopy. Another three years and he'll be rolling around on the floor in public in a puddle of his own urine (N.B. alcohol-induced wetting yourself is TOTALLY not the same as getting-kicked-in-the-bladder-at-self-defence-class wetting yourself).

After work I showered, put on my retro The Cure T-shirt, a little more kohl eyeliner than usual and a pair of black jeans for my date, then headed off (with a skip in my step) to meet

Vince at six thirty at our agreed rendezvous point (by the bridge on the lake in Manor Park). Even though I arrived half an hour early (as I always do), my date was there before me looking HOTTER than a phoenix's fart in the flames. In his fitted shirt and ripped jeans (the same ones with the hole at the top of his thigh), he had the presence of a movie star and I found myself feeling self-conscious and clumsy as he watched me approaching.

Oh God. I've forgotten how to walk. What do I do with my legs?

My whole body had become heavy, like a dead weight strapped to my chin. My knees kept buckling underneath me – it was exactly as if I were a baby taking its first unsteady steps towards its really SEXY father.

I'm walking like a constipated toddler.

I wasn't sure what facial expression to adopt either. Do I smile? Look seductive? Casual? Mysterious? In a state of discomfort and panic, I attempted all four expressions at once.

'Are you OK?' asked Vince, which revealed a tenderness and concern that instantly made him perfect boyfriend material.

Just LOOK at that thigh hole. I want to slip my finger inside and RIP it right open. OH GOD. Does that count as assault? Am I becoming a sexual deviant?

'I'm just a bit hot,' I replied quickly.

'I'll say!' he grinned, his eyes dropping down to my chest.

Oh God. Not more toothpaste dribble? I tried REALLY hard to keep it in my mouth this time.

Vince and I wandered through the park in the hazy, late

afternoon sunshine. I was certain that the people we passed by must have been laughing at such a mismatched pair. Vince Aston-Granger is a Winner. Blossom Uxley-Michaels is a Weirdo. And in exactly the same way my sister Breeze was never troubled by her unfortunate initials, Vince wasn't bothered either. He has the kind of inner confidence that I can only dream of. I hoped that by spending time with him a little bit of his self-assurance would rub off on to me.

On our leisurely stroll to the cinema to see *Bite Me – Dusky Dark Part II* (Vince has never seen it, but I've seen it SIX times already. I LOVE IT!), I learned everything about him. He's almost seventeen, goes to Gresham Park Sixth Form College, hates all subjects apart from art and music and taught himself to play guitar when he was just eleven. His parents don't understand him and his favourite bands are Bloody Minx, Steel Dragon and ancient, but cool dance acts the Prodigy and the Chemical Brothers. Our conversation flowed easily as we ambled along (and at one point we were actually holding hands!!!!). Suffice to say that by the time we arrived at the cinema, I was one hundred per cent, totally and utterly in love.

THE ~~KISS~~ NORK TOUCH.

I am not a kissing expert. I have had one slightly drunken snog with Matthew Ludlow at a party on a beanbag. Other than that, I've occasionally practised kissing on my Josh Raven poster (which now has a small soggy hole in the corner of his mouth) and I'm slightly ashamed to admit that I did ONCE try to snog

Boris my pink rabbit (but I almost choked when a clump of pink fluff got caught in my throat, which would have been the most humiliating way to die). So, when Vince turned and looked deeply into my eyes after a brilliant evening, a combination of fear, excitement, lust and plain 'I haven't got a clue what I am doing' came bubbling up from the pit of my stomach.

Whatever you do, don't puke in his mouth. That would be THE WORST.

My heart was thumping loudly in my ears. Vince seemed to be studying every single pore and blackhead on my face.

Please don't look at my top lip. I forgot to bleach my moustache.

He gently pushed a strand of my hair back and tucked it behind my ear.

He's looking at my ear in a weird sexy way. Is it waxy? I never check my ears. OH GOD, WHAT IF IT'S WAXY.

He tenderly ran his forefinger across my cheek and down on to my neck.

I don't know where to look. Oh God, we've made eye contact.

His mouth curled into the most intense, soft smile I had ever seen in real life. I'd seen it before though, a few times when Nigel the sexy Vampire in the *Bite Me* films goes in to kiss his pretty mortal lover.

I can't bear it. If you're going to kiss me, JUST KISS ME.

But as I waited expectantly with my eyes closed, I was surprised to feel the touch, not of his lips on mine, but of his hand ON MY NORK.

OH NO. This isn't right.

Instinctively I stepped back. For a moment Vince looked shocked. Then he smiled and nodded.

'Playing cat 'n' dog yeah?' he said. 'That's cool. I like a bit of fun.'

I don't know that game? Is it like British Bulldog 1-2-3?

Vince began to back away with a big grin on his face. 'We'll do it again then little pussy cat?' he said.

Say something witty Blossom.

'Meow?' I offered.

'WOOF,' he replied with a growl.

So does this mean we're 'an item' now?

FRIDAY 15TH JULY

I woke up officially A GIRLFRIEND. Well, Vince hasn't actually *asked* me yet, but after last night I think it's safe to assume that we are more than just good friends. With hindsight, I think the nork-touching was just a Scale Of Shame *Level 5* incident (Awkward Physical Contact) and should probably be forgotten. I'd imagine that Vince is probably curled up on his bed cringing at his accidental faux pas, wishing he could rewind the clock and just kiss me as he'd originally intended.

Neither of us are going to the fourth heat tonight as he's got something else on and I'm a bit grumpy and pre-menstrual, but I am seeing him again next week. I'm counting down the days (and hours. And minutes. And seconds. And milliseconds).

TOP 10 THINGS I LOVE ABOUT
VINCE ASTON-GRANGER

1. His hair. Messy and blonde. Lovely.

2. His eyes. Blue and intense. Lovely.

3. His thighs. Firm and lovely. Lovely.

4. His nose. Long and perfect. LOVELY.

5. His lips. Full and kissable. LOVELY.

6. His bum. Lovely, lovely, LOVELY.

7. His voice. Deep and sexy. LOVELY.

8. His dress sense. Casual and cool. LOVELY.

9. His hands. Big and strong. LOVELY.

10. The hole at the top of his jeans. LOVELY, LOVELY, LOVELY, LOVELY, LOVELY.

Walter came into Blue Nile just after one thirty. I sat behind the counter with my chin in my hands and watched him absentmindedly rearranging sheet music and twanging the individual strings of random guitars as he skulked around the shop. After ten minutes of 'browsing', I decided to break the silence.

'So Matthew says that Joel Scott and Ama Badu got through in the singer/songwriter heat last night.'

Walter didn't reply.

'He thought Joel was a bit too twee, but Ama was pretty awesome – like Tracy Chapman, but less grumpy.' I continued.

Walter looked at me in disbelief.

'I've been lending him albums so he'll stop being so

139

musically illiterate,' I explained.

Walter remained schtum for another few seconds. 'I'm not jealous you know,' he said finally.

'I know,' I replied, trying to sound sympathetic. 'Biceps that muscly would look really stupid on you.'

Leon's arms are more contoured than an ordinance survey map of the Lake District. Soooo hot!

Walter scowled underneath his fringe.

'You think Petrina fancies him?' he mumbled.

I thought of the globules of spittle that had collected in the corners of my best friend's mouth when she'd been watching Leon playing bass on stage in his leather trousers.

'Don't be daft,' I lied.

Walter muttered something under his breath (either 'I hate him' or 'potato' – I didn't quite catch it), then grumped off out of the shop.

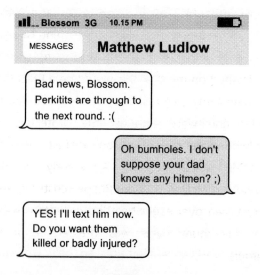

.ıl. Blossom 3G   10.15 PM

MESSAGES   **Matthew Ludlow**

Bad news, Blossom. Perkitits are through to the next round. :(

Oh bumholes. I don't suppose your dad knows any hitmen? ;)

YES! I'll text him now. Do you want them killed or badly injured?

✳ ✳ ✳

Oh how I envy Kirsty Mackerby. She gets to have her breakfast AND lunch at McDonald's – FOR FREE. But my raging green-eyed monster was tamed a little when Kirsty slipped me and Petrina some free McChicken Sandwiches and fries when we popped in for lunch on Saturday. Watching Kirsty shovel the greasy fries into the pop-out cardboard container, it suddenly dawned on me that this would be a BRILLIANT way to rebel against my parents. They've despised McDonald's for decades and were amongst the protesters on the infamous 'worldwide day of action' against the American fast food chain back in the 1980s. Apparently Dad, who was wearing a Ronald McDonald 'Grim Reaper' costume, suddenly had to wrestle an over-eager bearded collie that was trying to mount my mum (who was dressed as a mouldy cheeseburger).

'Do you reckon I could get a Saturday job here?' I asked Kirsty.

'Nah,' she said shaking her head. 'Everyone wants a McDonald's job. We get literally hundreds of applicants every week. I only got the job cos my cousin is "doing it" with the Regional Manager.'

Kirsty checked nobody was listening, then leaned across the counter and said in a low voice, 'One time, literally in the heat of the moment, they actually "did it" over the deep fat fryer.'

'Oh my God. Has your cousin been disfigured for life?'

'It wasn't turned on at the time, Blossom.'

I knew that. I totally wasn't thinking about burnt buttocks.

Sitting alone, blowing the wrappers off a handful of straws at a high table was Mei Miyagi and, after getting our food, we went over and joined her. At that moment, Paulette Dempsey walked in. Things might have been awkward between me and Paulette after the Dempsey Love website photo, but it was nothing compared to the strained atmosphere between Mei and Paulette. They've have been on frosty terms ever since last term (when Paulette's on-off boyfriend Max Burcott had a fling with Mei, causing Mei to break up with a distraught Kirsty), so when Paulette approached our table the tension was like being at Centre Court for the Ladies' Wimbledon Verbal Tennis Singles Final.

Dempsey to serve.

'I want to buy Mei's Gay Soirée.'

Ooh. Miyagi wasn't expecting that shot.

'What? Are you mad?'

Miyagi manages a backhand return.

'Seriously. I see fast cash potential.'

A lovely drop shot from Dempsey.

'It's not a business, it's not for sale and, even if it was, I wouldn't sell to you because you're a jealous, twisted, manipulator with suppressed homosexual issues.'

And a great recovery from Miyagi. Love fifteen.

'I'm NOT a lesbian. I'm asexual.'

Fifteen all.

'No wonder Max wanted to do sex with me.'

Great volley from Miyagi. Fifteen thirty.

'He wasn't interested in your lesbo ways. He wanted a rack of pure woman like me.'

Thirty all ('rack of pure woman'?).

'Are you kidding? Max has been sending me flirty texts ever since the party at Kirsty's house. Thank God she hasn't seen them. They're filthy.'

Ooooh. Just inside the base line. It's a good job Kirsty is out of earshot right now. She was utterly devastated when Mei and Max were discovered together in Kirsty's parents' bed a few months ago. It was a huge scandal. Thirty forty.

'Who cares? I dumped him ages ago. And he told me it meant nothing anyway, that you were just an easy lay.'

Deuce.

'That's not what he said in his texts.'

Advantage Miyagi.

'Yeah, well at least I don't look like a MAN.'

A low shot from Dempsey. Deuce.

'I've got great cheekbones. Why don't you just face the fact that you fancy the pants off me?'

Ow! Paulette is totally lost for words (does she really fancy Mei?) Advantage Miyagi.

'That's right, Paulette. Keep dreaming of my lady parts.'

Oooff! There's no way back from that. Game, set and match Miyagi.

Mei leaned across the table and kissed Paulette hard on the lips, then grabbed her bag, waved to Kirsty (who had just thrown a scoop of French fries all over herself upon witnessing Mei's public smooch) and strode purposefully out of McDonald's. While Paulette was left stupefied, catching flies with her open mouth, Petrina and I sank our teeth into our freebie chicken burgers and marvelled at Mei's extraordinary sexual confidence. She could make even a threefold-vow-taking-no-sex-whatsoever-or-God-will-be-very-very-cross Catholic nun want to sleep with her. Not me though of course. My erotic thoughts lie solely with the hot singer of a dance-punk band called Bumskulls.

I walked into work this morning listening to the new Bloody Minx album. As usual I found myself doing that thing where I pretend that I am in a music video as I walk down the street.

MY TOP 5 IMAGINARY WALKING MUSIC VIDEO SCENARIOS

1 THE BROODING WALK. If I'm a bit pre-menstrual, I like to walk in time to the beat of a moody song with a sullen (yet sexy) expression on my face. I especially enjoy this imaginary video if it is dark and raining hard enough to get droplets of water running down my cheeks.

2 THE PIED PIPER WALK. This is usually when I'm in a great mood. I strut along in time to an uplifting track and imagine that I am gradually joined by more and more people. At first it's just a couple of kids. I smile at them – they're cool. Then a gospel choir wearing long white robes join me, singing in their joyful, happy way. Next a group of students from a performing arts school tag along. They climb on top of cars in their colourful (and revealing) dance wear and do star jumps and back flips and all kinds of astonishing acrobatics. Finally all the office workers in their suits spill out on to the streets and dance about as if it's their last day on earth. And I walk away, content in the knowledge that I have brought a sense of gladness into the world.

3 THE 'L'EAU DE PULL' WALK. All the hot boys and foxy girls that I pass can't resist my hypnotic, wiggling hips and sensual scent of womanliness. As I lip-sync in time to the music, they fall at my feet and I have to step over their limp bodies that lie across my path. Even the stray dogs and nut-seeking squirrels in the park catch a whiff of my extreme sexuality as I go by. I am totally irresistible.

4. THE HOMELESS ALCOHOLIC WALK. I am a down-and-out wino. My hot lover has left me for a slanger and I am a mess. I stagger about the pavement (still in time to the music) and bump into the fences and bushes that I pass.

5. THE PROSTITUTE WALK. I only do this if there is NOBODY around. I imagine I'm a high-class hooker looking for business in a New York back street. A police car rolls up and I think I'm going to be arrested. But really the HOT policeman wants to pay for my services (N.B. THIS IS NOT A WEIRD PERVERTED SEX FANTASY. It's an artistic interpretation of my mood).

Today I did the Pied Piper Walk, even though I have just got my period and have had to take a Feminax to dull the cramps. Nothing could alter the fact that I was feeling great and didn't mind who knew it. I strutted along, surrounded by an imaginary crowd of FIT, sequinned-clad, goth break-dancers who instantly dissolved as I removed my headphones at Blue Nile.

Upon entering I found Dad merrily playing 'The Cuckoo's Nest' on a melodeon while Roger, the Squire of the Border Morris Dancers (dressed in normal clothes), jigged and pranced about in front of him. The traditional folk instrument had been shipped over especially from Germany. While they fawned over the it, I went over to the vintage 1960 cherry-red Gibson ES-335 guitar and softly stroked its smooth fret board. I couldn't help but think that, if Vince were a guitar, he'd be this exact model: elegant, toned, suave and SEXY. I stood gazing at the Gibson for much longer than I intended and by the time I'd realised that I was ACTUALLY perving over a guitar, Dad and Roger had both left the shop for lunch. I don't think they'd even realised I was there. Our boss Nile was behind the counter now, back from his Jamaican holiday and full of energy. He nodded acknowledgement then came round to join me in front of the guitar.

'Played by Chuck Berry,' he sighed. 'And I have that authenticated.'

'Cool,' I said.

'My mum had an affair with him, you know,' he said proudly before leaning in close and whispering, 'I could be his son.'

I wasn't too sure how to respond. On previous occasions he's told me that he could be the love child of Nile Rodgers, Jimi Hendrix, Michael Jackson and Stevie Wonder. His mum was a backing singer back in the day and was apparently a bit of a goer.

Nile took the guitar from the stand and held it towards me.

'Would you like to play her?' he asked.

Do my loins yearn for VAG?

I took the guitar in my hands. It was everything I'd ever dreamed of.

I lie on the cliff top in the sunshine, engrossed in The Harlot Mistfang Chronicles Part 1 – *the worldwide best-selling Vampire novel that I have written. It really is an AWESOME read. Alongside being in a huge, internationally-acclaimed electro-rock band, I am also a writing genius.*

The blissful peace and quiet is disturbed by the sound of a helicopter. I look up. The helicopter is heading in my direction. I squint and shield my eyes as it comes to land right next to me. My hair is flapping all over the shop. I cannot see the face of the pilot, but the door opens and I watch Vince Aston-Granger, the global dance superstar from Bumskulls, step out wearing Ray Bans and a shiny, cherry-red suit that is absolutely NOT cheap and tacky and off the hanger from a high street store. It's a slim-fitting and perfectly-tailored vintage suit that was once worn by Chuck Berry, Nile Rodgers, Jimi Hendrix, Michael Jackson and Stevie Wonder (it has been dry-cleaned and sterilised so there is no chance of catching chlamydia or anything nasty from it). I stand up as he walks towards me. He is holding out a box of Ferrero Rochers. They are my ABSOLUTE FAVOURITES.

I open the box and reluctantly offer him one. God, I hate sharing my nutty balls of perfection.

But Vince shakes his head. 'No thanks,' he says. 'I have a nut allergy.' WOWZOIDS. I will never have to share a box of yumminess with him EVER.

He takes off his shades to reveal his blue eyes that are oozing lust and love in equal measures. I ADORE his oozey eyes.

'Will you marry me?' he asks as he stands before me.

I pause a few moments for dramatic effect.

'Yes,' I reply.

He can't disguise the pure happiness that is now written across his blemish-and spot-free face. In the helicopter I notice that the pilot has removed his sunglasses. MATTHEW LUDLOW?!!! He is shaking his head. God, he's annoying.

I ignore him. Vince takes my hands and spins me round. My feet lift off the ground. Round and round we go in circles. We are a (slightly smaller and less metal) mirror image of the helicopter propellers that spin over our heads. We are The Ring of Love. The never-ending Circle of Life. And as I gaze into his (slightly blurry) face, I know that my life is complete.

We stop spinning. Vince takes me in his muscly arms and kisses me passionately on the lips. And then just when I think my life couldn't be any more perfect, he steps back and says, 'I have something to show you.'

For one brief moment, I fear that he might reveal he has Elephantitis of the testicles or something, BUT I need not worry. Instead he begins to make a primal, rhythmic sound from his mouth. The compass of my loins jerks suddenly as it pulls towards the magnetic attraction. VAG is beatboxing. Beautiful, throbbing gulps resonate from his larynx. I watch with uncontrollable desire as his sexy Adam's Apple bobs up and down, like a sexual kick drum, and I cannot stop myself from lurching forward and clamping my lips around it. And as I suck on his laryngeal prominence, I know that I am the happiest girl alive (although there is a vague worry in the back of my mind that I may have strayed into pervert territory).

END OF WEEK 28. MY TABLE OF ACHIEVEMENT

SHAME LEVEL PEAK	*Level 9 (Tena Lady on foot) + Level 8 ('I sit on the face') = 17*
GUITAR PRACTICE	*4hrs 3 minutes (Bring on the quarter-final)*
PARTY INVITATIONS	*0*
SNOGS	*1/2 (An accidental nork touch counts as half a snog)*

Is it right to feel sunny and bright (and hopelessly in love) when everyone else's relationship is falling apart? When Andreas surprised Breeze with an elegantly wrapped bottle of *Organism* (her favourite organic-no-chemicals perfume) she flipped her lid, accusing him of giving 'guilt gifts'. Meanwhile, Walter's blatant moodiness over Leon has escalated into a huge, Grand Canyon-size rift with Petrina. It's all looking pretty bleak where love is concerned. EXCEPT FOR ME because I'm skipping my Self Defence lesson to go on a proper real-time, grown-up date with Vince!!!!!!!!!

I know most girls my age would spend the day having facials and getting their nails done if they were spending an evening alone at Frankie's Diner with a SEX GOD, but that's not really my style. I'm still trying to give up biting my nails and I don't like people fingering my face or smearing it with avocado mousse slime. So in preparation I decided to drop in on Gayle to see if she would put a single pink stripe in my fringe.

'You sure you don't want a short crop?' she asked as I sat down in the chair. 'Cos you really do look like a Pygmy Marmoset monkey.'

'No,' I replied firmly. 'Just a pink stripe.'

'Like a punk badger?'

'Umm . . . I suppose.'

'Scrotum-dyeing is becoming very popular you know.' Gayle wandered off to the magazine rack, where she pulled out *National Geographic* again.

'Here you go,' she continued as she opened the magazine. 'The Vervet monkey. It's got a bright turquoise ball-sack. Look at that.'

She thrust a picture of a monkey in all its colourful goolie glory in front of my face.

'Nice,' I stammered.

'It's becoming quite popular in the fashion world. Won't be long before it spreads to the high street. Then it'll be lady parts too. I reckon a dash of Vervet Monkey Blue would really go with your colour.'

'How do you know?'

'Eyebrows,' she said sagely.

Then a long silence as I worked out exactly what she meant. *OH!*

I felt violated. 'Just a pink stripe please, Gayle.' I checked my eyebrows in the mirror. SHE WAS RIGHT. All this time I've been walking about showing off my private parts on my face without even realising!

And so, having once again skipped my Monday night self-defence lesson, I rocked up outside the cinema with my new pink hair stripe, dressed in black jeans and my skinny, black Glastonbury Festival T-shirt. It's funny – the last time I went to Frankie's Diner with a boy was a couple of months ago when Paulette set me up on a blind date with Matthew Ludlow. (And what a disaster that turned out to be. He burped vodka fumes in my face, then threw me over his shoulder in a fireman's lift and ran around town until I was almost shaken unconscious.) This date was going to be different, though. Tonight I would lay the foundations of a proper relationship.

Vince was already there when I arrived (I LOVE that he is an early bird too) and casually playing with his iPhone. He looked so ridiculously handsome in his fitted, red checked shirt and blue jeans that my (already bubbling) stomach lurched violently and for one awful moment, I thought I would sick up on his blue Adidas trainers. But the moment passed as I noticed his tidy, light-brown eyebrows. Thanks to Gayle, I knew what was going on inside his trousers, which was oddly calming.

Dinner was amazing. We talked over our burger and chips as if we'd known each other forever – he loves Bloody Minx, can appreciate the genius talent of Josh Raven and thinks jazz music was invented by Satan. And he isn't afraid to dish out a compliment.

'You've had your hair done,' he said right after he'd fed me one of his chips.

My cheeks began to flush. It's a well-known scientific fact that blushing is essentially a facial erection. When you are talking to an attractive person and you turn a bright shade of red, it's so OBVIOUS that you fancy them. I wish it was as easy to conceal a facial erection as it is to hide a trouser tent though.

'It's cute isn't it?' I said, hoping that I was managing to receive the food in a suitably seductive manner rather than looking like a dribbly spoon-fed baby.

'You should wear brighter clothes,' he grinned.

'I prefer darker shades of grey.' I popped one of my chips into his mouth and watched him masticate.

You could cut diamonds with that jaw. Or really big logs.

'Why do you always cover up your legs?' he enquired as he pushed six more huge chips into my mouth. 'I bet you'd look good in a skirt.'

My mouth is crammed to maximum capacity with chips and Vince has just told me he'd like to see my legs. I LITERALLY couldn't be happier (unless I had a box of Ferrero Rochers in front of me for my dessert – that would be the icing on the cake).

'You don't by any chance have a nut allergy do you?' I spluttered through my colossal gobful of fries.

'Nope,' he replied. 'But I am allergic to responsibility.'

Well, it was worth a shot.

'Can you beatbox?' I asked hopefully.

'No. But I can do armpit farts.'

Not quite as erotic as beatboxing, but it'll do.

After sharing an enormous chocolate fudge ice cream sundae, he walked me all the way (two miles) home. I'm not going to lie, when he took hold of my hand, I honestly felt as if my feet lifted off the ground. By my own scientific calculations it appears that the magnetic force of love is stronger than that of gravity (Sir Isaac Newton will be spinning round amongst the earthworms and dung beetles knowing that his law of gravitation has been trumped by a secondary school Weirdo).

We stopped outside my house. The inevitable was about to happen.

'I've really enjoyed tonight,' Vince said softly. He was looking at me intensely, as if he was studying my features for some kind of important face exam. I quickly ran my tongue across my brace to check there wasn't any chip debris stuck in the metal.

He's going to kiss me.

He tucked my hair back behind my ear. 'You'd look great with a short crop,' he whispered.

Has he been talking to Gayle?

And then he leaned in and kissed me. This time I was prepared (I had spent most of late Sunday evening snogging Boris my rabbit and pulling pieces of pink fluff from my mouth with tweezers, but it was definitely worth it as my technique had noticeably improved). It was an excellent snog. I know this because I totally lost track of time, forgot where I was and didn't even worry about stray visible tongues. I was totally immersed in the moment. Until . . .

OH MY GOD. His hand has accidentally found my nork again. He's going to be mortified. Should I tell him or save him the embarrassment and act like nothing's happened?

I pulled away from the kiss and faked a shiver.

'Oooh, it's a bit nippy out here,' I said, rubbing my arms and trying to make my teeth chatter.

'I'll say!' Vince grinned. He moved back towards me. I wanted to kiss him again, but I'd suddenly become VERY aware of my surroundings. Poor Vince clearly has some kind of hand-eye-nork co-ordination impairment. I felt that it would be unkind to put him in a situation where he might have another setback, especially in public where Mr Parkin at number 34 might appear with a camping chair and a packet of Pringles at any moment.

'What's up?' he asked looking disappointed. 'Do you want to go somewhere more discreet?'

Perhaps he has body Tourette's or some kind of involuntary nork-clutching syndrome.

I smiled and kissed his cheek as softly as I could.

'It's OK,' I said kindly. 'I'm the least shallow person I know. I'm deeper than a really deep wishing well.'

Vince looked as if he was going to say something but I wanted to save him the awkwardness of having to explain his condition to me, so I blew him a kiss, turned and walked away. It almost broke my heart, but I knew it was for the best.

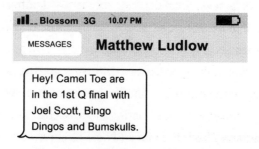

```
ıll ._ Blossom 3G    10.07 PM              ▆▆▃
MESSAGES      Matthew Ludlow

  Hey! Camel Toe are
  in the 1st Q final with
  Joel Scott, Bingo
  Dingos and Bumskulls.
```

It was the ultimate betrayal – instead of meeting me at midday as usual, Petrina went for lunch with Leon behind Walter's back. Leon – the uber hot Bumskulls bassist with the onstage presence of a sexy, wild panther dressed in leather. When I asked her if she'd considered Walter's feelings – I mean, we'd both witnessed Petrina's tell-tale excess saliva excretion when she was talking to Leon – she went on the defensive, adamantly denying that anything untoward went on. According to her, they just had a friendly chat in Joe's Café about the new Skadi manager (who Petrina thinks hates all women owing to the fact that he repeatedly uses the term of endearment 'sweetie' rather than calling any female employee by her actual name). Petrina has asked me not to say anything, which has put me in a horribly awkward position. Do I lie to Walter (who I've known since we were seven when he rescued me from the apple tree to which I'd been tied) or do I stay true to Petrina (who released us from the boiler room on our first day at secondary school after we'd been locked in by the slangers) and keep quiet? With this new dilemma weighing on my mind, alongside the worry that I am dating someone with an 'involuntary wandering hand condition' *and* the fact that Camel Toe would be directly competing against Bumskulls in the quarter finals, it's no wonder I had trouble concentrating as we rehearsed in Petrina's living room.

'Shall we take a break?' asked Petrina as I played yet another bad note. Feeling exasperated, I threw Cassiopeia on to the sofa and took a custard cream from the open pack on the coffee table.

'Would you still love Walter if he unintentionally groped melons in Skadi?' I was testing her reaction with a clever hypothetical question.

Petrina frowned. 'Of course,' she said. 'I can cope with weird fetishes, but I absolutely will not put up with childish bouts of jealousy. Walter does NOT own me.'

'To be fair, Petrina, Leon is one of the hottest boys either of us have ever spoken to. It's no wonder Walter is feeling a bit insecure.'

Petrina rolled her eyes. 'If I'd have known he was a controlling, clingy quimboid then I'd never have got with him in the first place.'

I was beginning to feel uncomfortable. Petrina was being a bit unsympathetic. Walter isn't possessive or untrusting – in fact far from it – but when your first proper girlfriend is getting a lot of attention from a ridiculously-proper-real-time-hot rock god, a nudge of reassurance really wouldn't go amiss.

When I arrived home, I set about rearranging the brand new (signed!!!) Josh Raven posters that Poptastic Management had sent me. I'm trying to mix up the Josh posters with a few other band posters (Bloody Minx, The Horrors, The Cure) as there is a small chance he might drop by for a baked potato on his way to Pete Hartley's recording studio. I wouldn't want Josh to think that my room was some kind of shrine to him. That would just be too weird. I positioned my life-size cardboard cut-out of Josh next to my bed, drew my Josh Raven curtains and lay down on my Josh Raven duvet to listen to the new Josh Raven album (*Dark Lover of the Night*) in my new room. And then my enjoyment was interrupted when the door flung open.

'He's definitely having an affair, the cheating baboon!' My sister never minces her words.

I was the voice of reason. 'Andreas really doesn't seem the type.'

'ALL men are the type,' growled my sister as she threw herself on to MY bed.

If Andreas has cheated on my sister, I will KILL him. This is my room now and I'll do whatever it takes to protect it – even if it means murder.

'OK,' I said calmly. 'What proof do you have?'

'My intuition,' said Breeze, tapping her rapidly flaring left nostril (which is presumably where she keeps her intuition). 'And it's never been wrong.'

'What about the time your intuition made you call 999 and claim that a UFO had crash-landed in the high street, causing death and devastation?'

'How was I to know it was a live art performance? The tomato ketchup really looked like blood.'

'And remember when your intuition told you that Walter had a massive crush on me?'

Breeze's 'gut feeling' caused me to spend three panic-stricken weeks, trying to compose a speech to inform Walter that I loved him as a friend, but absolutely NOT in a sex way. When I finally read it to him one lunch break he laughed and said snogging me would be as 'gross as snogging his nan', which I did NOT take kindly. We might not have found each other sexually attractive, but a more complimentary let down wouldn't have gone amiss (e.g. 'you're beautiful and sexy Blossom, but I only have eyes for Petrina).

Breeze hauled herself from MY bed and paced barefoot across my room.

'Well I've also compiled a dossier of evidence,' she growled. 'And it's massive.'

She ran out of my room and returned a few moments later

with a huge hemp-paper journal which she opened and thrust into my face.

'Item number 43,' Breeze read out loud. 'Andreas has been noticeably touchy-feely in public.'

'Andreas is always "touchy-feely in public"', I stated.

'Yeah but he used to only do it when he wanted to have it off,' she retorted. 'Which I admit is most of the time BUT for the past few weeks he's been doing it even when he isn't sexually aroused.'

WAY TOO MUCH INFORMATION.

'That furry oaf is definitely up to something,' she continued. 'And I intend to find out what.'

She walked over to my favourite Josh Raven poster (the one where his wet shirt is open, revealing his sexy howling wolf tattoo) and scrutinised it up close.

'What a dick,' she said.

It was obvious she was channelling her pent-up anger with Andreas at my hot poster, so I bit my lip and didn't say a word. After almost sixteen years of living with my sister, I know better than to venture into an unplanned argument with her. She's always been a bit emotionally unstable.

✳ ✳ ✳

The sound of my mother shouting, 'Get off me you filthy rozzer!' woke me from a deep, contented sleep. My radio alarm clock told me it was 6.56AM, a little earlier than I would have liked, but as today was quarter-finals day and I had a lot of preparing to do before I set off for work, the wake-up call was probably not such a bad thing.

'Shut it, you slag. You're nicked.'

That sounds like my dad.

'Oink, oink. It's the fat pig in blue,' yelled back Mum.

'Spread em, punk,'

'No darling,' said my mother. 'You're an English bobby, not a New York cop. I'm very aroused right now, you know?'

I pulled back the curtains to see what on earth was going on. What I saw down below, gave me the BIGGEST SHOCK OF MY LIFE (even worse than the static shock that Breeze gave me after she'd rubbed her Eskimo socks on the carpet in front of Great Aunt Edna's electric fire. I had to wear a plaster on my earlobe for a week). Mum was wearing her 'Frack Off Mother Frackers' T-shirt and my father was dressed in a shoddy, fancy-dress policemen's uniform. He had Mum pushed up against the camper van and was handcuffing her hands behind her back whilst she pretended to protest.

'Are you going to handcuff me to the rhododendron bush?' she said in a suggestive tone.

'If you're lucky . . .'

OH MY GOD. This is utterly disgusting. I am DEFINITELY going to puke.

I drew the curtains again the moment I saw Dad rolling up a copy of the *Daily Mail* into a makeshift truncheon. I'd brought that newspaper home to annoy them, but somehow it had turned me into an accidental sex play contributor.

I needed to up my rebellion game before their midlife crisis really came into (organic) fruition. I briefly thought about getting myself pregnant, but then I imagined how much my mum would enjoy strapping a baby grandchild to her bosom in a tribal print papoose. I needed another plan.

Matthew Ludlow called into the shop with tonight's quarter-finals running order. Camel Toe were billed second, followed straight after by Bumskulls, which made me feel nervous.

When I first found out that we would be in direct competition, I texted Vince to ask if he minded being up against me and Petrina. His reply was simply *it's a dream come true*, which was very sweet and sensitive but I still wasn't sure how he really felt.

I wondered if he was as desperate to win as I was. Sure, I wanted Bumskulls to put on an awesome performance and go through as well as us, but I couldn't pretend that I didn't hope with all my heart that Camel Toe would get into the final and win.

Matthew was extremely complimentary about my new pink hair-stripe, saying that it was 'really pretty' and 'made my eyes sparkle'. It's good to know that even a hardcore alcoholic like Matthew can sometimes see beyond his boozy bubble cocoon to flatter a friend. Not that he was actually drunk for once. In fact he looked fresh-faced (no spots) and smelt of his unique but lovely 'chocolate-covered baby' scent.

Petrina was meant to come over straight after work to run through the set, but she sent an offish text saying that she had a headache and would be a bit late. Matthew arrived on time for the run-through as planned.

'Oh hey,' I said, opening the front door. 'Petrina's been delayed.'

'Yeah, I know,' he replied, leaning his skateboard up against the porch. 'I just rode past her and Leon sitting in Joe's Café.'

'Are you sure?' I asked in disbelief. *Petrina wouldn't lie to me.*

'One hundred per cent,' he confirmed. 'Those canary yellow Skadi uniforms are disgusting.'

Oh Petrina. How could you?

Feeling hurt, and with band rehearsal postponed, I decided to focus my mind on compiling an 'essential playlist' for Matthew to listen to on his phone. He genuinely hasn't got a clue about music, which is a little disconcerting seeing as he's the manager of my band, so I downloaded twenty brilliant tracks to try and spoon-feed him a bit of basic musical knowledge. There is still a long way to go, but as a result of today's lesson, Matthew is now at least 'aware' of Led Zeppelin, Radiohead, Bloody Minx and The Cure. After only an hour he knew all the words to Josh Raven's 'Moonlight Stalker' and was wearing my retro The Cure T-shirt (which revealed a little of his midriff and looked quite good on his slim physique). So successful was my tutoring that I'm considering one day opening my own Rock School, (to educate and inform musically clueless teens), where anyone who breaks the rules of conduct will be forced to sit in a soundproof room and listen to an hour's worth of 'freestyle jazz'. That would be the most effective form of discipline EVER.

'Nice hair,' said Walter, who had entered my bedroom without us hearing. He seemed bemused at the sight of Matthew jumping up and down on my bed playing air-guitar to a Josh Raven track. I was delighted to see Walter – the rift between him and Petrina had left me in an uncomfortable no-man's territory and I'd missed him and his stupid fringe enormously. I leapt up and almost knocked him over with my enthusiastic hug. Walter's uncharacteristically loud chuckle was halted abruptly when something on the wall caught his eye.

'You been snogging your poster?' he asked, clocking the soggy, torn corner of Josh Raven's mouth. Matthew stopped air-strumming and bounced over to take a look for himself.

I'm going to KILL Petrina. That was a confidential girlie secret. Now I look like a paper-licking pervert.

'Walter! How ARE you?' I screeched in a panic. Walter shook his head and slumped down on to my bed, automatically picking up my pink rabbit and hugging him close to his chest. I prayed that he wouldn't notice the balding, sodden area around Boris's mouth (SHAME).

'She's seeing that guy Leon,' he said. 'I can sense it'.

I glanced over at Matthew, who had put his headphones

back on and was continuing his education (Radiohead). I willed him to keep his gob shut.

'Has she been meeting him secretly?' Walter continued.

Monsieur Ecclestone is right again. Psychic gypsy extraordinaire.

I couldn't see his eyes through his fringe, but I knew they were sorely pitiful.

There is no way I'm going to be the one who breaks Walter's heart by telling him about Petrina's illicit rendezvous.

'God, no. Absolutely not. She'd never do that. Ever. Even though he is drop dead sexy HOT and could have any women he desired at the click of his fingers. No.'

Was that convincing enough?

Walter's body crumpled.

'She could do so much better than me,' he mumbled.

'Don't be daft,' I said softly. 'Petrina adores you.'

Walter hauled himself back on to his feet, letting Boris drop to the floor. He turned to me as if he wanted to say something, but then changed his mind and walked silently out of my room. I felt awful. By staying loyal to one friend, I had betrayed another. A kind, gentle, caring friend. With an unbearable sense of guilt growing inside, I looked to Matthew for a bit of compassion and understanding. Matthew. The boy wearing my ladies retro band T-shirt, who had flung off his headphones and was now crouching on the sill ready to jump out of the open window.

'Please don't tell Walter,' I called after him.

But Matthew had already sprung outside like an Urban Ninja,

efficiently negotiating the silver birch tree, rhododendron bush (where Mr Parkin's tortoiseshell cat Tinkie likes to do its business) and fence, before landing nimbly in our front garden, just as Walter emerged from the house. I watched the two of them disappear down the road side by side and all I could do was hope that Matthew would see sense and not risk hurting Walter any more than he was already.

'It's NONE of your business,' Petrina YELLED as we set up for our delayed rehearsal a short while later. 'We're just friends.'

'Then why did you lie to me and tell me you had a headache?' It was a reasonable question.

'Because I knew you'd react like this.'

'If it was a normal guy, like . . . Matthew Ludlow, it would be different. But Leon is a snake-hipped, leather-clad, bass-wielding Demi-God of Rock.'

As if to highlight my point, the corner of Petrina's mouth began to pool with spittle.

'Ha! See?' I said, pointing at her face. 'It's a reflex action.'

Petrina wiped her sleeve across her mouth. 'Does Walter know?'

'I don't think so, unless Matthew has said something.'

'It means nothing,' she glared. 'I'm just thirsty.'

And so we ran through our set in total silence, which turned out not be such a bad thing after all. It's amazing how a bit of anger and resentment can have such a positive effect on a performance. No wonder so many successful bands have punch-ups and violent disagreements amongst themselves – it all adds to the energy of an explosive live show.

FIRST QUARTER FINAL

**1. BINGO DINGOS 2. CAMEL TOE
3. BUMSKULLS 4. JOEL SCOTT**

SECOND QUARTER FINAL

**1. SOVEREIGN NRG 2. AMA BADU
3. LIQUID MAGGOT 4. PERKITITS**

Everyone was at the golf club venue later that evening. Matthew, Bob Ollox, my parents (embarrassingly Dad had a Border Morris Dancers rehearsal afterwards, so was dressed in his full 'blacked-up' costume), Breeze and Andreas, the slangers, Felix and Toby, Mr and Mrs Olsen, Paulette, Kirsty and Mei were all members of the sold-out audience. The only person who was noticeably absent was Walter. But, to be honest, he seemed to be the furthest thing from Petrina's mind as she spent most of the evening chatting to luscious Leon.

Once again, Matthew had proved his loyalty to me and hadn't told Walter about what he'd seen. But Walter's imagination had been eating him up, so it was probably a good thing that he wasn't there in person to witness his girlfriend's blatant flirting. He'd already broken the speaker in my phone earlier when he roared at me after I'd asked how he was feeling. I had enough to cope with as it was without worrying about losing my hearing. Vince was being extremely tactile and my fears that his hand-eye-nork-co-ordination-impairment might flare up were intensified when he kissed me so passionately during Bingo Dingos set that my family couldn't fail to notice (they were also standing RIGHT NEXT TO US and watching intently). In their typically right-on way, Mum and Dad both gave me a double thumbs-up and Breeze gestured that Vince was a 'ten out of ten'. Only Andreas showed any sign of disapproval, glaring angrily at him, like the over-protective big brother that I never had (or particularly wanted).

After telling me that I should have worn an outfit showing off my legs to better my chances of winning the quarter-final, Vince gave me a long good luck kiss and I made my way on stage with Petrina.

It was a weird performance – not our worst, but definitely not our best. Perhaps it was the growing hostility that had been creeping into our friendship, or maybe it was simply a case of nerves, but our usual onstage magic just wasn't there. Not that anyone seemed to notice, with great comments from the judges and rapturous applause from the audience, Camel Toe seemed to be triumphant once again.

The irritation on Fiona Tittledown's face was apparent for all to see when Felix strode over to congratulate me.

'You sounded really cool,' he said. Whilst perhaps not quite as flawless as Vince, Felix Winters, with his tousled brown hair and intense eyes, was still ninety-nine-point-nine per cent perfect.

'Thanks,' I replied as casually as I could.

'Nice T-shirt,' he added, gesturing at the *Ludlow's Luxury Loos – drop your anchor in comfort* slogan embroidered across my back. He winked over at his best friend Toby, who had his arm draped lazily around Lucy Perkins' shoulders.

'Band image is important,' I said wisely.

Felix nodded in agreement and right then Margo Tittledown pranced out on stage to introduce Bumskulls. She was wearing a turquoise, shoulder-padded jumpsuit with an orange belt flaunting her tiny waist. With her huge blonde helmet hair and overstated jewellery, she looked like a blinged-up Formula 1 driver.

As Vince and his proper, real-time sexy ensemble began their set, my mind started to wander. I'm pretty much over my Felix infatuation now, but what if I was put in a life or death 'Snog, Marry, Kill' situation with him, Vince and Josh Raven? Contemplating this dream scenario almost BLEW MY MIND

♥ SNOG ♥

HOT BOY	PROS	CONS
VINCE	He is an AMAZING kisser.	I would only be allowed to snog him and whilst right now that's fine, what if in a year or so I wanted to do the sex?
FELIX	Fiona would HATE it.	He might make me talk about his love of Star Wars during/after the snog.
JOSH	He is GORGEOUS and it would be über-cool to say that I've snogged an international rock star.	He's a promiscuous groupie snogger and probably has sexually transmitted herpes of the mouth.

♥ MARRY ♥

HOT BOY	PROS	CONS
VINCE	I would get to wake up next to him every day. Plus I already know what our children, Mancake Junior and Josh Adonis, will look like. It would be cruel to take away their lives before they've even been conceived.	ZERO!!!!!!!!!!
FELIX	Fiona would HATE it.	He might have a hidden sex fetish and ask me to dress up as the little green goblin or the hairy bear from Star Wars.
JOSH	We'd live in a massive house with its own recording studio where Camel Toe could record albums.	He's gay and could never really be in love with me.

171

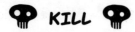 **KILL**

HOT BOY	PROS	CONS
VINCE	If I can't have him then nobody else will.	He is my soul mate.
FELIX	Fiona would HATE it.	He is proper, real-time hot.
JOSH	I would become a celebrity murderer like Mark Chapman, who murdered John Lennon.	No more Josh Raven music.

After a tough mental wrestling match with myself I settled on: snogging Felix, marrying Vince and killing Josh (but Felix only trumped Josh in the 'snog' category because of the mouth herpes situation).

Bumskulls were awesome. Vince, the dance-punk maestro, owned the stage and the audience were his powerless puppets. His trademark stage dive was once again received with enthusiasm and the crowd were calling for an encore long after the band had finished. He came to me straight away, all sweaty, wild-eyed and pumped full of adrenaline. He kissed my neck, took my hand and I found myself being lead outside into the darkness of the car park. In the background, Joel Scott had begun his acoustic set. It felt like one of those romantic film scene moments.

'This could be *our* song,' I said, leaning against the rough brick wall as the soft Spanish guitar sound floated around us.

'Yeah whatever,' Vince replied as he stroked my hair.

'I could make a playlist of tracks that can be "our" soundtrack,' I continued. 'Is there anything you want to put on it?'

Look at his sexy, sweaty face. If I were to lick off a droplet of his sweat would that make me a cannibal?

'No,' he replied bluntly. He was looking at me in that intense way again and, before I knew what was happening, he was kissing me – his hand moving straight to my nork.

Now what? Bat him away like a moth?

Just as the unease began to swell in my stomach, there came a strange wailing from above.

'Poncerama ooooooooooooooooh. It's no wonder that nobody really likes yooooooou.'

What the . . . ?

I looked up to see Matthew Ludlow balancing precariously on the edge of the golf club roof. In one hand he was waving a bottle of bright green, toxic-looking liquid (which I later discovered was crème de menthe, stolen from his parent's booze cabinet). Concerned for my unpredictable manager's welfare, I pushed Vince away. He glanced disinterestedly up at Matthew then focused on kissing me again.

'No, Vince,' I said firmly. His expression changed – a look of frustration and annoyance.

'Forget about him,' he said stroppily. 'He's an idiot.'

Instinctively I became defensive. 'He's my friend,' I replied as I freed myself from Vince's embrace. This was confusing.

Matthew's rude interruption had made me feel irritated and relieved simultaneously. How could that be?

'W-w-what you doing, you great p-p-pillock? Get down.'

Bob Ollox stepped out of the shadows into the lamplight, smoking a dodgy looking roll-up.

OH GOD. Was he watching us? I feel like I need to disinfect my modesty.

Matthew ignored him and carried on singing the rousing song lyrics that I had written for all the Weirdos in the world. I'd never heard him sing before and was surprised to discover that he had quite a nice voice.

'What's that you're d-d-drinking?' Bob asked. 'It's not got n-n-n-nuts in it has it? You'll make yourself sick again.'

Matthew has a mild nut allergy?

'You attention-seeking idiot,' yelled Vince quite aggressively.

But Matthew seemed unperturbed as he continued to share his song with the summer night sky. Bob, however, slowly turned his shaved, tattooed head, his eyes glaring with such blatant animosity at Vince that my Mancake felt no other option other than to retreat back into the safety of the golf club. I desperately wanted to follow him, but felt obliged to stay and help Bob. It took us another ten minutes to coax Matthew down from the roof, by which time any compassion that I might have felt had disappeared, especially as he dribbled all over my shoulder. Bob hugged him tight, as if he were his own son and led him off towards the van. I'm thinking that a stint in one of those hardcore Thai Buddhist rehab centres where they enforce a daily puking session in the Vomiting Temple, is probably on the cards. Matthew's parents could easily afford the fees.

I arrived back inside just in time to catch the end of Joel Scott's last song, another slow, dreary ballad. Petrina was engrossed in conversation with Leon, Mum was dancing alone with her eyes closed, head thrown back and arms aloft (I pretended not to know her) and Fiona was playfully stroking Vince's cheek as they giggled by the bar, their foreheads so close they were almost touching.

Wait! Rewind . . .

FIONA IS STROKING VINCE'S CHEEK?

He was looking at her in that intense way – the way he'd looked at me just fifteen minutes ago. When Felix returned from the toilet, they quickly moved away from each other.

Right then I understood exactly how Walter must have felt at the sight of Petrina lustfully drooling over Leon. Blinking back the burning tears that had caught me by surprise, I averted my eyes. I never thought I'd be the jealous type – always assuming that I was open-minded and generally cool. But seeing the first boy who had ever shown an interest in me now showing the same interest in Fiona Tittledown hurt me in a way that I'd never felt before.

It was obvious, of course. Who had I been trying to kid?

Vince was so completely out of my league. What would a proper real-time HOT Winner want with a Weirdo like me when he could have someone as popular and beautiful as

Fiona at the click of his fingers?

Vince re-joined me on stage along with Petrina and the rest of the quarter finalists. But now it felt like nothing mattered anymore. I didn't care when the crowd went crazy after Margo Tittledown announced that Bumskulls were through to the semi-finals, nor did I feel excited when Pete Hartley gave me and Petrina a huge hug as Camel Toe were told that they'd be joining them. I went through the motions of embracing and high-fiving everyone around me and managed to smile when Mum kissed me and said how proud she was. And I laughed when Breeze smacked the back of my head and told me that I was 'pretty cool for a massive Weirdo'. But all I really wanted was to go home, crawl into bed and go to sleep forever.

From: Noodlebrain12
To: RavenGirl007
Sent: July 21st 23:53:10

Hey!
I have a question for you. Is Narnia a real place?
Cheers,
Noodlebrain12

From: RavenGirl007
To: Noodlebrain12
Sent: July 21st 23:57:22

No. Why?

RavenGirl007
P.S. I was almost asleep.

From: Noodlebrain12
To: RavenGirl007
Sent: July 21st 23:59:01

I thought the train I'm on right now was going to Narnia.
Never mind. This must be the one that goes to Hogwarts.
Cheers,
Noodlebrain12

From: RavenGirl007
To: Noodlebrain12
Sent: July 22nd 00:01:01

You're a bit mad aren't you?
RavenGirl007

From: Noodlebrain12
To: RavenGirl007
Sent: July 22nd 00:01:43

Bum drops!
Noodlebrain12

After arriving half an hour late for work, I dragged myself
to McDonald's for a lonesome lunch-for-one (where Kirsty

Mackerby snuck me TWO free Big Macs and a chocolate milkshake due to 'the sadness in my eyes almost breaking her heart'). Then after work I curled up on the sofa underneath my duvet to watch *Bite Me – Dusky Dark Part 1* for the twentieth time. My mood was lifted slightly when I read online that the third film in the trilogy has just begun filming, but even the thought of more gratuitous topless shots of Nigel the sexy vampire couldn't completely banish the overwhelming feeling of darkness that had wrapped itself around me.

Listening to maudlin, self-indulgent songs to ease the melancholy of heartbreak is a teenage rite of passage, although up until now I hadn't had the opportunity to try it out for real. But now that I was genuinely suffering, I was able to listen to the twenty-five-track 'heartbreak playlist' that I had started eighteen months ago (I update it with new songs every few weeks) and I'm pleased to report that listening to dreary songs about rejection and anguish is TOTALLY effective. I allowed myself to wallow in wonderful, sonic self-pity for hours and enjoyed it so much that I intend to do it again every night for the foreseeable future.

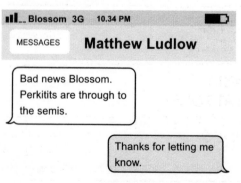

I'm really sorry about last night. :(

That's ok. Maybe you should visit the Vomiting Temple.

Cool! Is that a nightclub? It's a date. When shall we go?

Nooooooo. It's a place where alcoholics go to sick up booze.

Oh. Right....think I'll give it a miss.

 SEND

END OF WEEK 29. MY TABLE OF ACHIEVEMENT

SHAME LEVEL PEAK	*Level 3 (snogging in front of my parents while they made 'phwooar' gestures was pretty mortifying).*
GUITAR PRACTICE	*I'm working on bar chords. This week I will attempt to master F#m.*
PARTY INVITATIONS	*0*
SNOGS	*Vince accidentally touched my nork, then RIPPED out my heart.*

MEAD MOON

ALSO KNOWN AS MOON OF CLAIMING,
ROSE MOON, MOON OF THE MIDDLE SUMMER
BUCK MOON

The atmosphere between Petrina and me was tense. I'd spent the entire weekend wallowing in my pit of gloom, but when I arrived at her house it seemed that she was in an even worse state than me. Although she claims not to be the kind of person who needs to keep tabs on her boyfriend, she was constantly checking her phone and even asked me to text her in case it wasn't working. It was a tricky situation – I'd tried to remain impartial, but having seen Vince flirt so outrageously with Fiona, I couldn't help but side fully with Walter. Vince could at least plead 'inappropriate touching disease' as his reason for behaving like a quimboid, but Petrina had no excuse at all for sneaking around with Leon. We mechanically ran through the Camel Toe set without speaking. There was no doubt about it – we sounded lame.

One of us had to rise above the situation.

'Whatever's going on between us,' I reasoned after an hour and twenty minutes of verbal silence. 'We've got to leave it at the door.'

I am SO mature.

'What? Like a pair of dirty, soiled boots?' Petrina's tone was aggressive.

'Remember Glastonbury before you compare our friendship to a pair of poo-covered wellies,' I said. 'At least we were happy then.'

'We need a gimmick,' said Petrina ignoring me.

'What kind of gimmick?' I asked.

We couldn't afford the hydraulic crane that we wanted to lift Petrina and her keyboard above the audience's heads. Or the giant radio-controlled hamburger that would slowly open to reveal Camel Toe standing on a stage made from a massive gherkin.

'A simple stage dive into crowd surf?' Petrina suggested.

'Vince does that already in the Bumskulls set.'

'Yeah, but you don't often get girls doing it.'

She was right. Although we somehow managed to leave our poo-covered wellies at the door, it was an awkward, laboured hour that we spent choreographing a stage dive that we would then work into our set. All the greatest rock stars have done it at some point. How hard can it be?

My parents are going away on a yoga retreat in a week and have agreed to let me stay behind to look after the house. HOME ALONE!!!!! And while they're gone, I'm going to throw a party to celebrate my sixteenth birthday. I was going to do it secretly without telling them (a proper act of teenage rebellion) but Mum had already bought twenty-four bottles of (organic) lager and fifteen family-sized packets of vegetable crisps for me in preparation. I'm not entirely sure if having the approval of my parents for a night of debauchery and hardcore partying is cool or just plain weird, but I'm excited about it all the same. To make sure that the evening runs smoothly without any hiccups, I've put together a Party Planning Committee comprising of me, Walter and Matthew. (Petrina was so touchy at band practice that I daren't approach her about it.) Matthew is a self-declared 'Party Expert' – he's had loads of brilliant parties and has offered to help organise it. First up I created an online events page, inviting everyone in my year at school.

AUG 6	PARTY!!! PARTY!! PARTY!!

 Invited by Blossom

 You're invited to celebrate Blossom's 16th Birthday

On: Saturday 6th August

 7.30-11.30pm

So bring a drink and your dancing shoes.

I've sent a text to Vince (but have had no reply yet) and Paulette has agreed to promote the event in return for me advertising her Dempsey Love website. This is going to be the best party EVER, even if Mum has insisted on us having a doorman in case things get 'out of control'. (She clapped her hands gleefully as she said 'out of control' as if this was exactly what she hoped would happen.) She suggested that one of the 'Johns' might be the man for the job, but I immediately said no. I really wasn't comfortable with the idea of ex-convict John Clinton or John Hawthorne the flasher or John Baker the drug dealer acting as my doorman. Instead I have promised to find a suitable (less horrendous) person for the job.

Breeze and my mum are worse than the Spanish Inquisition. After we'd had dinner at Breeze's flat, they both decided to come with me to my self-defence class. On the way there, I was subjected to a painful interrogation about my physical relationship with Vince, during which Breeze mentioned the time she caught pubic lice from a bearded herbalist named Dusty. Even though I was adamant that I wouldn't need them any time soon, Mum maintained that 'safe sex is paramount' and insisted on pulling in at a petrol station to buy me a packet of condoms (as if I would take contraceptive advice from two women who between them have utilised the NHS sexual health clinic more than anyone else I know).

The church hall was full and Kenny was impatiently pacing up and down when we arrived even though we were only three minutes late. After initially refusing to believe that I was Mum's daughter ('but how could someone so feeble come out of someone so resilient?'), he paired us all up, putting Petrina and me together. She didn't protest, but then she didn't give me a friendly greeting either. We had to go back over what we'd learned so far – first up was fending off a male attacker.

'WHERE?' Kenny yelled at the top of his voice.

'BALLS,' we all shouted back.

'LOUDER,' he added. 'Burst his eardrums. THEN . . . twist and pull.'

I continued to scream 'BALLS' as loudly as I possibly could, then reached down and pretended to yank and rotate Petrina's imaginary scrotum.

'OW!' yelled Petrina totally over dramatically. 'That hurt.'

'How could it?' I snapped. 'Your testicles aren't even real.'

'Yeah, well you did it too hard.'

I wasn't going to argue. It had been like this between us all evening. At one point Petrina had deliberately elbowed me in the stomach although she claimed it was an accident.

Equally horrendous to the distinctly bad vibes between me and Petrina was having to bear witness to Mum flirting with Kenny the meathead. She was already in high spirits seeing as tonight was a full moon (the Mead Moon) and the weather was clear for her monthly naked moon-dance, so watching her publicly parading her sexuality in a women's self-defence class was almost as bad as it gets. I say 'almost'. Worse was to come.

After dropping Breeze back at her flat, we arrived home to find Dad eagerly changing out of his Morris dancing costume, preparing for the moon dance. I wanted to make myself scarce for my parent's intimate monthly ritual, so I knocked up some beans on toast and a cup of tea, then retreated upstairs. To find my mum stark naked in my room was nothing unusual – she and Dad are always wandering around the house with no clothes on. I don't particularly like it, but I'm certainly used to it. She was facing my Josh Raven poster (the soggy-mouthed one) when I walked in.

'He really is a cutie isn't he?' she said. 'Though a little bit smooth and clean-cut for me. I prefer them rough and ready.'

She turned round to face me and I instantly noticed that she was holding my wooden paddle hairbrush in her hand.

OH. MY. GOD.

'W . . . W . . . WHAT ARE YOU DOING?' I stammered almost spilling my beans all over the cream carpet.

'Oh, I couldn't find my hairbrush,' she said waving mine in the air. 'I always like to make sure I'm neat and tidy before the moon dance.'

And then she continued to comb her ENORMOUS bush with MY hairbrush.

'You don't mind do you?' she asked rhetorically. 'I might get one of these myself. Doesn't yank at the pubes as much my Tangle Teezer.'

Oh my eyes, my eyes, they're bleeding.

Then she threw the brush on my bed and walked out of my room as if nothing REVOLTING had happened. I wonder if John the therapist does hypno-counselling to erase mentally disturbing images of parental nudity? Or am I just going to have to burn that pubicly contaminated brush?

It'd been almost a week since my heart had been RIPPED APART by Vince and, having to deal with the Petrina situation as well, I felt more miserable than I've felt in my entire life. In an effort to cheer myself up I asked Nile if I could have another strum on the cherry-red Gibson ES-335 when I got into work this morning (after I'd nipped into Boots to buy myself a new hairbrush). That elegant guitar was the only thing that I knew would take my mind off Vince (who still hadn't called or sent me a single text to apologise). However, when I arrived, the Gibson wasn't in its usual place.

'Where is it?' I asked Dad who was standing behind the counter.

Dad shrugged. 'Sold, I guess.'

Nile appeared from the back room holding a 'translucent ochre-yellow' (with leopard pick guard) Hohner MadCat Telecaster guitar. It was stunning (but not as stunning as the absent guitar of my dreams).

'This one was actually played by Prince,' he said, proudly placing it in the central display holder that once held my beloved Gibson ES-335. 'Do you know my mum once slept with Prince? He could be my father.'

'Where's the Gibson?' I asked desperately.

'Sold it a couple of days ago.'

Seeing how distraught I was, Dad came over and gave me a big hug and for a brief moment, as I snuggled up against his chunky knit cardigan, I felt comforted. With my head rested against his chest I gazed out through the window just as Fiona and Vince walked past together.

Nooooo! Get away from her! She's riddled with ticks and ear mites.

Without a beat, I was up and out of the shop door. And there they were. Fiona (wearing huge sunglasses and a baseball cap pulled down low over her face as if she was a Z-list pop star in disguise) and MY VAG arm in arm, looking very much like a young couple in love.

'VINCE!' I hadn't intended to shout. It just kind of came out automatically.

Fiona leapt away from him as they stopped and turned back towards me. There was a look of surprise on his face.

'Hey!' he grinned.

WOWZOIDS! He's hotter than a randy firefly's scrotum.

Behind him, Fiona side-shuffled under the awning of a shop front and pulled her cap down even lower in an attempt to make herself less visible.

'I didn't know you and Felix had split up.'

Fiona was inching ever further away (though not far enough for my liking).

'We err . . . haven't,' she stuttered. 'I just bumped into Vince on the street. Nothing dodgy. All above board. Felix totally wouldn't mind.'

LIAR, LIAR! CROTCHLESS PANTS ON FIRE!

'What you up to?' asked Vince in his uber cool way.

'Erm . . . I was just . . . looking at our new Hohner MadCat Telecaster guitar,' I said, trying to sound as casual and non-jealous as possible.

'Like Prince plays?' he asked, moving towards me.

Ah-ha! The intoxicating allure of the mighty guitar. Come to me, my pretty.

'Yeah,' I stated, more confidently. 'He's actually played this one.'

'No way!'

Gotcha!

Vince started walking towards me with an expression of pure excitement. 'Can I see?'

Fiona's face dropped as she realised she was no competition for the sheer awesomeness of a Telecaster. I gave her a (fake) consolatory smile as Vince stepped into the shop to be with me. Not her. Me. ME ME ME!!! My heartbreak almost forgotten, I knew I would feed off of this one small victory for weeks – the two of us, sitting on the shop counter, examining the merits of the best guitars out on display. The sight of Fiona's defeated expression had momentarily brought me a sense of contentment and I was able to push the miserable thoughts of my broken friendship and Vince's previous betrayal to the back of my mind.

When it was time for me to leave, I asked Vince if he wanted to go on for a milkshake in Joe's Café, but he said he had to meet someone. For a moment I was tempted to follow him just in case he was off to see Fiona again (though not in a jealous-psycho-stalkerish way of course), but Nile stopped me in my tracks by making me do a stock take.

I proudly performed The Prostitute Walk on my way home with 'Moonlight Stalker' as the soundtrack blaring from my headphones. I felt more sexually confident than ever before and was trying to incorporate an aggressive swagger into my walk that didn't make me look like a prison warden. My imaginary music video hooker was an empowering role that I think I managed to perfect and by the time I'd walked the two miles home, I reckon most people wouldn't have been able to pick me out as the imposter in a line-up of real prostitutes.

The following day was quiet in the shop. We only had one customer all morning – a man in his early twenties with a bowl haircut who'd been playing 'Greensleeves' repeatedly on a recorder for over an hour. So when the shop door opened and Paulette walked in wearing a cropped Dempsey Love vest top and black leggings, I was as relieved to see her as I was annoyed.

'You are never going to find love in here,' she said shaking her head as she looked at the Greensleeves man.

'It's OK,' I smiled confidently. 'I'm already "seeing" someone.'

But am I though? Are Vince and I actually going out?

Paulette seemed concerned. 'You need to get a grip, Blossom. Sex dreams aren't real.'

WHAT?

'That's by the by,' she continued. 'Let's talk business. I'm working on a "dating tips" page for my website that offers advice to dating couples. I want to shoot a short film next week and as the face of Dempsey Love I need *you* to be the star.'

A film star? ME?

'Err . . . I don't know. I'm really bad at acting,' I said, desperately searching for an excuse. Paulette's already put my bare norks out there for the world to see, so God knows what part of my body she has her sights on now. 'When we did the school production of *Oliver!* Mrs Carrington said I was the most unconvincing London orphan she'd ever seen.'

'That's because you were delivering your lines in a Pakistani accent.'

'It was supposed to be cockney.'

Paulette folded her dimpled arms. 'It's OK. You won't have to act, you've just got to be yourself.'

For some reason (loyalty/boredom/curiosity/stupidity – delete where applicable) I found myself agreeing to Paulette's request.

When my phone rang that evening, while I was watching Josh Raven videos on YouTube, I was delighted to see Vince's name flash up on the screen.

Play it cool Blossom. Calm yourself.

I picked up the phone.

'I LOVE YOU VINCE!'

Nooooo.

'Eh?'

'Nothing. How's . . . it going?'

Good recovery.

'Yeah cool. So do you want to meet for a drink after you finish work tomorrow?'

'IS A FROG'S BUM WATERTIGHT?'

'Eh?'

'I mean . . . Yes, that would be nice.'

'Cool. See you in Joe's Café.'

I waited for him to hang up before I whispered 'Marry me, my one true love . . .'

'Eh?'

Noooo! KILL ME NOW! He hasn't hung up!

'Err . . . it's a . . . hymn . . .' I blurted.

Quick, make up a tune.

'Marry me, my one true love . . .

You're a red-footed booby and I'm a turtle dove.

Your sweet scent takes my breath away . . .

What have you stepped in to smell this way?'

Vow. Freestyle singing in rhyming couplets is really hard.

'See you tomorrow then Vince . . . Vince?'

Oh. He's hung up.

Paulette is still refusing to reveal the secret formula for the online 'Dempsey Love Calculator'. She claims to have been given the ancient tried-and-tested mathematical equation by a Witch Doctor who she met at a safari park in Wiltshire. The spooky man warned her that if she ever reveals the secret formula to anyone else a plague of human-sized hornets will sting her to death. It sounded totally viable to me, so I spent a bit of time playing around with different love combinations.

Blossom + Vince = 8%
VAG + BUM = 3%
Blossom + VAG = 11%
BUM + Vince = 9.5%
Blossom Uxley-Michaels + Vince Aston-Granger = 7%
Bee + Vee = 54%

Breeze has moved back home AGAIN. Feeling suspicious, she followed Andreas yesterday afternoon as he walked the short distance into town. He apparently met a woman (who Breeze recognised as Tania, the Movie Nights London club manager) outside the cinema, kissed her on both cheeks and then Breeze watched in horror as they looked at a menu in the window of the swanky restaurant Garden of Vegan. She was so infuriated that Andreas would dare to have an affair with another vegan that she left immediately so as not to embarrass herself in public (it's never stopped her before). She went back to the flat, packed up some things and called Dad at work to come and pick her up (which he did, like the slave to my sister that he is).

But Breeze's love life was no concern of mine, especially now that I was back 'on' with Vince. My chocolate milkshake was both the most delicious drink I'd ever tasted and the most annoying as I sat gazing at him across the table, listening as he raved about a new Fender American Standard Tele in Mystic Blue that he was saving up for. You see I just couldn't find a way to suck the straw without it looking suggestive. Ever since Vince caught me eating a phallic banana, every type of food seems to have the potential to appear rude.

TOP 5 FOODS THAT I WILL NEVER EAT IN PUBLIC AGAIN

1. Banana
2. Ice lolly
3. Plums
4. Cadbury's Creme Egg
5. Haggis

In the end I puckered up and sort of kiss-sucked the straw. It popped out of my mouth and I quickly retrieved it with my tongue. Vince stopped talking abruptly and leaned across the table with a smile on his face.

'Game on, again?' he purred.

What game is that then?

'Of course,' I replied, hoping he'd give me a clue into what exactly we were about to play.

'I should warn you, I'm the master of this game,' Vince

grinned. 'And I always catch my prey.'

Ah-ha! I get it! I haven't played this since I was a kid.

'Well, I've always been pretty good at this game too,' I said as I got to my feet. I took the straw out of my empty glass and absentmindedly licked off the last drops of milkshake. 'You better start counting.'

Vince winked then sat back in his chair and watched as I walked out of the café. I ran across the road and found THE BEST HIDING PLACE EVER – inside a clothes-recycling bin. In fact it was such an awesome hiding place that I was still crouching inside two hours later. Vince might be a proper real time hot Mancake, but he is totally rubbish at hide and seek.

Andreas pulled up outside our house, early evening. He was on his way to his Movie Nights club dressed as Spiderman and, aside from the skin-tight Lycra exposing way too much in his downstairs department, it was a huge relief to see him. The sooner Breeze and her massive oscillating blow holes moved back in with him, the better. It's like she's got a bad case of PMS (Permanent Moody Syndrome).

'Come with me,' he yelled from the open-top, James Bond-replica Aston Martin.

Breeze was leaning out of my bedroom window, looking angry. 'Go away you bushy boar,' she screamed back.

Andreas was standing on the driver seat with his hands on his hips. 'You miss me and my manliness. Come home.'

The door of number 34 opened and Mr Parkin rushed outside. 'Have I missed anything?' he called to me, looking worried.

I shook my head. 'She called him a "bushy boar"', I replied.

'Phew. I've heard that one before. I'd hate to miss a new one.' Mr Parkin nipped back inside and re-emerged a few seconds later with a tube of Pringles and his camping chair.

'You're nothing but a lying, cheating, longhaired baboon,' shrieked my sister.

Andreas beat his chest with his fists. 'We all sprang from apes,' he yelled.

'Yes, but you didn't spring far enough,' Breeze spat.

Mr Parkin clapped his hands in delight. 'Good one!' he exclaimed.

Andreas squatted down and rearranged his goolies. I felt a bit of sick come up into my mouth. 'I'm the only man you need,' he said.

Breeze shouted back, 'Yeah but you'll never be the man your mother is.'

She slammed the window shut causing the whole house to vibrate with her rage.

Half an hour later and she was driving off into the sunset with Spiderman in his Aston Martin convertible. Love is weird.

END OF WEEK 30. MY TABLE OF ACHIEVEMENT

SHAME LEVEL PEAK	*Level 3 (Mum buying condoms for me).*
GUITAR PRACTICE	*I've given up on bar chords. My fingers are clearly the wrong shape.*
PARTY INVITATIONS	*1 (does an invitation to my own party count? I think so).*
SNOGS	*No actual snogs, but I am back on with Vince.*

WEEK 31
TOTALLY LEGAL

It was Dempsey Love filming day and Paulette had set up her kitchen as a kind of intimate restaurant. She'd blocked out the natural light by pinning sheets over the windows and had tried to create a romantic vibe with a candlelit table laid for two. Sitting on one of the chairs picking his nose was a small, ginger-haired boy. His expression of sheer determination as he rummaged around inside, turned to that of triumph as he retrieved the prize and placed it carefully on his tongue.

'Simon, that's disgusting,' said Paulette. 'Go away.'

'I am having my snotty snack at the table,' he replied nonchalantly. 'It's the chef's special.'

'Blossom's date will be here in a minute, so hop it and watch TV.'

WHOA! I have a date? But how did she get Vince's phone number?

Paulette took a five-pound note out of her pocket and waved it in front of her little brother.

'Gotta keep him sweet,' she said to me. 'He designed and coded my website. He's one of those freaky child prodigies. A technical genius.'

Simon stuck out his lip as he snatched the cash from

his sister and climbed off the chair. He looked up at me (still munching on his bogey)

'You smell funny,' he said.

RUDE.

'Why, what do I smell of?' I asked.

'Farts,' he said, before pottering off to watch TV.

He might have had a point. Being trapped in a confined space all day with a vegan (Dad) and a spicy food fanatic (Nile) did have some violently pungent consequences. 'So what's all this about a "date"?' I asked Paulette.

'Mei will be your dinner partner today,' she said, not quite managing to look me in the eye.

'But . . . Mei?'

Paulette sighed. 'She was the only person available at such short notice'.

'You don't even like her.'

Paulette's issues with Mei have almost reached fever pitch over the past few weeks.

'I never let emotions get in the way of business,' she said firmly. 'Anyway, I've asked Mei to butch up for the film.'

Before I could consider what 'butch up' actually meant, the doorbell rang and I was able to see for myself. Mei Miyagi stood on the doorstep wearing a sharp, tailored, slim-fit black suit that hung perfectly on her sporty physique. Her hair was slicked back and she'd drawn on a bit of stubble with eye pencil that gave her an air of masculinity and sophistication. I'm not going to lie – with her firm jaw-line and intense brown eyes she looked hotter than a strip club on fire.

'All right, Mei?' I said self-consciously.

Mei frowned. 'Marco,' she said in low voice. 'My name is Marco.'

Oh God. I'm all confused. I think I find her attractive. BUT only as a man. When Mei is a woman she does nothing for me. What does this mean? Am I a hetrobian? A homohetrual? A lesbatarian? WHAT DOES IT MEAN?

I wondered if this was a watershed moment in my life when my suppressed lesbionic feelings were finally rising to the surface. But from the back of my mind an image of Josh Raven in the 'Moonlight Stalker' video, where he is standing topless (his proper real time sexy nipple ring in FULL view) underneath a gushing waterfall, kept appearing and after a few moments he was joined in the cascading water by Vince who was TOPLESS too! After a bit of thought, I came to the conclusion that I am 98% heterosexual and 2% homohetrual.

The actual filming itself seemed to go well. All Mei and I had to do was sit at the table eating spaghetti bolognese while Paulette shouted directions at us, e.g.

• 'Gaze into each other's eyes as if they were delicious Maltesers.'
• 'Make love to the pasta. No, Mei NOT literally – I mean look at it with a sexy face.'
• 'Lick your lips seductively as if they were smeared all over with Branston pickle.'

However, the afternoon ended in a bad way when Mei stormed out of the house after Paulette refused to pay her any 'repeat fees' saying theirs was purely a 'buyout' agreement. I didn't really have a clue what they were arguing about although I'm slightly annoyed with myself for settling on a 10% discount membership to Dempsey Love Online and a 'Before you make love physically, show it mentally' badge as payment for my services. I really need to wise up on business matters.

Matthew still hasn't told anyone about seeing Petrina and Leon together in Joe's Café. As a result, Walter's suspicions are still unconfirmed and it's only his own speculative thoughts that he has to go on (which are of course right!). He hasn't texted Petrina for days and is keeping himself to himself. But the knock-on effect of Petrina's unspoken betrayal was not only eating at Walter, but at me and even Matthew, who says the situation is making him feel uncomfortable. I'd agreed to catch up with the boys for a Party Planning Meeting in McDonald's. With the way things were between us, I still hadn't asked Petrina to join the committee. As much as I wanted to include her, I'd fill her in on the details at the next best opportunity but right then, I had no idea when that might be.

Walter and I were already stuffing our faces with the free burgers that Kirsty had given us when Matthew arrived.

'Vince is with Fiona Tittledown,' he said.

Surely he wouldn't meet up with her again? Vince is with me now . . . I think.

'Don't be silly,' I replied with a gob full.

'It was definitely him. On the high street,' he said adamantly.

'It's probably just his doppelgänger,' I laughed, turning to

Walter. 'Remember when we saw *my* double that time when we were queuing for tickets at the cinema?'

Walter grinned. 'How could I forget? The likeness was uncanny.'

'Of course, it would have been preferable to have a female double,' I said, cringing a bit at the memory. 'Although it's safe to say that I do look hot with a goatee.'

'Yikes,' exclaimed Matthew.

'But you see? Everyone has a doppelgänger and I think you've just seen Vince's.'

Wowzoids! IMAGINE! Two Vinces!! I could hold hands with both of them on either side of me. I could kiss one and then the other. I could walk with each of my hands on one of their bum cheeks. I AM AROUSED. Oh God. Does this mean I am a three-way sexual pervert?

'I suppose,' Matthew mumbled as he sat down. 'Anyway, we need to plan your party. It's less than a week away and already over a hundred people have said they're coming online.'

'HOW MANY?'

My mind was suddenly filled with terrifying visions of drunken thugs and criminals gatecrashing my party, trashing the house, weeing in the plant pots and puking all over Polystyrene Stonehenge.

'It's OK,' Matthew chipped in. 'I'll ask Bob to be the doorman. He used to be a bouncer at a rough bikers club in Leeds where they fought each other all the time with chains and axes.'

'I feel safer already,' said Walter.

Our party planning duties were shared in the following way.

WALTER: DJing and music (Matthew did volunteer but he is still in the infancy stages of his musical education). I will of course have final say on the playlist.

BLOSSOM: Food.

MATTHEW: PA system, security and drink (although he is under STRICT instructions NOT to bring any spirits on to the premises).

PETRINA (?): Decorations (the weather looks set to be good so it'll be a garden party. Petrina will – hopefully – relish the challenge of decorating Polystyrene Stonehenge).

Matthew Ludlow sits behind a desk wearing a white suit with no shirt underneath. I am surprised to see that he is quite muscular and doesn't have the pigeon chest that I was expecting. I feel my cheeks begin to flush. (It is NOT a scientifically proven facial erection. There are exceptions to the rule and right now I am simply feeling a bit warm.)

'I can guarantee you a place in the final,' says Matthew, blowing cigar smoke out of his mouth.

'Don't you know smoking kills?' I shout.

'I didn't know you cared,' he smiles.

'I don't,' I reply. 'I just don't want a dead manager.'

Right then the door to Matthew's office is flung open and Vince walks in.

'You don't need him,' says Vince. 'You need me as your manager. You WANT me.'

Matthew makes a peculiar noise as he clutches his throat with his hands.

'Help me,' he gasps. 'I'm dying.'

Did he just swallow his cigar? You see – smoking really does kill. Vince holds his hand out towards me.

'Come with me,' he whispers in a proper real-time sexy voice.

Matthew Ludlow slumps on to his desk. I know I should help him but the hole at the top of Vince's thigh is winking at me. I swallow hard and feel myself redden. My face is publicly aroused. Damn it.

'Don't do it, Blossom. He only wants you for your flat chest.'

I look back at Matthew. His strawberry-blonde hair has become damp with sweat. I feel a strong urge to reach out and softly stroke his forehead. But Vince is like a strip of Velcro and I'm like an expensive cashmere jumper. As our hands touch, I don't want to snag my woolly body by pulling away.

'I'm sorry, Matthew,' I say. 'The Mancake and I are meant to be together.'

But my apology is wasted as Matthew has already died.

Later that afternoon I went over to Petrina's house to talk through the party plans, but she stood in the doorway and didn't invite me in.

'So, are you OK being in charge of decorations?' I asked from the doorstep.

Petrina pushed her glasses up on to the bridge of her nose. 'I'll cover Polystyrene Stonehenge with fairy lights and candles,' she said without actually looking me in the eye. 'It will look enchanting.'

'Sounds great,' I replied.

There was a long, awkward silence.

'Erm . . .' I was trying to fill the gap. 'Do you want to come over and practise the stage dive with me later?'

'OK,' Petrina replied curtly. She turned away and closed the door behind her. I don't know if I can exactly name the emotion that I felt at that moment, but it was one of the most horrible sensations I'd ever experienced.

To: rachel.ferloine@poptasticmanagement.com

Sent: August 2nd 07:22:01

From: Blossom Uxley-Michaels

Subj: STAGE DIVING

Hi Rachel,

Hope you are well and not snorting too much coke off the toilet seat at the office!!!!!!!! ROCK 'N' ROLL!!!!!!!!!

Anyway, I was hoping you could help me out. We've got through to the semi-finals in the Battle of the Bands competition and I would like to incorporate a stage dive/crowd surf into the Camel Toe set. I know Josh often stage dives (in a really sexy way that kind of looks like he's humping the heads of the audience) and I wonder if he could give me some tips to make my stage dive as good as his (although I don't want to head hump).

Many thanks,
Blossom Uxley Michaels

P.S. It's my birthday tomorrow (not that I'm hinting or anything. Although if you have a spare guitar or drum kit lying around the office then I'll gladly accept it as a gift).

To: Blossom Uxley-Michaels
Sent: August 2nd 17:07:28
From: rachel.ferloine@poptasticmanagement.com
RE: STAGE DIVING

Dear Blossom,

Thank you for your email. It's always enlightening to hear from you.

I have called Josh on your behalf and he has these tips for you:

1. Make sure your trousers are on securely to avoid embarrassment.
2. Always search for the part of the crowd where there are the most hands in the air to catch you.
3. Jump for distance rather than height. You don't want to come down on the crowd like a ton of bricks.

4. If in doubt, make sure you have a friend in the crowd who will catch you.

Josh also wants you to be the first person to know that he will be one of the judges for the Battle of the Bands Final. He wishes you the best of luck with the semi-finals and hopes to see you on stage at the final.

I hope this helps and 'happy birthday' for tomorrow!

Best wishes,
Rachel Ferloine

Management Assistant
Poptastic Management

P.S. I don't do drugs and neither does anyone else in the Poptastic Management office.

After last week's involuntary display of violence, I decided not to go to self-defence (again!) and persuaded Petrina to come over for a band rehearsal instead. The mood between us was still unpleasantly frosty, but now that we knew Josh Raven would be one of the finalist judges we were able to be professionally civil with each other. After we ran through our set, I practised stage diving while Petrina supported me with her hands to help me glide through the air. It was as if we were in *Dirty Dancing*, training for the pivotal scene where we had to do 'the lift' in front of hundreds of people. I must take note of Josh Raven's first piece of advice – 'make sure your trousers are on securely to avoid embarrassment'. Even so, I will NOT be wearing my brown Scooby Doo pants. I will instead buy a brand new pair of attractive, yet functional knickers that will secure my modesty should the worst happen. A stage-diving rock star can never be too careful.

After practising the F#m bar chord on Cassiopeia in my bedroom for forty minutes, I decided to give Vince a call.

This time I will absolutely NOT act like a prize quimboid when I speak to Vince. Just act normal when he answers. As if you're speaking to a parent.

"Ello?'

'Hi Dad!'

Arrrrrrrgggghhhhhhh!

'Eh?'

'Nothing! It's me . . . Blossom.'

'Oh right . . . what's up?'

'I just thought I'd ring and say hi . . . see how you are . . .'

'Yeah . . . can't complain.'

The way he copes so positively with his wandering-hands disease is so inspiring. I must remember to nominate him for The Pride of Britain Awards.

'Look, I gotta go,' he continued. 'You want to meet up tomorrow?'

He has SO remembered my birthday.

'God YEAH.'

But I really hope he doesn't want to play hide and seek again. I was in that bin for hours before I realised he'd gone home.

AUGUST 3RD. I AM SIXTEEN YEARS OLD

Mum woke me up at 8 o'clock this morning singing the rude version of Happy Birthday (Happy birthday to you / Though you make us all spew / Get plastered, you bastard / Happy birthday to you) holding a cup of tea and a small present, carefully wrapped in green paper, tied with a silver bow. With bleary eyes I sat up and gratefully received my gift.

'Thanks, Mum.'

She sat down on the bed next to me and softly flattened my wild bed hair. 'I can't believe my baby is all grown up,' she smiled.

'I can't drive or vote,' I said.

'But you can have sex. And sex is what makes the world go round.'

Just what I want to hear first thing on my birthday.

I began to unwrap my present. It was a small, rather beautiful wooden box, with hand-carved woodland creatures decorating the lid. I wondered what could be inside. A necklace? A bracelet? Mum looked on eagerly as I carefully opened the lid of the box. Inside was a transparent plastic bag filled with dried green leaves.

Mum clapped her hands excitedly. 'Now that you're sixteen, if you choose to try marijuana, that's absolutely fine. But there's a lot of dodgy stuff around these days. You need a reliable supplier, so I got this from your dad's friend John Baker. He only deals in the best.'

She took the bag that I was still holding between my thumb and forefinger and sniffed it deeply. 'It's good stuff – just don't leave it lying around the house. It's been a long time since your dad and I got stoned so if we see it, we'll definitely smoke it.'

HOW CAN I EVER REBEL AGAINST THESE PARENTS?

Later on after breakfast, I took the bag of cannabis outside and tipped it into the rhododendron bush where Tinkie was in the middle of doing her business.

Walter dropped by as I was getting ready to meet Vince in Manor Park. I was having a NIGHTMARE. I'd no idea which T-shirt to wear, my cut off black jeans were dirty (the washing machine is broken after Mum's hairbrush accidentally got put in on a wash and her hair clogged up the filter. HER HAIR!), I had three new spots on my chin, there was a piece of marmalade rind stuck in my brace that I couldn't pick out and the pink stripe in my hair was wildly out of control (it looked like a run-over flamingo had crawled into my hair to die). Walter solved one of my problems with his BRILLIANT birthday present: a Poncerama T-shirt that he'd designed himself.

When the doorbell rang, with everyone else in my family out at work, Walter offered to answer it. I heard a little bit of low mumbling and then two sets of footsteps climbing the stairs.

'Happy birthday,' said Petrina walking into my bedroom in her canary-yellow Skadi uniform, her blue eyes avoiding my gaze behind her heavy-rimmed glasses.

'Do you know there's a tortoiseshell cat running about on its hind legs in your front garden'?

I thought of the cannabis that I'd discarded in the

rhododendron bush and felt a bit irresponsible. Walter stood sheepishly in the doorway, his long, dark fringe masking his entire face as he looked down at the floor. The tension between the three of us was so intense you could almost reach out and twang it (I imagine 'tension' to look like a steel guitar string). And the atmosphere between my two best friends was not so much frosty as positively Ice Age with no sign of a big thaw in the foreseeable future. Petrina handed me a card, inside which were a pair of tickets to see King Quiff playing live in a few months.

MY TOP 5 SIXTEENTH BIRTHDAY PRESENTS

1. & 2. (joint first) Poncerama T-shirt/King Quiff tickets.

3. Vegan eight-hole purple DM boots from Breeze and Andreas. I LOVE these. They would have been in first place if they'd been made of leather – my feet are definitely not vegetarian. They're proper meat-eaters just like the rest of me.

4. Why Men Are like Dogs from Aunty Claire (which I can't wait to read).

5. A joke 'plastic turd' key ring from Uncle James.

And then of course there was the bag of cannabis weed from my parents – which is only marginally better than the eco-friendly water bed that they got me for my fourteenth birthday. It was made from recycled wetsuits and rubber dinghies and was the most uncomfortable mattress EVER. It burst after only a week, flooding my bedroom and forcing me to sleep on the sofa for the next two months. Thankfully I have the two best friends in the world (at least I *think* Petrina is still my best friend), who got me the most awesome gifts I could have even asked for. If only we could all kiss and make up so Petrina and Walter could double date with Vince and me. But as things stand, Petrina can barely tolerate being in the same room as me and still can't even bring herself to look at Walter. She only hung around for another painful five minutes before making her excuses and leaving. Walter was resting his forehead on the windowpane, his long fringe pressed up against the glass as we watched her walk down the front drive. It was 28°C, but she yanked her Skadi fleece zip right up over her chin and plunged her fists deep into the pockets. It's always cold in Petrina's world.

Two hours later – perked up a little by my cool new T-shirt and vegan eight-hole purple DM boots – I arrived at the park to meet Vince. I imagined that he'd planned a surprise birthday picnic or something, with scotch eggs, crisps, Coke and cake. And I also couldn't help but wonder what he might have bought me as a present. Chocolates, perhaps (*God I hope I've mentioned that Ferrero Rochers are my favourite*). Or maybe some cool jewellery, like a handmade necklace? Or a beautiful song that he's written especially for me? The suspense was almost too much to bear, but thankfully Vince was already waiting for me, casually leaning against an oak tree, wearing a white Steel Dragon T-shirt and those super-sexy-I-want-to-stick-my-finger-into-that-thigh-hole-and-rip-it-open-like-a-shameful-pervert jeans. (Come to think of it, he's always wearing those jeans. Either he never washes them or he makes holes in all his trousers. Whatever the case – they are HOT!). He smiled and my insides melted.

His teeth are so white and straight, like two neat rows of Piriton Hay-fever tablets.

'Hey!' he said.

GOD I LOVE HIM.

'Hi!' I looked down at the plastic ASDA bag in his hand.

'Oh yeah,' he said holding out the bag towards me. 'I bumped into your idiot friend Matthew on the way here and he told me that it was your birthday.'

Gratefully I took the bag from his hand and opened it. Inside was a tiny, bright pink miniskirt (size 8). The label was still attached

'Erm . . . thanks,' I said, pretending to be thrilled. It was two sizes too small and about the width of my belt.

'Why don't you slip it on?' he asked with an incredibly sexy wink. 'You've got great legs.'

NOOOOOOOOOO. I'm going to look like a prostitute.

'OK,' I said feeling terribly uncomfortable, but desperately wanting to please him. And then two minutes later I was stepping out from behind a tree wearing what can only be described as a pink bum bandage. It clashed with my purple DM boots, but least it went with my hair stripe.

'Wow,' Vince yelped as I walked towards him. His eyes were stuck fast on my legs. It was at this exact moment I realised that I hadn't shaved them for TWO WEEKS. 'You look amazing.'

No I don't. I look like a Yeti in a nappy.

But Vince didn't seem bothered. Instead he gave me that intense look, before kissing me so passionately that it LITERALLY took my breath away. I suppose if I had to die by a form of asphyxiation then this was as good a way to go as any. But then as his hands moved down towards my bum (through no fault of his own, I know), I became all too aware that my buttocks had broken out of the barracks. In the middle of a crowded park. In broad daylight.

OH MY GOD. I did not foresee this situation. Which knickers am I wearing? Please let them not be my brown Scooby Doo ones. Please . . . please . . .

I pulled away from Vince. 'Shall we go for a walk?' I requested. 'Or go and get something to eat?'

I'd been so excited all day that I'd not eaten and was beginning to get really hungry (especially now that I realised Vince hadn't arranged a surprise birthday picnic). But Vince wasn't hungry for anything apart from me apparently.

'Nah,' he whispered. 'Let's go somewhere more private.' With his hand still on my escaped bum cheek, he began to gently steer me towards some bushes.

OK. Now is the time. I'm going to have to talk to him about his progressive hand-eye-nork co-ordination disorder.

I pulled myself slightly away and looked him directly in the eye. 'I know about your condition,' I said as reassuringly as I could.

'What?'

I took hold of both of his hands. 'I know it's not your fault, but you need to know . . .'

Just say it Blossom. Sometimes you just have to be cruel to be kind.

'You keep on accidentally grabbing my nork,' I blurted.

'Accidentally?' Vince smiled.

A lot of people laugh when they're embarrassed. Poor baby.

'Look, it's OK,' I continued as kindly as I could. 'I totally understand.'

He pulled me towards him and . . . HIS HAND IS THERE AGAIN!!!

'You see,' I said, pointing at his wayward hand that had once again parked itself on my chest.

'Come on, Blossom,' he said impatiently. 'I've had enough of the chase. You're sixteen now. You can do . . . anything.'

I'd been expecting him to be embarrassed and full of remorse but instead he seemed annoyed. The cogs of my mind clunked into motion.

'Wait . . . so you knew what your hand was doing all along?'

'Errr . . . yeah?'

'So you don't have a terminal-involuntary-nork-touching-disease?'

216

'Huh?' Vince took hold of my wrist and began to pull me roughly towards the bushes. 'Come on,' he said. 'Let's go and celebrate your birthday.'

The wave of anger that rushed through my body at that precise moment took me completely by surprise.

I feel VIOLATED. What would Emmeline Pankhurst do?

'You did what?' asked Walter an hour later in my kitchen (he'd rushed over at a moment's notice).

'I yelled "BALLS", then grabbed hold of them, twisted and pulled,' I explained. 'It was as instinctive as breathing.'

Walter nodded, seemingly impressed. 'That Kenny guy really taught you well.'

'But Vince isn't ever going to speak to me again,' I said, my chin sinking deeper into my hands.

'He's a nork-grabbing quimboid,' said Walter quite angrily (for him).

I looked down at the cheap pink skirt that had ridden up to completely reveal my BROWN SCOOBY DOO knickers. Vince Aston-Granger might be the most beautiful boy I'd ever set eyes on (with lips as soft as mega expensive goose feather pillows from John Lewis), but he'd well and truly overstepped the mark. I knew in my heart that a boy that handsome would probably never look twice at me again and I hoped it hadn't been my only chance at finding true love.

Nork-Grabbing Quimboid
By Blossom Uxley Michaels and Petrina-Ola Olsen

Look at him there,
His body ripped and his bum so yummy.
Standing there,
Without a care,
My chest gets tight and my guts go funny.

He'll woo you until your skin shudders.
But his only desire is to touch up your udders.

He's a nork-grabbing quimboid,
As welcome on my body as a haemorrhoid.
A nork-grabbing quimboid,
With icy cold fingers like an android. (Pronounced and-er-oid)

See him there,
His eyes like magnets, they'll paralyse ya.
Standing there,
With shiny hair,
Seductive groin that will hypnotise ya.

But don't trust a man with small hands.
He'll rub them all over your mammary glands.
He's a nork-grabbing quimboid,
As welcome on my body as a haemorrhoid.
A nork-grabbing quimboid,

With icy cold fingers like an android

He seems like an angel, but his heart is like steel
Don't trust those eyes,
Cos he just wants to cop a good feel.

To highlight the fact that this was intended to be an aggressive song, I discarded my guitar chord book and invented a brand new chord of my own. A sort of half bar chord, that doesn't sound so much angry as utterly FURIOUS!

From: Noodlebrain12
To: RavenGirl007
Sent: August 3rd 23:50:22

Hey!
How's it going? It's been a while!

Cheers,
Noodlebrain12

From: RavenGirl007
To: Noodlebrain12
Sent: August 3rd 23:53:31

Hi!
I've split up with my boyfriend today so I'm not feeling

so great. To be honest I've had a pretty crap few weeks. By the way, you do know it's nearly midnight?

RavenGirl007

From: Noodlebrain12
To: RavenGirl007
Sent: August 3rd 23:55:01

Hey!

I'm sorry to hear that. Your (ex) boyfriend is obviously an idiot. This is the best time to check out the night sky. I'm sitting on the roof of my house right now looking at the stars. It's beautiful out here.
I bet I could cheer you up.

Cheers,
Noodlebrain12

From: RavenGirl007
To: Noodlebrain12
Sent: August 3rd 23:58:00

Thanks, but I don't think ANYONE could make me smile right now. Not even a star-gazing fruitcake like you!!
RavenGirl007

From: Noodlebrain12
To: RavenGirl007
Sent: August 3rd 23:59:59

Hey – watch who you're calling a fruitcake!
9 out of 10 voices in my head agree that I'm completely sane.

Chin up, pancake lips!

Cheers,
Noodlebrain12

From: RavenGirl007
To: Noodlebrain12
Sent: August 4th 00:00:23

LOL!! You are totally bonkers!
RavenGirl007

From: Noodlebrain12
To: RavenGirl007
Sent: August 4th 00:00:51

Ha! I knew I could make you laugh.

Cheers,
Noodlebrain12

My parents have gone away and Breeze is back in the flat with Andreas, which means I'm FREEEEEEEEEEEEEEEEEEE for four whole days!

It feels strange being alone in the house – well, I'm not really alone, as Walter has moved in with me for the duration.

I had planned to do all the things that I'm not able to do with my parents around, but seeing as they are so liberal-minded, there really isn't much that's off limits in our house. In fact the only thing I could think of was to have a poo in the downstairs toilet with the door open whilst changing the TV channel with the remote control. And even then, if my parents had been home, they probably wouldn't have minded as long as they weren't watching Question Time.

N.B. I performed this small act of rebellion BEFORE Walter arrived to drop his stuff off, obviously.

I instinctively ran to the door when Petrina walked past the shop window on her lunch break. Our relationship might have been strained, but I still loved her and missed her so much that it felt as if a bit of my heart had broken off. Nile gave me the thumbs-up, so I dashed out immediately hoping to join her as if things were normal again.

'PETRINA!' I shouted.

She turned around and seemed a bit flustered to see me.

'Can I come with you?' I asked hopefully.

'Umm . . .' Petrina wasn't exactly being hostile, but she was definitely acting strangely.

'Hi Blossom,' said a voice from behind me. I turned around

and saw Leon (who'd apparently just been to the cash point) smiling warmly at me. I was astonished at how he still looked proper real-time hot even though he was wearing a revolting canary-yellow, supermarket uniform.

'We're just going for lunch,' he continued. 'Want to come?'

Petrina looked at me with an expression of being TOTALLY RUMBLED. The guilt on her face was clearer than an eye-bogey viewed through a magnifying glass (I tried this once and I was surprised to see that up close mine looked like a tiny, beautiful black dragon. Eye-bogey art could catch on one day).

'No,' I replied a little more abruptly then I intended. I know I'd seen Petrina and Leon together before at the Battle of the Bands, but seeing them parading their feelings for each other before me so blatantly was like having ice cubes rubbed all over my front teeth until I got brain-freeze. 'I never thought you could do this to Walter. Not in a million years'.

Leon was standing so close to Petrina that their arms were almost touching. If I squinted I could just make out the electrical charge of sexual chemistry that was crackling between them (or it might have been a stray canary yellow thread from Leon's Skadi uniform).

'I haven't done anything,' said Petrina defensively.

I looked at Leon (with his cheekbones so sharp you could shave your legs on them). Could my best friend, who I thought I knew inside out, really be two-timing Walter??

'I'm still coming to your birthday, right?' said Petrina, perhaps a little anxiously.

I smiled weakly. 'Of course.'

'A party? Am I invited?' asked Leon, who seemed oblivious to the tension between Petrina and I.

OVER MY DEAD BODY. Walter would be devastated.

'Of course!' *Damn those cheekbones for making me so weak.*

I watched as Leon and Petrina walked away together, trying hard to read their body language. They weren't actually holding hands yet they were definitely close enough for their auras to be touching.

And so forty minutes later I found myself sitting in Joe's Café, waiting for Matthew, who was inevitably running late. He finally turned up at quarter-past twelve holding a huge, black bin-liner inside which was a big rectangular object. His face was paler than usual, with dark shadows smudged underneath his eyes, yet his smile was broad and infectious the moment he saw me sitting at the table.

'Hi, sorry, sorry, sorry . . .' he said, trying to catch his breath. 'Couldn't run for the bus carrying this, so I had to walk.'

He placed the bin bag on the floor and slumped down into the seat opposite me.

'So did you have a good birthday?' he asked.

I shifted uncomfortably as I recalled my horrendous date with Vince. It had left me feeling embarrassed and naïve and, although I know what he did was unforgivable, there was a part of me that still felt guilty (not to mention embarrassed), that maybe I had led him on.

'Umm . . . it was OK.'

Matthew was playing with the bottle of tomato ketchup in front of him. 'I bet Vince bought you something amazing right?' he said.

HA! If only he knew.

'Yeah,' I lied.

Matthew seemed to be squirming in his seat.

Yuck. I hope he hasn't got worms.

He reached under the table and pulled out the huge black bin liner. 'I've bought you a present,' he said without actually looking at me. He discarded the bin bag on the floor to reveal

225

an ENORMOUS long red box, which he placed carefully on the table. He sat back in his seat and, as he reached to stroke down the sides of his hair, I noticed that his hands were trembling. I really hoped it wasn't the 'DT shakes', which can be caused by the sudden withdrawal from alcohol. If Matthew intends to kick the habit by going cold turkey then he's going to need the help of those Buddhist Monks and their Vomiting Temple.

'I hope you like it,' he said, his voice so quiet that it almost became a whisper.

I lifted the lid of the red box.

OH. MY. GOD!

I reached inside with both hands and gently lifted out the vintage 1960 cherry-red Gibson ES-335 guitar from Dad's shop – the one played by Chuck Berry. I held it aloft in front of me, my own Sword of Excalibur. The Axe of Rocktalibur.

'It's beautiful,' I sighed.

I checked it was in tune, and then struck a G chord on it. The sound was rich and full. I followed it with a C chord and then an Am and then:

'Poncerama, everybody thinks you're weird,
With your bowl cut hair and your silly bum-fluff beard.'

Together, Matthew and I sang Poncerama in its entirety and, by the second chorus, the whole café was singing along with us. It was a real life 'Pied Piper Music Video' moment. Even Joe himself was swinging his tea towel above his head as he sang the words.

'Poncerama oooh, Poncerama oooh,
'Poncerama oooh, Poncerama oooh,
'Poncerama oooh, It's no wonder that nobody really likes you.'

And then, just as we got to the bridge, Matthew did something that I'd never seen him do before. Something special. Something tremendous. Something that I LOVE almost as much as the Gibson ES-335 guitar and Ferrero Rochers. Matthew Ludlow began to beatbox. And he was good. In fact, he was excellent. His vocal bass was ridiculously heavy and his high hat clean and fresh. His rhythm was impeccable, his timing precise. I looked on in awe as his Adam's apple rose and fell hypnotically to the beat of its own drum.

God I would like to clamp my lips around that laryngeal lump of loveliness . . . Wait. No. This is Matthew Ludlow – school clown and professional drinker – we're talking about, not some international sex god. I am SO on the rebound.

As we finished our spontaneous rendition of Poncerama, the customers in Joe's Café gave us a huge round of applause. We proudly took a bow and sat back down, Joe immediately rushing over to give us two chocolate milkshakes on the house.

Matthew looked at me sheepishly. He didn't seem quite as pale anymore, his cheeks were flushed and his eyes sparkled with amusement. I stroked the elegant guitar that I held in my hands. It was everything I'd ever dreamed of – all my aspirations and hopes right there, in a shiny, cherry-red, guitar-shaped package.

'You know I can't accept this,' I said sadly. Matthew's

disappointed expression made my chest feel funny. 'It's the most thoughtful, perfect gift anyone has ever bought me,' I continued, running my fingers along the fret board. 'But you shouldn't be spending that kind of money on me. It must have cost thousands.'

'Don't worry about the cash,' said Matthew. 'I've got access to Dad's account whenever I want it. I wanted to buy you something special.'

I stood up and moved round to Matthew's side of the table. 'One day, I'll buy this myself,' I explained. 'When *I've* earned it. But until then . . . '

I handed the guitar back to its reluctant owner and then reached into my own pocket.

'And *I've* got something for you,' I said, holding out the joke plastic turd key ring that my uncle James had bought me for my birthday.

Such was the expression of pure wonderment on Matthew's face; it was as if Jesus Christ himself had laid a special sacred poo in the palm of his hand.

WOWZOIDS. Why Men Are Like Dogs *is right – young men really do respond well to silly plastic treats in the same way that a puppy goes nuts over a fake bone. I wonder if Matthew would fetch it if I were to throw it across the café.*

Impulsively, I kissed Matthew on his cheek. He always smells so good, which is unusual for an alcoholic as they're meant to smell of urine and extra strong lager.

SATURDAY 6TH AUGUST. PARTY TIME!!!!!

The garden looked brilliant – like a kind of scaled-down Glastonbury Festival. There was bunting strung up in the branches of the trees, flags blowing in the breeze, funny sign posts and the dreaded Tent of Evil (minus the missing square that had got stuck in my hair at Glastonbury) had been erected (ha, ha!!!) in a corner of the garden and labelled as the Tent of Love which is code for 'The Snogging Tent'. Petrina had silently done an excellent job of decorating Polystyrene Stonehenge with coloured fairy lights and red and purple paper lanterns emitting a warm, welcoming glow (which sort of made up for her cold, subdued greeting when she turned up at my house). A Happy Sixteenth Birthday banner hung upon the Heel Stone and Walter had set up the decks with Matthew's help on the central Altar Stone. To be honest, the bubbling excitement and anticipation had a pacifying effect on Petrina and Walter, who were doing a pretty good job of being civil to one another, exchanging pleasantries and even laughing together when Walter tripped over a cable and fell into a bush.

7.20PM Bob Ollox arrived and took up his position as 'doorman' at the front of my house.

7.24PM I managed to convince Mr Parkin at number 34 that Bob was not a member of the English Defence League here to spread hatred and violence in our street.

7.30PM Walter began his set with a segue of uplifting guitar-band tracks, carefully selected by me to make sure our guests arrived to a feel-good festival vibe.

7.32PM Matthew cracked open his first beer of the evening.

7.33PM Matthew demonstrated how to express the emotion of happiness through the medium of dance.

7.43PM Matthew cracked open his second beer.

7.44PM Petrina checked with Bob that nobody had tried to get into the party and been turned away. (They hadn't).

7.50PM Leon arrived after apparently being subjected to a traumatic full body search by Bob. Petrina greeted him with an elbow nudge (which by her standards was practically having it off in public).

7.51PM Walter played a track called 'I Hate Your Guts' by Steel Dragon that was definitely NOT on the agreed playlist.

7.55PM Matthew tried to high jump over the washing line and almost garrotted himself.

7.56PM Leon said that he'd forgotten to feed his next-door neighbour's cat and left.

8.11PM Mr Parkin positioned himself in his front garden with a flask of tea to keep an eye on Bob, who was now sitting by my front door swigging from a bottle of Jack Daniels.

8.28PM Petrina and I opened a beer each. We drank together in silence.

8.36PM Mr Parkin accused Bob of 'aggressively staring at him' and threatened to call the police.

8.37PM Bob pinned Mr Parkin to his own front door and drew a penis on his face with a Bic Biro.

8.44PM The police arrived outside number 34 and cautioned Bob.

9.01PM Petrina and I opened another beer.

9.05PM I sent a text to Mei Miyagi asking where she and Kirsty were.

9.09PM Got a reply from Mei saying that she, Kirsty, Paulette, Max, Felix AND JUST ABOUT EVERYONE ELSE were at the last-minute 'awesome' garden party thrown by Lucy Perkins.

9.10PM I asked Mei if Vince was at the party.

9.11PM Mei replied. Vince was there, having just been punched in the face by Felix, who'd caught him kissing Fiona.

9.12PM I demonstrated how to express the emotion of anger through the medium of dance.

9.23PM Bob and Mr Parkin swigged from the Jack Daniels bottle with their arms draped around each other's shoulder, singing 'Anarchy in the UK' by the Sex Pistols. Turns out Mr Parkin is an ex-punk and they were both at the Pistols' infamous Lesser Free Trade Hall gig in Manchester in 1976. Who'd have thought it?!!!

9.54PM Petrina, Walter, Matthew, Bob, Mr Parkin and I did the conga up and down the street seven times until Mr Parkin's bowels started giving him jip.

10.03PM Another beer.

10.13PM Matthew climbed over next door's fence and fell into their pond where he then spent ten minutes trying to catch the expensive koi carp in his underpants.

10.34PM Petrina pointed out the Titania star that Walter had bought her for her birthday.

10.47PM Bob took me aside while the others danced around Polystyrene Stonehenge to the sound of Josh Raven.

'He's a g-g-good kid,' he slurred nodding over at Matthew

(who appeared to be dry-humping the Altar Stone). 'Heart of gold.'

'He makes me laugh,' I replied, realising that I was feeling quite squiffy.

'H-h-he makes e-e-everyone laugh,' he said with a sad look on his face. 'I just wish someone would make h-h-him smile too.'

'What?' I couldn't quite believe that Bob was trying to tug at the emotional heartstrings for Bridge Mount's biggest lush. 'I'd smile all the time if my parents were as loaded as his and bought me everything I ever wanted!'

Bob continued watching Matthew (who was now climbing up on to the roof of our garage to retrieve his trousers, which he'd just thrown up there). 'Just because a person's p-p-privileged, doesn't mean he feels loved.'

I wasn't entirely sure what Bob was on about, but I had noticed that the tattoo of a raised middle finger on his forehead was slightly off centre. I wondered if it bothered him as much as it was bothering me.

'He loves his mum though,' I said. 'He's always rushing around buying stuff for her.'

Bob turned and looked me in the eyes. 'Wise up, Blossom,' he said in a slightly scary tone. 'His mum's never there. She's spent most of her life in S-S-S-Sandhurst Park.'

The psychiatric hospital?

'His dad can't cope,' he continued. 'S-s-so he jets around the world making m-m-money so that his sons can have "everything they n-need".' Bob spat out the last words of the sentence as if he'd just swallowed poison.

We both looked up towards the garage roof where Matthew had taken off all this clothes apart from his pants and was gazing up in wonder at the starlit sky. 'WE'RE ALL SO TINY!' he yelled at the top of his voice. 'WAAHOO!'

'Be gentle with him, Blossom,' Bob whispered softly. 'He's fragile.'

I wasn't quite sure what Bob meant. I don't think I have the sheer physical strength to actually break Matthew's bones. Not that I'd want to of course – I am a pacifist and will only ever use violence in self-defence (e.g. if somebody attempts to grab my nork again).

END OF WEEK 29. MY TABLE OF ACHIEVEMENT

SHAME LEVEL PEAK	Scooby Doo pants on show, pink bum bandage, hairy legs, twisting Vince's goolies, calling him 'dad' on the phone, nobody coming to my party . . . I'll just round it off to a neat Level 9.
GUITAR PRACTICE	Not so much this week as I've been far too busy publicly humiliating myself
SNOGS	I don't want to talk about it.
PARTY INVITATIONS	Let's not rub it in, OK?

WEEK 32
FAME

SCANDAL: Paulette snogged Mei Miyagi at Lucy Perkins' party at the weekend.

Matthew and I dropped into McDonald's for lunch shortly after my parents returned from their yoga trip. They brought me back a massive chunk of Amethyst Quartz crystal that had been 'infused with the positive energy of a Yoga Guru' to help me 'learn how to love myself and how to receive love from someone special'. Quite frankly, I can't see how a lump of purple rock will help my love life – unless of course it has the same properties as Kryptonite and can render 'nork-grabbing quimboids' powerless. In which case, I'll keep it in my pocket as a lucky talisman.

Kirsty Mackerby was so utterly distraught that yesterday's Gay Soirée was cancelled. Apparently at the party, after a glass of what Paulette thought was fizzy wine (but was actually fizzy grape juice), she lost all her inhibitions and started vigorously twerking in front of Mei, who had turned up dressed as Marco. Next thing they'd both disappeared, only to be discovered half an hour later kissing at the end of the garden by a devastated Kirsty. The poor girl was so upset that she got my McDonald's order wrong FIVE times (as if I would ask for a bean burger!). Eventually the manager got so fed up with the customer complaints that she told her to take the rest of the day off (not that I complained – that would be heartless when I was getting my food for free).

To: Blossom Uxley-Michaels
From: cupidsowner@Dempseylove.co.uk
Sent: August 8th 16:45:07
Subj: Dempsey Love Film

Dear Blossom,

Please find attached a transcript and a link to the Dempsey Love film. I was working on it until 4AM last night. Your acting skills took a LOT of editing. But I'm a slave to my business and I seek perfection. I'm like my father – I will work and work until my arse literally drops right off. (My dad told me that he once worked so hard that he had to go to A&E to have his bum sewn back on. That's the kind of dedication and commitment to business that I aspire to.) The film will be online tomorrow.

One other thing – don't think for a moment that I haven't noticed the way you are flirting with

Marco in the film. I've zoomed RIGHT in on your eyes and I know LUST when I see it. Well I think I had better make myself clear – keep your dirty thoughts to yourself. MARCO IS MINE. ALL MINE. MINE.

Regards,
Paulette Dempsey

Marco? Doesn't she mean Mei? And what's going on anyway? Up until Lucy's party, Paulette and Mei couldn't stand each other. It was clear to me that Paulette had lost the plot a bit and channelled ALL her insecurities and jealous rage into the final edit of the film (her voiceover sounds quite deranged). When this goes online, I'm going to be the laughing stock of Bridge Mount Secondary School AGAIN (even in the holidays).

DEMPSEY LOVE DATING TIPS RUNNING ORDER
V/O = VOICE OVER (PAULETTE DEMPSEY)

OPENING TITLE: 'DATING TIPS' MUSIC BED – ROBBIE WILLIAMS – 'LET LOVE BE YOUR ENERGY'	V/O
SHOT OF GOLDEN STATUE OF CUPID FIRING AN ARROW THAT I HAVE MADE MYSELF WITH PLASTICINE, PRITT STICK, FERRERO ROCHER WRAPPERS AND A PIECE OF MACARONI AS HIS WILLY.	'Hello. I'm Cupid. The God of Desire and all things Erotic. By joining Dempsey Love Online Dating, you've confirmed that you're a pathetic loser in love. . . But you're not alone.'

CUT TO: CLOSE UP OF BLOSSOM'S FACE. SHE HAS PASTA SAUCE AROUND HER MOUTH.	**V/O** 'This is Blossom. She couldn't find love if it vommed in her face.
CUT TO: CLOSE UP OF BIG SPOT ON BLOSSOM'S CHIN.	She has acne.
CUT TO: CLOSE UP OF THE PIECE OF CARROT STUCK IN BLOSSOM'S BRACES THAT SHE DOESN'T KNOW ABOUT.	She always has food wedged in her braces.
CUT TO: BLOSSOM'S ANNOYING LAUGH.	And her laugh sounds like a constipated dolphin. But, with a bit of help from me, even a hopeless case like Blossom can find love. Here's how:'
CUT TO: BLOSSOM AND MARCO HAVING A ROMANTIC CANDLELIT DINNER. **TITLE: TIP 1.** BLOSSOM IS STUFFING HER FACE WITH FOOD. MARCO LOOKS APPALLED. HE DOES NOT FIND THIS DISPLAY OF GROSSNESS ATTRACTIVE.	**V/O** 'Tip one. Don't be one of those modern girls who "eats whatever she wants".'
TITLE: TIP 2. BLOSSOM IS JABBERING AWAY. MARCO LOOKS BORED AND IS YAWNING.	**V/O** 'Tip two. Don't talk utter rubbish. Your date doesn't want to hear self-obsessed bilge.'

TITLE: TIP 3. DON'T CRY. BLOSSOM IS CRYING HYSTERICALLY. SHE LOOKS LIKE A MENTAL CASE. MARCO IS HORRIFIED. HE GETS UP AND LEAVES THE TABLE.	**V/O** 'Don't be a cry baby. Just because you've got your period, it doesn't mean you should get all hormonal. Control yourself.'
TITLE: TIP 4. DRESS TO IMPRESS ZOOM INTO SHOW BLOSSOM'S UNFLATTERING WHITE T-SHIRT THAT MAKES HER TINY BOOBS LOOK LIKE A COUPLE OF PARACETAMOLS ON AN IRONING BOARD. CUT TO: CLOSE UP OF MY FABULOUS, AMPLE BOSOMS IN MY WONDERBRA (MAKE SURE MY FACE AND TUMMY CANNOT BE SEEN). CUT TO: MARCO LOOKING DELIGHTED AT MY CHEST.	**V/O** 'Blossom's chest is like a five-year-old boy's. To enhance her lack of boobage, she should wear a push-up bra.'
TITLE: TIP 5. **NO PROSTITUTION** BLOSSOM LOOKS THRILLED AS MARCO PAYS THE BILL. HE TURNS AND SMILES AT HIS DATE. BLOSSOM LICKS HER LIPS SUGGESTIVELY LIKE A DIRTY SLAPPER.	**V/O** 'No one likes a prozzie. Don't let your date pay for the meal otherwise you owe them favours afterwards.'
CLOSING MUSIC: **MICHAEL BUBLÉ -** **'HAVEN'T MET YOU YET'**	

Notable points to consider:

1. I finished the rest of my spaghetti bolognese AFTER we'd wrapped. I had no idea Paulette was still filming. I ate it quickly before it got too cold.

2. I DO NOT HAVE ACNE.

3. Mei was yawning because she'd been up till 2AM the night before, having an in-depth text disagreement with Kirsty Mackerby over whether Sofia Santana, who plays Molly in the 'Bite Me' vampire film series, is gay or not.

4. I was not crying. I had just accidentally poked myself in the eye with my fork and it really hurt.

5. My period is not due for another ten days. I was therefore DEFINITELY not premenstrual.

6. Paulette MADE me lick my lips. She said they were dry and cracked like an old lady's nipple and needed lubricating.

7. WHAT IS ACTUALLY WRONG WITH MY LAUGH?

8 Robbie Williams and Michael Bublé? Ugh. Paulette has the worst taste in music ever.

✳ ✳ ✳

FIRST SEMI FINAL

AMA BADU VS. CAMEL TOE

SECOND SEMI FINAL

PERKITITS VS. BUMSKULLS

Of course I'm relieved not to be facing Vince or the slangers in the next round, but if we do manage to get through to the final, it's going to be Awkwardo City. Whether we're facing Bumskulls or Perkitits, it'll be a battle to the very last breath. First up, though, Camel Toe have to get past Ama Badu, who will be a tough opponent to beat. Still, the dream of playing at the Kaleidoscope Festival, where Steel Dragon, Josh Raven, Bloody Minx and King Quiff are all in the line-up, is a MASSIVE incentive, ensuring that we'll put everything we've got into our performance.

Despite our rocky relationship, Petrina and I are determined to put on our best performance yet. We've choreographed a 'fool-proof' stage dive – Walter will be standing directly in front of the stage, ready to catch me, (Walter is the most reliable, consistent person I know, so for once I feel confident about my Shame Level remaining fairly low for the next couple of days). Our carefully planned five-song set is:

1. THE MAN WITH AN EGGY BEARD
2. LUTRAPHOBIA
3. NORK-GRABBING QUIMBOID
4. YOU'RE SO GAY
5. PONCERAMA

My stage dive is scheduled to take place during the second chorus of 'Poncerama', when Walter will be in position and Petrina will take over lead vocal duty while I surf the wave of adulation. Quite frankly, I can't wait to see the look of surprise on the faces of the slangers (and on Vince's if he's there)!

I stand on top of the Scottish hillside in my horse-drawn chariot, surveying the enemy. I am wearing a bodice with pointy metal bra cups. They give me woman power. Behind me my fearsome army of four stands strong. Petrina is my formidable general. Matthew Ludlow is wearing a tunic. His legs are nice. Walter is also wearing a tunic. I do not look at his legs. It would be like perving at my brother.

The enemy approaches on horseback. Fiona and Lucy look like a pair of buxom wenches. Their helmets are rubbish. In fact I think they're wearing a couple of colanders on their heads. I pull down the visor of my far superior golden helmet with wings that stick out either side. Behind the slangers, Vince, Leon, Felix and Toby are trying to arrange themselves into an arrow formation. They are too stupid to realise that they need an odd number to make them look pointy.

'ATTACK,' I shout. The others jump on the back of my chariot and, with our guitars held aloft, we charge towards the enemy.

The twanging sound of fast picking, fierce shredding and uber speed soloing vibrates through the air and it all gets a bit icky. Yes, there is blood. Yes, there are bits of yucky intestines and brains strewn across the highlands, BUT this is the Battle of the Axes and there can only be one winner.

Suddenly, there is a deafening ring and I realise that I've been struck by a bitchin' sweep-picking flurry. My ears begin to bleed. I look around for support from my army, but they are all dead.

'You're going down,' sneers Fiona as she paces towards me with her tacky, neon pink, junior guitar from Argos. Her fingers are fast, but the real driving force comes from Vince. His Fender American Standard Tele is like an extension of his own body – a Mystic Blue penis substitute. He holds it arrogantly and I am annoyed that he is waving it in my direction. I may not have the nimblest fingers in town, but I can sing and strum now like the baddest mutha. And as I improvise a ferocious riff on my cherry-red Gibson ES-335, Vince and Fiona are forced to cover their ears.

'Arrrrrggghhh,' they cry, dropping to their knees.

Ha! I am a rock GODDESS. And as I strike the opening chords of 'Poncerama', it's clear that I will soon be victorious. Vince's ears can't take it any more. They begin to spin like the propeller on a hand-held fan, faster and faster until they break free and shoot off into the air. A pair of golden eagles swoop down and gobble up those perfect lugholes. They can't believe their luck. Fiona looks on in horror until she too can take no more and her stupid, dumb head explodes into a zillion gunky pieces.

And I survey the carnage, knowing that I have won the Battle Of the Axes and will go down as one of the greatest women in history alongside Boudicca, Emmeline Pankhurst and Molly from the Bite Me vampire film trilogy (she may be mortal, but she can take out a group of psycho vampires with her bare fists and throw an angry wolf across the forest as if it were a fluffy Frisbee).

SEMI-FINAL DAY

In the space of three minutes, Paulette Dempsey has singlehandedly turned me into the laughing stock of not only the entire school, but also THE ENTIRE COUNTRY. I woke up today at stupid o'clock (6.43AM to be precise). I was nervous about the semi-final so I went downstairs, made a cup of tea and switched on the TV. My parents frown on commercial breakfast television saying that 'it fuels middle England's insatiable appetite for spreading fear and hatred', and this small act of rebellion made me feel strong inside. The ruddy-faced male presenter with a beer gut was introducing the next item on a 'teenage dating tips' film that had gone viral overnight, with over a million views. And the next thing I saw ON NATIONAL TELEVISION was ME. With a huge spot on my chin and a piece of carrot dangling from my braces. And there I was again, laughing like a constipated dolphin, sitting opposite 'Marco' Miyagi who looked utterly bored (but unbelievably attractive). Oh, and then there was Paulette Dempsey (seizing the opportunity for a bit of self-promotion by wearing a pink Dempsey Love T-shirt) sitting on the sofa chatting candidly to Mr Beer Gut and his foxy female co-host.

My life couldn't possibly get any worse . . . could it?

Brambledown Golf Club was becoming a bit like a manky old T-shirt that's covered in tomato ketchup stains and has a permanent faint whiff of B.O., but you won't throw away because ~~Felix Winters~~ someone once told you it was cool

(Everyone has one of those right?).

Pete Hartley was getting out of his flashy, black sports car as we pulled up in the car park. He was smoking a huge cigar and wearing offensively small running shorts and his trademark Hawaiian shirt.

He waved at us as we all piled out of Bob's van. 'Hey guys! Good luck tonight. Hope you've got something special in the bag cos that Ama girl's a belter.'

Well that's done wonders for our confidence. Thanks, Pete.

I hoped he hadn't seen the Dempsey Love film on Breakfast TV this morning.

'Have you checked your brace for any stray carrots Blossom?' he grinned cheekily.

Arrrrrrrrggggghhhhhhh.

Petrina wasn't there, having chosen instead to get a lift with her mum, but Matthew and Walter weren't perturbed by Bob's remarks in the slightest.

'You'll be great,' said Matthew with certainty. 'You've got the talent, the songs – you're the real deal.'

'Not to mention "the gimmick",' said Walter, whose fringe was looking particularly long today. There's going to come a point where he'll have to cut it – it's beginning to look like he's screwed his head on back-to-front.

We'd told Matthew about my surprise stage dive and he'd been sworn to secrecy to create maximum impact when I executed the move at the end of our set. Matthew and Walter had both been really sweet about my mortifying morning TV performance, saying that nobody our age watches TV at that time of the day anyway (apart from THEM obviously), but so far I hadn't heard a word from Petrina. She's the only person who could have made me feel better and right now I was missing my best friend more than ever.

The venue was PACKED. I'd never seen so many people squeezed into one room.

'I see you've brought your secret paramour,' I said scornfully to Petrina, who'd slipped in quietly with Leon without saying hello.

Petrina ignored my not so subtle dig. 'Nice that everyone's come to see *you*,' she said, looking around with a hint of irritation in her voice. 'Clearly breakfast TV is very popular with teenagers these days.'

OH GOD NO!

I scanned the room and, sure enough, wherever I looked people were pointing and giggling in my direction. It was nothing I hadn't experienced before (the constant name-calling I faced at school had become imbedded in my DNA), but on a scale of one to ten on the insult scale, the taunts were up there in the tens alongside past favourites such as Pork Tit Bumface and Bumface Poopy Pants.

'I'm scared Petrina. I've got a bad feeling about tonight,' I said.

It was true. I had a strange sensation of impending doom growing inside of me. I'd imagine this was how Nostradamus felt on a daily basis. He must have had dangerously high blood pressure.

'Pull yourself together,' snapped Petrina in a tone that

she'd never used with me before.

My chest tightened. 'Why are you being like this?'

'Why am I being like this?' retorted Petrina. '*You* basically accused me of being a scarlet harlot when I arrived.'

'How dare you!' I said in a very slightly raised voice (I'm not usually one for confrontation). 'I would NEVER use the phrase "scarlet harlot". It's what old people say.'

Although, I'll admit, 'Scarlet Harlot' would make an excellent song title.

Petrina dismissed me with a flick of her hand. 'You can think whatever you want,' she said.

'Well if it's all so innocent, then why the sneaking around behind Walter's back?' I asked.

'Walter doesn't own me,' she said defiantly. 'So what if I've been meeting Leon for lunch every so often?' I looked past my angry friend as a dark figure crept up behind her.

'Shut up!' I hissed at her with intent.

But Petrina didn't get the hint. 'Who lit *your* tampon fuse?' she jeered. 'And what are you looking at?'

She turned around just in time to meet Walter's fringe-obscured eyes. For a moment it seemed as though he was going to say something, then his head dropped and he shuffled away. It was horrible to see him so hurt.

'Walter, wait . . . !' called Petrina, but Walter had already disappeared into the crowd.

'You've got to make it better,' I pleaded. 'You've broken his heart.'

She fixed her eyes back on me. 'He's always had insecurity

issues,' she breathed, her voice now barely audible. 'But *you?* You know me better than anyone.'

She looked away, but I could tell from the way her voice cracked at the end of the sentence that she was crying. Petrina doesn't cry. In fact she hasn't publicly shed a tear since she was eight years old. A group of her classmates were giving her the birthday bumps in the church hall when a 'pudding-faced' boy called Eddie Arnold whipped off her knickers in front of everyone, causing her to cry continuously for three solid hours. If I was Petrina's mum I'd have whisked her off to the nearest child psychologist straight away, but the damage had already been done. In those three hours she must have cried out an entire life's worth of tears until there was nothing left. And now I was the one who had made her cry again after all this time. I am officially a heartless, MASSIVE QUIMBOID.

'I'm sorry . . .' I whispered, but it was too late. Petrina had already disappeared back into the crowds.

I found Walter sitting on the ground in the car park. He was throwing pieces of gravel against the tyre of Margo Tittledown's silver Mercedes. I sat down next to him, not knowing what to say now that he'd had confirmation that Petrina had been going behind his back.

'I'll still help with the stage dive,' he muttered.

'Thanks,' I replied. 'You're a good friend.'

We sat in silence for a few more moments before I got pins and needles in my foot and hobbled back inside.

I tried to put my horrible argument with Petrina out of

my mind as Ama Badu took to the stage. She'd improved enormously since the heats – now confident without being arrogant, and with sublime folky songs and a breath-taking voice. I watched her from the side of the stage willing her on, yet sort of hoping that she'd hit a wrong note and not perform to her absolute best. Towards the end of Ama's set I'd noticed Walter waving his arms about at the back of the venue in some kind of animated conversation with Fiona and Lucy. This was unusual for two reasons:

1. The slangers don't like to associate themselves with a Weirdo like Walter.
2. Walter never moves animatedly. It's the equivalent to his use of words – he uses minimum words for maximum impact and it's the same with his movement. Less is always more with Walter.

Before I could work out what was actually going on, the crowd erupted into rapturous applause as Ama finished her flawless set to a standing ovation from the judges. It was going to be difficult to top that performance, especially since Petrina and I weren't speaking. I watched anxiously as Bob Ollox set up the Camel Toe equipment, knowing that this was one of the most important moments of our lives – only two more performances stood between us and the Kaleidoscope Festival. My nerves were so shaky that I was wearing two Tena Lady pads (which I had Sellotaped securely to my gusset to ensure no embarrassing fall-outs), but, right then, waiting for our big moment and with my stomach churning pugnaciously, I began to wonder if a pair of rubber pants might have offered more substantial protection.

After four heats and two quarter-finals, Margo Tittledown had relaxed a little on stage and was openly using words such as 'dudes', 'OMG' and 'outa sight', so when she introduced Camel Toe as the 'hip, rad and totally groovy Camel Toe', a little part of me died inside. Clearly the sight of a helmet-haired, fortysomething-year-old woman in a white twin-set and pearls trying to 'get down with the kids' had ruffled Toby Richmond's feathers as well, because he hurled an empty plastic Coke bottle which smacked Margo right in the middle of her Botoxed forehead. I hoped that this wasn't an indication of things to come during our set.

TOP 5 WORST THINGS THAT COULD HAPPEN AS CAMEL TOE PERFORM ON STAGE

1. Someone throws a bottle of urine at us with no lid on.

2. Someone gobs at us on stage. According to Bob, back in the 1970s a punk singer caught conjunctivitis after someone's spit landed in her eye and another singer got glandular fever after he swallowed some dribble on stage. GROSS.

3. I forget the words.

4. I forget how to strum and sing simultaneously.

5. I wet myself.

Of course, the absolute worst thing ever would be if Petrina didn't join me on stage at all, but just as I was beginning to think the worst, she appeared beside me.

'Let's do it,' she said flatly.

'Petrina,' I blurted out as we were about to walk on stage. 'I miss you . . .'

But she'd already gone ahead. I followed in her shadow to the loud taunts of: 'It's spotty Bumface the constipated dolphin' and 'All right, carrot teeth?'

It was strange. I'd been taunted and teased for so long that insults had become as effective as candy floss bullets – yet standing on stage at the semi-finals, every single heckle felt like a knife to my heart.

We powered through our first song on autopilot (there's a lot to be said for rehearsing), hitting all the right notes and doing all the right moves. The painful animosity between Petrina and me had knocked the wind out of my sails, though not quite enough for me to ignore the slangers, who had predictably positioned themselves at the front of the stage in an effort to put us off our stride. Fiona's attempts would have been in vain, had it not been for the fact that she was snogging Vince's face off (with her eyes open so that she could enjoy the reaction on my face). I hadn't even realised that he was in the venue, let alone 'hanging out' with a stupid, dumb slanger (I'm guessing Felix *must* have known what was going on between them by now). Alongside them, Lucy Perkins was the filling in a HOT boy sandwich with Toby on one side and

Leon on the other (although she was so wrapped up in Toby she didn't even seem to have noticed the other gorgeous boy beside her). I could tell that Petrina had noticed them – she was looking cross and had to keep wiping the corner of her mouth with her sleeve. But my attention kept getting drawn back towards Vince (who was wearing his filthy, smelly, but oh-so-sexy jeans with the thigh hole). Seeing him stirred mixed emotions in me – part of me despised him and his DELIBERATELY wandering hand (that was now resting comfortably on Fiona's MASSIVE chest), but the other part felt sick that he had chosen her over me.

Our second song, 'Lutraphobia', came to an end.

'I want to dedicate this next song to a special guy,' I said into the mic, as we were about to begin our newest song. There were a few cheers and a wolf-whistle from somewhere in the crowd. Fiona and Vince were still snogging (PUKE).

'This guy was proper real-time HOT,' I shouted to more whistles from the audience. 'But turns out he wasn't such a nice guy. In fact, I would go so far to say that he was nothing but a NORK-GRABBING QUIMBOID!'

And then we began playing our newest song. Its catchy chorus had everyone singing along almost immediately. Astonishingly, Vince didn't appear to twig that he had been my artistic muse and, much to the annoyance of Fiona, he was shouting along with the chorus too.

From 'Nork-Grabbing Quimboid' we segued smoothly into 'You're So Gay' and then ended with a fired-up rendition of our seminal crowd pleaser 'Poncerama'. As we approached the second chorus, I knew what I had to do. We'd run through this choreographed sequence so many times that it was almost instinctive. The crowd were euphoric, clenched fists punching the air. A torrent of rock 'horn hand' gestures rippled across the room, a tsunami of energy surging towards me. This was my moment. I had to ride the wave and become one with the music. I stood on the edge of the stage and closed my eyes, feeling the energy ebb and flow through my body. I felt myself sway with the current that pulled me gently off my feet. And I dived head first into the crowd where I thought I saw the top of Walter's head.

I am floating . . . I am floating . . . OH MY GOD. That's NOT Walter. That's the back of a girl's head. WHERE IS HE?

The audience seemed to move as one as all the heads and arms beneath me shifted to the sides. It was as if I were a younger, lady version of Moses, the sea of people parting, leaving only a fast-approaching, hard, sawdust-covered floor. The noise of the crowd died away as they waited for the impact.

Oh my God, oh my God. Have my front teeth shattered into a million pieces?

I scrabbled about on the floor trying to get myself back on to my feet. There was no sign of Walter. Why wasn't he there ready to catch me? Have I broken my face?

What hot guy will ever want to go out with a gummy-mouthed teenager?

'Blossom, are you OK?' It was my mum. She was helping me to my feet.

My fingers . . . my fingers . . . they're mangled. The digits of my right hand are dangling like a string of limp Cumberland sausages. How will I ever be able to play the cherry-red Gibson ES-335 guitar of my dreams again?

'I'm going to kill Walter.' Petrina's face was like a raging Viking warlord's as she marched off in search of him.

Matthew, who had rushed over from the bar, had his arm around my waist and led me gently towards a chair.

I'll have to learn to strum with my stump (after my fingers have been amputated) or practise plucking the strings with my teeth (except I can't because I HAVE NO TEETH).

Turns out that I hadn't lost any teeth, nor were my fingers broken. Other than my mortally wounded dignity I was perfectly fine. While the audience laughed and the slangers jeered, I glanced over at the two judges, who were huddled over the table deep in discussion. I'd messed it right up. Who was I trying to kid? How could Spotty Bumface the Constipated Dolphin / Ham Hooters / Braceface / Weirdo Gothbag / Daylight Dodger / Bumface Poopy Pants (select insult of your choice) ever win a battle of the bands competition? What on earth was I thinking?

My parents fussed around, squeezing drops of Rescue Remedy into my mouth and buffing my aura to restore my 'inner calm' (which was almost as embarrassing as falling flat on my face).

Matthew squatted down next to me as I slumped into the chair and buried my head into my hands.

'I've ruined our chance,' I whispered. 'I've destroyed all that credibility we've worked so hard for by being a ginormous quimboid. I've let Petrina down, I've humiliated her . . . she must totally hate me.'

Matthew put his arm around my shoulder and I caught a waft of his spicy-hot-chocolate-covered-baby scent. It smelt strangely comforting.

'Don't be daft,' he said softly. 'How could *anyone* hate you?'

But, with Petrina and Walter nowhere to be seen when I needed them most, Matthew's kind words weren't enough to convince me.

Petrina reappeared about ten minutes later, but still without Walter. Perhaps the sight of her lustful glances at Leon had been too much and he'd decided to go home. She kept her distance from me as we stood on stage with Amu Badu awaiting the judges' final verdict. She was only a couple of feet away, but it felt like a hundred miles. I quickly scanned the room: Mum and Dad were giving me the double thumbs-up (CRINGE), Paulette and Mei Miyagi (not dressed as Marco) seemed to be holding hands (though I couldn't quite see), Kirsty was alone leaning against the wall and throwing occasional glances at her ex-girlfriend. Breeze and Andreas (who was dressed as The Joker from Batman) were arguing by the fire exit. Bob was trying to coax Matthew down from on top of one of the giant speakers. Lucy had her head thrown back in an apparent fit of laughter at something hilarious that Toby had said. Vince was up at the bar and Fiona was leaning across the judges, whispering something into her mum's ear. By the way she kept smirking at me, it was obvious that she'd been thrilled by my public humiliation. Fiona Tittledown's compassion had obviously been traded in along with her heart and soul when she'd made her pact with Satan (though, if I'd been the one making a deal with the devil, I'd have asked for much longer eyelashes than Fiona has – hers are just a tad on the stumpy side).

'It's been a tough decision guys,' Pete said into the microphone. 'Ama, you began on a high and maintained the standard throughout. Utterly mesmerising.'

Ama looked bashfully down at her feet

'Camel Toe,' continued Pete. 'I've seen better performances from you. Your usual spark wasn't there tonight and, of course, there was Blossom's unfortunate incident.'

There were a few sniggers from the audience, none louder than those coming from the mouths of the stupid slangers.

And then came the moment we'd been dreading. I had to resist the urge to reach out and grab Petrina's hand. She hates physical contact at the best of times, but with her animosity towards me so apparent, I feared the touch of my fingers might have forced Petrina to decontaminate herself in a bath of diluted Witch Hazel.

'So, after careful consideration,' announced Margo Tittledown, who had taken hold of the mic. 'I'm delighted to announce that the winner of the first semi-final is AMA BADU!'

The sound of the crowd erupting into rapturous applause deafened my ears. Ama's wide-eyed surprise seemed genuine – she was a humble and unpresumptuous winner and thoroughly deserved to beat us. But I felt as if I'd been winded, like the time when Breeze dropped a bale of hay on to my chest at a folk festival after I'd put a fly that I'd just killed inside her vegan sandwich. (It was dead already and didn't have fur, four legs, a tail or the normal number of eyes that animals have, which means it didn't count as actual meat. FACT). I congratulated the winner with a sour taste in my mouth and a head full of shattered dreams. But what was even worse was that Petrina didn't say a word to me. She just jumped off the stage and walked away.

It was only after all the fuss had died down that I noticed my phone vibrating in my pocket. Eleven missed calls and five texts.

'Oh my God, quick,' I yelped at Matthew who had come to offer his condolences. 'We've got to rescue Walter before he turns into a cannibal and eats a dead Rastafarian.'

'. . . What?' said Matthew.

'Never mind,' I said. 'I'll explain later. Come on,'

We eventually freed Walter from the cupboard a whole fifty-five minutes after the slangers had locked him in. They'd subjected him to a violent tickling interrogation where he had no other choice other than to reveal our tactics for the stage dive. Walter was sitting in a puddle of disinfectant with the shaft of a Vileda Super Mop (that he'd mistaken for a dead Rastafarian) wedged in between his teeth. It would seem that in extreme circumstances, Walter would last for just under an hour before he was forced to turn to cannibalism.

From: RavenGirl007
To: Noodlebrain12
Sent: August 10th 23:28:22

Hi!
How's it going? I've had the most awful day EVER. I know this sounds a bit forward, but do you fancy meeting up sometime? I could do with a little spark of happiness right now.

RavenGirl007

From: Noodlebrain12
To: RavenGirl007
Sent: August 10th 23:30:45

Hey!
Sorry to hear you're feeling low. I would TOTALLY love to meet up – but I feel like I'd be being disloyal to someone else. She doesn't know I'm interested and I'm probably just being an idiot, but it wouldn't feel right. By the way, I've somehow come home tonight with a hedgehog in my pocket. What should I do?

Cheers,
Noodlebrain12
P.S. Are you drunk? You're not going to kill yourself or anything are you?

From: RavenGirl007
To: Noodlebrain12
Sent: August 10th 23:57:22

Ahhhhhhh! You are soooooooo cute. Whoever she is, she's a very, very lucky girl. I hope I find someone as lovely as you one day.

RavenGirl007
P.S. Put the hedgehog into a cardboard box with an old towel for the night. Make sure it has water and a little bit of cat food. Then ring the animal rescue centre in the morning.
P.P.S. I'm not going to kill myself and I'm not drunk.
P.P.P.S. Are YOU drunk?

From: Noodlebrain12
To: RavenGirl007
Sent: August 10th 23:59:45

Yes. I'm drunk.
Cheers,
Noodlebrain12

I woke up with a shock. Breeze was snuggled up into the crook of my neck, her massive crater-like nostrils threatening to suck me inside with each deep intake of breath.

WHAT THE?

Gradually, as my brain emerged from its morning fug, I began to recall last night's events. After the semi-final, my sister and Andreas had rowed in spectacular fashion, which wouldn't be unusual, had Breeze not collapsed on her knees in floods of tears in the car park. Like Petrina, Breeze NEVER cries. She's about as emotional as a blacksmith's steel anvil. Andreas screeched off in his Aston Martin leaving my parents to scoop another distraught daughter up from the floor and take her home with us in the camper van.

'I told him *no more lies*,' said Breeze quietly as we sat together in the darkness. 'And he said he *had* been secretly seeing Tania.'

Andreas may be many things – hairy and horny to name two – but I'd never had him down as a cheat. He adores my sister. Or so I thought. I'd almost fallen asleep when Breeze tiptoed into my room and lowered herself silently on to my bed. I waited a few moments to assess the unfamiliar dynamics before I sat up. Hugging her knees to her chest, with her hair sticking to her tear-streaked face, she looked like a little child. My chest tightened as I pushed back a strand of her hair and tucked it behind her ear.

Breeze looked at me with her red eyes. 'I thought he was different,' she continued, her voice trembling. Feeling out of my depth and not knowing the right words to say, I rested my head against my sister's. 'Vulnerable' was not a word that I would ever associate with her, but right then I felt the need to protect and comfort her as best I could.

'Vince is an idiot you know,' she said quite unexpectedly.

'You know you can do much better than a creep like him.'

Wow. Breeze is being nice to me. She should have her heart broken more often.

'There's someone out there who will love you for who you are, even though you're an animal-murdering, frigid weirdo.'

Or maybe not.

And so tonight was the second semi-final. Perkitits vs. Bumskulls. Who do you support when you can't stand either of the bands? But seeing as Camel Toe weren't in the competition any longer, I didn't see the point in going along to watch.

And are Camel Toe still Camel Toe anyway? Petrina isn't replying to my texts, so I have no way of knowing what is going on. Matthew came into the shop at midday to take me for a 'cheer-up-lunch', which was very lovely of him, but I must have been dreadful company. The only thing that made me feel vaguely better was hearing that Petrina was devastated too. Matthew bumped into her on her way to Skadi and said she looked terrible. He tried to console her by telling her that the winners of these competitions always get forgotten and it's the runners-up who have the most success. But she wasn't having it, saying that the Kaleidoscope Festival would have been 'the greatest platform ever'. She's right of course, but retreating into one of her 'blue funks' again really isn't going to help. The last time it happened was in Year 9 when Lucy Perkins pulled down Petrina's woolly tights in a hockey lesson. I think the trauma triggered a flashback to the 'Eddie Arnold birthday knickers incident' and it resulted in her wearing a black veil over her face for two whole weeks. Even though she claimed she was trying out a radical new look, I knew she was really using it to express her stifled emotions. She might not openly cry in public, but she isn't cold-hearted. In fact, for all her outspoken, forceful, political spiel and no nonsense approach, Petrina is actually extremely sensitive.

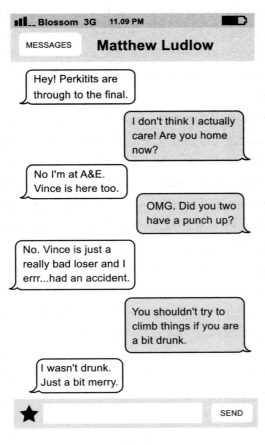

I later found out that the power mysteriously went off in the middle of Bumskulls' set (Matthew claims to have seen the slangers acting suspiciously next to the mains box), causing Vince to go berserk. He publicly dumped Fiona (apparently calling her 'an annoying cling-on'!), before smashing up his equipment and eventually putting his fist through a signed framed photograph of Tiger Woods (much to Margo Tittledown's horror). Matthew also said that Petrina hadn't been there to support Leon. For the sake of Walter, I'm glad that she didn't watch Bumskulls, but I can't help but worry that her absence is a sign that she's retreated into a deep blue funk again.

I've had to switch my phone off all day. Ever since Paulette outed me as 'desperate and single' on breakfast TV I've had endless calls from teen magazines and websites wanting to get an exclusive with me. Mum has even had to unplug our landline as journalists had somehow managed to get the number. And they'd been badgering Petrina and Walter, who had thankfully made themselves unavailable. Shame the same can't be said for some of my other so-called 'friends' who were clearly more than willing to speak to cool teen lifestyle website Koolbitzmag.com

KOOL BITZ MAGAZINE

News, Showbiz, Health, Love

Class weirdo Blossom Uxley-Michaels (age 13) couldn't get a boyfriend, no matter how hard she tried. Eventually she turned

to teen dating agency Dempsey Love ('the most effective pathway to true love on the internet'). Dempsey Love helped acne-riddled Blossom find a date with 57-year-old homosexual Marco Miyagi, proving that there is a match for everyone no matter how offensive your laugh is or how much half-chewed food you have stuck in your brace. A close friend said, 'I've always thought Bumface . . . I mean, Blossom, was too weird to get a date with anyone at all. To be honest, I'm still too shocked to comment.'

I'm going to have Fiona Tittledown and Paulette Dempsey arrested for treason or defecation or whatever it's called when you tell blatant LIES. The blasphemous article has been shared by 'friends' on pretty much every social networking site I can see. I've tried to explain that a) I wasn't looking for love and b) I am SIXTEEN, but nobody cares. (N.B. Mei genuinely doesn't mind being mistaken for a man. In fact she has taken to wearing a fake moustache every so often as it makes her feel liberated. I wish she wouldn't. She looks great with facial hair. TOO GREAT.)

Despite last week's glitch, Mei's Gay Soirée in McDonald's has become the weekly event of the summer. In fact, it's proved so popular that there are now over eighty regular members.

To avoid any more hurt and humiliation, poor Kirsty has asked her manager if she can work Saturdays from now on rather than Sundays, when she'd be subjected to seeing Mei and Paulette together as a new couple. Regardless of the way she's been treated, Kirsty is still very much in love and is convinced that Paulette is only using Mei as a way to develop her business.

I worry about Kirsty – there don't seem to be any other lesbians working in McDonald's (perhaps it's the phallic-shaped French fries that put them off), so she'll have a tough time trying to find a new girlfriend. Mei, being the confident outgoing girl that she is, will never have trouble finding a new partner. Since getting together with Paulette, she seems to have taken on the persona of 'Marco' more and more frequently.

But I have noticed that whenever Mei touches her new girlfriend, Paulette appears to slightly pull away. It's a very subtle rejection that most people wouldn't spot, but I've been observing closely (though NOT in a weird voyeuristic pervert kind of way – I'm watching for the sake of my friend Kirsty, who is facing a possible local shortage of lesbians).

'Hey, Bumface,' called Lucy. I was sitting with Walter enjoying a burger when she walked past our table with Fiona, the two of them sucking their milkshakes over-suggestively through straws (which made me want to VOM). 'Next time you attempt a stage dive, maybe you should wear armbands to keep you afloat.'

Lucy still thinks she's a comedian then.

I stood up angrily. 'I would have been fine if you two hadn't locked Walter in the cupboard.'

Walter tugged at my arm, trying to get me to sit back down.

'I have no idea what you're talking about,' sniggered Fiona.

'You sabotaged our set and then you sabotaged Bumskulls'. You're just a couple of low-life cheats.' After all that had happened to me, I was absolutely FUMING.

'Face it, weirdo, you're just jealous,' snapped Fiona. 'We're natural winners and we've got this competition in the bag.'

'What do you mean?' I asked.

Fiona laughed and raised her angry, over-plucked eyebrows. 'My mum paid for the Honey Dome venue. The sponsors are *beyond* delighted with the high-profile platform.'

The Honey Dome is one of the most prestigious music venues in the UK where all the greats have played at some point – from Jimi Hendrix and The Cure to Josh Raven and Steel Dragon. To be able to perform there in the final, a place seeped in so much awesome music history would be MIND-BLOWING. I was sooooo jealous.

'Are you saying that your mum has already won the competition for you?' I asked.

Fiona flicked her blonde hair away from her face. 'I'm just saying that it pays to know the right people.'

I wonder if anyone has ever been killed by the power of telepathy?

END OF WEEK 32 MY TABLE OF ACHIEVEMENT

SHAME LEVEL PEAK	*I think I have exceeded myself in terms of shame this week. I have reached Level Infinity.*
GUITAR PRACTICE	Plenty
SNOGS	*Let's just not even go there.*
PARTY INVITATIONS	*Who invented this stupid Table of Achievement anyway?*

When Matthew charged into the shop, out of breath and red-faced, I assumed something awful had happened. Ten seconds later Petrina walked in wearing her supermarket uniform and the black veil.

THE BLACK VEIL? Petrina was in a worse blue funk than I'd realised.

'They let you wear that at work?' I quizzed.

She might have been in an emotional state, but it was clear by the tone of her voice that I hadn't been forgiven. 'I told them I was exercising my right to freedom of expression and if they didn't let me, I'd contact Amnesty International and the *Guardian,*' snapped Petrina.

'This had better be REALLY important,' she scowled at Matthew, who had collapsed on the counter in a sweaty heap. 'I'm missing my lunch break for you.'

'What's going on?' I asked, not having an actual clue.

'I dunno,' said Petrina. 'I got a text from him saying to meet him immediately as it was super urgent.'

Matthew lifted his red and blotchy face. 'I ran all the way here,' he wheezed. 'I wanted to tell you the news in person.'

Petrina's arms were folded and her foot was tapping

impatiently. 'What news?'

Matthew took a deep breath, 'Pete Hartley called,' he explained. 'It seems that Ama Badu isn't who she claims to be.'

What she's a Russian killer spy?

'She's not really seventeen,' panted Matthew.

'What?' questioned Petrina. 'How old is she?'

'Try adding on another thirty-seven years.'

Wait up . . . thirty-seven plus seventeen, that's . . .

Petrina gasped.

So seven plus seven . . . that's fourteen . . . carry the one . . .

'The rules of the competition state that all contestants must be under the age of eighteen,' Matthew clarified. 'So Ama's been disqualified.'

Three plus one, plus the one that I've carried over . . .

'So wait . . .' said Petrina, pausing to get her head around the situation. 'Does that mean . . .?'

'SHE'S FIFTY-FOUR!' I couldn't believe it.

Petrina and Matthew looked at me.

'Blossom, has it really taken you that long to do the maths?' asked Petrina.

'You know I'm no good at mental arithmetic.'

Matthew clapped his hands excitedly. 'Do you know what that means?' he smiled.

I will never be an accountant?

'Camel Toe is through to the final by default!'

Petrina screamed and pulled the veil dramatically from her face.

OH. MY. GOD!

KALEIDOSCOPE PRESENTS

BATTLE OF THE BANDS

FINAL

 V S

JUDGES:

PETE HARTLEY (LEGENDARY PRODUCER OF STEEL DRAGON)
MARGO TITTLEDOWN (OWNER OF BRAMBLEDOWN LEISURE GROUP AND KEEN POP MUSIC LOVER)

AND INTRODUCING SPECIAL GUEST JUDGE

JOSH RAVEN

WEDNESDAY 24TH AUGUST
VENUE: THE LEGENDARY 'HONEY DOME'
DOORS 8PM
FREE ENTRY

THE PRIZE:

- *THE OPPORTUNITY TO PERFORM A FULL SET, LIVE ON THE MAIN STAGE AT THE KALEIDOSCOPE FESTIVAL*
- *ACCESS-ALL-AREAS VIP FESTIVAL PASSES*
- *LUXURY ACCOMMODATION IN A GLAMPING YURT*
- *RECORDING TIME AND MASTERING OF A SINGLE AT PETE HARTLEY'S RECORDING STUDIO WITH AN ACTUAL RELEASE DATE AND PROMOTIONAL SCHEDULE*

Sponsored by   **Ludlow's Luxury Loos**   **CAK ENERGY DRINKS**   **DUNGLEBERT'S BURGERS**

Having been woken at 7AM by the sound of my parents arguing, I got up and went downstairs, lingering outside the kitchen, deciding whether or not to enter as they continued to row.

'Ten THOUSAND pounds?' Dad said in an angry voice.

'Knowledge costs,' snapped Mum. 'And Shanty Farquhar is the most experienced Tantric Sex Teacher in the world. He's the Guru.'

That was the moment I decided to enter the kitchen, in the hope that their intimate (which is code for DISGUSTING) conversation would end. But of course, I was wrong.

'Well, Blossom,' said Dad. 'I hope you haven't inherited your mum's insatiable sexual appetite. Your poor future boyfriend won't know what's hit him.'

Oh God. Am I too old to be fostered out to another family? I'll sweep chimneys. Sweat tears in a workhouse. Anything.

Right then the doorbell rang and, quite frankly, I couldn't answer it fast enough. Receiving the recorded delivery of mum's new Rose Quartz Vaginal Energy Crystal couldn't have been a more welcome interruption.

The Battle of the Bands final is in just over a week and Camel Toe have a lot of rehearsing to do. There is only one problem – since Matthew told us the news, I haven't seen or spoken to Petrina (she is once again ignoring my texts). I called Walter and Matthew over an emergency meeting to discuss our possible options if Petrina has indeed left the band.

Option 1: Carry on as a solo act, renaming the band 'Camel' or 'Toe'.

Option 2: Continue as a duo, but dress up Walter in glasses and a blonde wig to pass off as Petrina.

Option 3. Ditto above but using Matthew as fake Petrina.

After careful consideration, we have decided on Matthew being the substitute Petrina. Not only is his fair skin tone closer to that of Petrina's, but I also want to attempt the stage dive again and will need Walter (who I've already rehearsed with) to be in the audience ready to catch me. The slangers aren't stupid enough to pull the same stunt twice, so Walter will be in position in the legendary Honey Dome mosh pit to prevent another humiliating disaster. Matthew rather cleverly suggested that we rehearse in the centre of Polystyrene Stonehenge so that: a) I can practise my stage dive off of one of the circle stones from a decent height, and b) I get used to playing in a place seeped in history.

Breeze came outside to watch us play a couple of songs. Normally she would have dished out a stream of insults as she watched me playing guitar, perched on the Altar Stone, while Matthew mimed along to Petrina's pre-recorded keyboard part and vocals (that she had programmed for me a while ago in case she couldn't make rehearsals). But the split with Andreas has left my sister a shadow of her usual self. It's almost as if my feisty, aggressive, confrontational sister has been replaced by a floaty, flimsy, gentle imposter. For once she didn't offer an opinion or give criticism, instead she sat down barefoot with a mug of camomile tea and listened quietly before padding back indoors. And yes, I know it sounds weird, but I wish the old hostile Breeze with her massive angry nostrils would come back. Not least because this new version has succeeded in REALLY annoying my parents. The 'new' Breeze went to church on Sunday morning and is now considering becoming a nun. When they found out, Mum and Dad went berserk. I can't believe that she's managed to finally find a way to rebel against our parents. This is MY time for rebellion. Breeze's time has passed – she isn't even a teenager any more. Nevertheless, I have to admit that conforming to a religious organisation is just sheer GENIUS. I wish I'd thought of that.

PROS AND CONS OF BEING A NUN

PROS

1. *No boy trouble*
2. *No unwanted pregnancies*
3. *No risk of a sexually transmitted infection*
4. *No panic in the morning that you have nothing to wear*
5. *An instant solution to those 'bad hair days'*
6. *A constant supply of free wine*

CONS

1. *I'd die a virgin*
2. *No kids*
3. *I'd have to give up Camel Toe*

4. I probably wouldn't be able to write my vampire novel series – the Harlot Mistfang Chronicles. I don't think the boss of the nuns would approve of sexy bloodsucking immortals murdering teenagers in the name of Satan.

So it seems that the pros outweigh the cons. This would have been the perfect way to rebel. *GOD I'M SOOOOO ANNOYED.*

I'd probably have to stop saying 'God' so much, wouldn't I?

Breeze has told our parents about me, Vince and the 'nork-grabbing incident', even though she'd been sworn to secrecy. She said that, in an effort to throw off the shackles that had been binding her down, she must free herself from all the secrets that she's been holding on to (her other confessions included: peeing on Mr Parkin's front porch late one night when she was drunk, using Mum's yoga mat barefoot even though she knew she had a highly contagious verruca and buying a copy of the *Daily Mail* once just to get the free *Psychedelic Love Songs of the 60s* CD that they were giving away). I am praying that my sister meets another man soon – this new, holier-than-thou REBELLIOUS Breeze is AWFUL.

My parents were naturally extremely concerned about my welfare, with Dad threatening to go and speak (peacefully) to Vince's parents, but when I explained how I'd dealt with the situation they couldn't have been more proud. So much so that Mum couldn't wait to tell Kenny how I'd been able to defend myself and in doing so 'preserved the honour of the feminist sisterhood'.

'This is solid proof that my self-defence techniques are the best,' said Kenny to his class. He cupped his hand to his cauliflower ear. 'What are they?'

'THE BEST,' we all shouted back (though not Petrina as she hadn't turned up).

'YEAH,' he shouted. 'What did you shout Blossom?'

'BALLS,' I yelled at the top of my lungs.

Kenny nodded approvingly, hands on his hips, surveying his group of women. 'Today, we're going to work on tits,' he said.

'Oh, I love it when he's forceful,' whispered Wendy, who I'd noticed was wearing more and more perfume each week.

Mum turned and glared at her with her fierce yoga eyes. My parents might have knocked the whole 'open relationship' fiasco on the head, but Mum still loves to flirt and did not like Wendy encroaching on her territory at all. Kenny was oblivious and teamed the two up as partners. I'm not going to go into massive detail, but it's safe to say that Wendy and Mum's animosity towards each other escalated as the class went on. Each self-defence move that they practised became more and more aggressive until Kenny was forced to physically pull them apart when Mum picked Wendy up and threw her over her shoulder, slamming her hard into the mat.

'IPPON!' screamed my pacifist mother with a demented look in her eyes. 'Ten points. A perfect throw. HA! Still got it.'

Apparently my mum was a black belt first dan in Judo at the age of eighteen. I had no idea.

When Andreas sent me a text at 10AM asking if I could meet him ASAP, I knew it must be important. Andreas doesn't emerge from his 'man boudoir' until after midday. Until my sister moved in with him, Andreas' apartment was the ultimate nightclub owner bachelor pad. It was decorated in black and red, everything was either super furry (e.g. shag-pile rug, faux-fur cushions, fake tiger-print bed throw) or super shiny (e.g. satin bed-sheets, black marble coffee table, squeaky leather sofa). He had everything the modern man could want – a separate fridge for beer, a fifty-inch TV mounted on the wall, a state-of-the-art surround sound system, a MASSIVE circular bed, a swimming-pool-sized Jacuzzi and a life-size golden statue of a naked woman with humongous norks. It was a pretty hideous apartment to be honest.

Then, with the arrival of Breeze, the bold colours and clinical surfaces gave way to colourful hemp-based materials, Indian throws, recycled wood furniture (plus her favourite Retro Hanging Bubble Pod Chair) and a whole range of potted house-plants (including my sister's beloved Ursula). Andreas' sleek bachelor pad became more like a Mongolian yurt.

But, after meeting Andreas in Starbucks, I was once again sure that, despite Breeze's dominant interior design preferences, despite her revolting vegan hamster food breakfasts and despite her general-all-round-annoyingness, Andreas still loved her with all his heart. With a little bit of my help Andreas hoped to win her back before she donned a wimple and kissed goodbye to her beloved Organic Naughty Knickers.

HOT OFF THE PRESS:

Mei Miyagi has been ceremoniously dumped after Paulette bought Mei's Gay Soirée for a discount price. Turns out Kirsty was right – Paulette *had* been using Mei to get to her business and as soon as Mei accepted the cash, Paulette publicly declared herself to be asexual again. Mei is absolutely distraught. She thought Paulette was really in love with her (or with Marco at least).

Since discovering she was pretty awesome at making money, Paulette has become a Ruthless Entrepreneurial Monster™. Her scruples have been sold along with her soul and she'll trample on whoever it takes to get to the top, be it Mei, me or even her own granny, who she scammed into giving a week's pension money in return for the promise of a date with Marlon Brando (who is not only a Hollywood movie star but is also dead). Her secret business motto (brutally discovered by Mei) is *Use, Abuse And Then Refuse*™. I don't think there is any point in trying to get back at Paulette for her nastiness as the good Lady Karma will have plans for her sometime in the future. I just hope that it's a public comeuppance that involves something stinky and messy. Hmmm. I wonder if Matthew Ludlow can puke on command?

END OF WEEK 33: MY TABLE OF ACHIEVEMENT

SHAME LEVEL PEAK	I AM TOTALLY OVER THIS STUPID TABLE OF ACHIEVEMENT.
GUITAR PRACTICE	I AM TOTALLY OVER THIS STUPID TABLE OF ACHIEVEMENT.
SNOGS	I AM TOTALLY OVER THIS STUPID TABLE OF ACHIEVEMENT.
PARTY INVITATIONS	I AM TOTALLY OVER THIS STUPID TABLE OF ACHIEVEMENT.

WEEK 34
THE FINAL

Having been returned by Matthew a couple of weeks ago, the cherry-red Gibson ES-335 was back on display in the shop. I walked up to it and softly stroked its fret, knowing that it could belong to me. Matthew's birthday present was the most thoughtful and generous (not to mention expensive) gift that anyone had ever bought me, but the Gibson wasn't mine to own – at least not yet anyway.

The bell clangs. I circle around the ring, as my opponent stares me in the eye. The crowd is chanting my name: 'Ball Twister, Ball Twister, Ball Twister,' they shout. I am filled with pride and confidence.

'You're going down,' says Dastardly Dempsey. She is wearing a midnight-blue catsuit with a gold lightning flash across the chest and a pair of spherical, gold deely-boppers are bouncing about on top of her head.

I lunge forward to pull her into a headlock. I'm so psyched that I don't even care when my silver leotard rides right up in between my bum cheeks. But Dastardly Dempsey is too fast. She lands a forearm smash on my cheek and my legs fly out from underneath me. I crash down hard on to the floor. Before I can get back up on to my feet, Dastardly Dempsey is climbing up the ropes. She's ready to jump. ON TO ME. She launches herself into the air. THE TRAMPLER SLAM™. It's her killer trademark move where she basically tramples over anyone who gets in her way. I am totally winded and rendered powerless, even though I have been working out and eating nothing but spinach and protein shakes for two weeks. The crowd is booing as Dastardly Dempsey's massive bottom suffocates my face. And then just as I think it can't get any worse, she high-fives someone else who has entered the ring. Someone wearing a tight, denim, body-stocking with a hole at the top of one thigh.

It's Vince 'The Nork-Grabber' Granger! Wait up, that's unfair. I didn't know it was tag-team wrestling.

Dastardly Dempsey stands up and I see The Nork Grabber's arm extending towards my chest, his fingers ready to grab my assets.

I know what I have to do. 'BALLS,' I scream at the top of my voice. As I go to perform my signature move the crowd chant my name. 'Ball Twister, Ball Twister, Ball Twister.'

The Nork Grabber crumples to the floor, groaning in pain. I see my opportunity to escape, but, before I can stand up, Dastardly Dempsey suddenly twists me roughly into the Boston Crab lock. I have the worst view EVER – she's clearly not wearing any knickers.

My fate is sealed. Two against one just isn't fair and I'm about to admit defeat when . . .

Someone jumps over the ropes, 'air-flares' across the ring and 'windmills' Dastardly Dempsey in the head with his spinning legs. She drops to the floor like a deadweight, directly on top of The

Nork-Grabber. The crowd cheers. They are both out for the count.

I turn to high-five my mysterious tag-team partner. He is wearing a shocking pink ladies swimming costume back to front and a purple, sparkly mask that covers his whole face. With those lean, muscular biceps, it can only be the world famous wrestler Felix 'The Fox' Winters.

'Thank you,' I say. 'Although as The Ball Twister, I could of course have handled the situation entirely by myself with my womanly wrestling ways.'

'I know,' says the voice that I recognise but is NOT that of Felix The Fox. Curiously, I reach out and pull off his mask.

'MATTHEW 'LIQUID MOTION' LUDLOW?! Of course! How could I have not recognised his signature killer breakdance moves?

Liquid Motion Ludlow drops to the floor, performs a few celebratory breakdance moves, then jumps over the ropes and disappears back into the cheering crowd.

I lap up the chants of 'Ball Twister' for a little while longer before I go back to my dressing room for a much-needed wee.

Carrying out a secret plan when it involved my now holy but still annoyingly stubborn sister, turned out to be quite tricky.

For the last week Breeze has been moping around the house, watching *The Sound of Music* on endless repeat and testing out different vegan fabrics as makeshift wimples. She also enlisted Mum's help in trying to learn yogic levitation, so that she can be the modern version of Christina the Astonishing. Breeze explained that Christina was a thirteenth-century nun who died from a seizure, but then rose out of her coffin during her funeral and floated up to the rafters, complaining that everybody stank of sin. I've been racking my brains trying to think what 'sin' would actually smell like. My guess is a mixture of raw sewage, B.O. and Petrina's rancid feet in the summertime.

All I had to do was get Breeze to the Garden of Vegan restaurant in town for eight o'clock.

'No,' said Breeze firmly. 'I'm practising my yogic flying with Mum tonight.'

The sight of my sister and mother jumping about the living room with their legs crossed while they watch *Eastenders* has become a disturbing, regular occurrence.

'Some fresh air and good food will do you good.'

'I'm fasting at the moment,' sighed my pale and pasty sister. 'I can only drink Camomile tea until I am cleansed.'

This new Breeze is so dreary. I need to fire her up again.

'Jesus wouldn't want you to be hungry,' I said. 'That's why he fasted for forty days and forty nights, so that the rest of us could eat Meat Feast Pizzas without feeling guilty.'

Is that right? Jesus fasted for our sins or was that Gandhi?

I could see that Breeze was beginning to get annoyed.

'Oh, come on,' I begged. 'It'll be fun.'

'Since when have you been "fun"?' asked Breeze. It was a fair question and one that I couldn't answer.

'I'm thinking of becoming a vegan,' I fibbed. My sister brought her face close to mine and looked straight into

281

my eyes. She inhaled deeply through her humongous sniff buckets.

'I smell BULL,' she wheezed. 'LIES.'

She's getting angry. My plan is beginning to work!

'I'm at an experimental age, Breeze,' I explained. *I'm going to have to really manipulate her now.* 'I want to step out of my comfort zone and you are so knowledgeable about all things vegan, organic and non-leathery. I need to explore how I can live my life without exploiting animals for their delicious meat.' *Mmmm burgers.*

Breeze eyed me suspiciously, but the 'false praise' approach seemed to be working.

'All right,' she said. 'But only if you try the Spicy Thai Vegetable Soup.' She smirked in a way that made me think that the word 'spicy' was probably a dangerously huge understatement.

'It's a deal,' I said, feeling relieved that I wouldn't actually have to try the dish myself. I can't handle spicy food at all. Once after eating a mild chicken korma takeaway I started sweating and shivering so profusely that Dad had to wrap me from head to toe in tin foil to stop any more of my body heat from escaping.

And so, just after eight o'clock, I arrived at Garden of Vegan with my sister, who thankfully had ditched her makeshift organic wimple for the night and, instead, had made herself look rather gorgeous. Once inside the waiter ushered us over to a candlelit table for two where Andreas was waiting patiently. He stood up as soon as he saw my sister and they faced each other without uttering a word; Andreas in his sharp, black, tailored suit, Breeze in her floaty bohemian summer dress. The most perfect, mismatched couple ever.

'You cheating BABOON,' screamed Breeze.

It's good to have my awful sister back.

'I did not cheat, you crazy, hippie WOMAN,' yelled Andreas.

Neither of them cared that they might be disturbing the other diners in the restaurant, so I felt obliged to whisper awkward apologies on their behalf.

'Why the texts? Why the "moro mou"?'

'I call everyone "moro mou" apart from you because you go MENTAL whenever I say it.'

'You deceitful fuzzy sasquatch!' screeched my irate sister.

'Chill out, moro mou.'

'ARRRRRRGGGGHHHHH! I saw you with her!' Breeze was shaking. 'Sneaking around together.'

'She was helping me plan your surprise,' said Andreas a little more quietly. 'Do you really think I would choose to eat in a place where the food is DISGUSTING'?

Breeze put her hands on her hips. 'What?'

Everyone in the restaurant looked horrified.

'All this green gunk makes me sick. I'm a carnivore, Breeze. I need bloody, vein-covered, protein-filled meat.'

A few of the customers had turned a little pale.

'But,' continued Andreas. 'I came here because you love all this veggie crap. And Tania helped me choose this . . .'

He reached into his pocket and, pulling out a small

283

black box, dropped down on to one knee. The other diners gasped with delight (though they still looked a little bit queasy).

'So, you tree-hugging, kumquat-muncher,' said Andreas holding out the ring. 'I love you and I want to marry you. Will you be my wife?'

Breeze's frown gradually softened and she smiled for the first time in weeks. Then she launched herself wildly on to her fiancé and they dry humped each other on the restaurant floor until the waiter was forced to pull them apart. I figured that this was probably a good time to leave.

CORN MOON

ALSO KNOWN AS DISPUTE MOON,
LIGHTNING MOON, MOON WHEN ALL
THINGS RIPEN, STURGEON MOON.

BATTLE OF THE BANDS FINAL

I've done something REALLY stupid.

I finally figured out how to rebel against my liberal-minded parents and put it into action. My epiphany arrived when a nasty image of my naked mum brushing her muff with my hairbrush popped into my head as I practised the chords of 'Nork-Grabbing Quimboid' on Cassiopeia this morning.

Of course! It's so obvious.

Fast forward two hours and I was lying on Gayle's table in the salon treatment room.

'Landing Strip, Triangular Armadillo, Heart-Breaker, Furry Yeti Paw, G-Wax or Hitler?' she asked matter-of-factly.

I had no idea this would be so complicated.

'Do people really ask for a "Hitler"?'

I wondered what type of woman would want the mark of a fascist dictator branded on her lady parts.

'God, yeah,' chirped Gayle. 'That girl in your class with the big boobies, Fiona Tittledown, comes in every four weeks for hers.'

Swallow the sick, Blossom. Swallow the sick.

In the end I opted for a 'Heart-Breaker' with a small vajazzle in the shape of a butterfly, knowing that my parents would totally disapprove. In their eyes, artificially altering the appearance of a female's 'Sacred Well' (BLEURRGHH) is a rejection of 'divine womanhood'. So basically I've defaced Mother Earth's muff with an excruciating buzz-cut and a handful of tacky stick-on plastic crystals.

But it seemed that my non-conformist (to my family) efforts

were in vain as Mum's reaction to the news of my vajazzle was:

'I'm so proud of you. Using your pubic mound as a canvas to express yourself, is so artistic.'

And not only that, I've come out in a terrible sore, red rash that itches like mad. If I scratch myself in public, everyone's going to think I have pubic lice. Just as well I don't have to stand on stage in front of a few hundred people wearing tight jeans then. Oh no . . . wait . . .

The thought of performing without Petrina in the Honey Dome was terrifying. It's a MASSIVE venue, done up with fortress-style walls and a black painted ceiling, covered in stars to make it feel as if you are outside in a castle courtyard. The floor sloped gently down to the stage to guarantee a great view from wherever you stood and the smell of stale, adrenaline-fuelled sweat seeped out of every pore in the walls. Standing in that enormous dark, empty room with Walter, soaking up the atmosphere before the sound checks, would have been an almost spiritual experience had it not been for the absence of Petrina and the presence of the slangers.

'Yuck,' complained Fiona. 'The floor is all sticky.'

'Beer, blood and sweat,' I said. 'Rock 'n' roll.'

'Yeah, well they could have given it an antiseptic wash before we arrived,' said Fiona, her shoes glitching each time she raised one off the floor.

Right, then the back door opened to reveal a RIPPED figure silhouetted against the bright daylight.

'Blossom, daaarling!' It was Josh Raven. Lucy's mouth dropped open and Fiona's eyes bulged wildly as if she'd developed a thyroid condition. Josh skipped over and embraced Walter and me tightly. I suppressed the urge to lick his neck when his delicious scent wafted under my nose.

He looked around him and threw his arms wide. 'Isn't it just wonderful?' he said. 'The ambience . . . the space . . . the acoustics!' And then, right there he launched into a spontaneous acapella version of his worldwide number one hit single 'Moonlight Stalker'. It was an incredible, surreal moment (I mean, it's not every day that Josh Raven performs a private show for you), but I still felt awkward and didn't quite know how to react without looking unnatural.

It seemed that nobody else shared my inhibited self-consciousness. Fiona was clapping eagerly, her grin veering into frenzied fanatic territory and Lucy started screaming hysterically and clawing at her own face. Walter casually nodded his head, his fringe swinging in time to the beat of Josh's tapping foot. I knew I had to do something instead of standing stock still, which seemed really rude and unappreciative while Josh sang his heart out.

So I nervously began clicking my fingers.

What am I doing? This is so uncool.

Walter shook his head in a 'What are you doing? That is so uncool' kind of way. I decided that a bit more conviction was in order, as if I really meant business. So I began to click my fingers on the other hand too.

288

Double finger clicking in front of JOSH RAVEN? Blossom, have you lost your tiny mind?

I bit my lower lip at the same time and added a rhythmic nod to make sure everyone knew I was really sincere. At this point, I realised with horror that Walter, Fiona, Lucy AND Josh Raven were now all looking at me as if I had totally lost the plot. Obviously, I was curling up and dying inside, but now that I was double-finger-clicking and nodding with such gusto, I'd committed to the cause and there was no going back. This was one of those horrible moments in life that I hope my brain will classify as a 'trauma' and subsequently bury at the bottom of my subconscious, where only an experienced psychotherapist will ever be able to uncover it.

As the venue began filling up, I paced anxiously around backstage with Walter trying to calm me down. Matthew had bought a new, long blonde wig from a party shop but he insisted on wearing it so that the hair hung over his face with the huge black-rimmed glasses over the top. He looked more like Cousin It from The Addams Family than a Norwegian keyboard maestro.

'This is ridiculous,' I said. 'We'll never pull it off.'

Matthew brushed his long, blonde hair over his shoulder. 'She might still turn up,' he said.

But I shook my head. Despite Camel Toe getting through to the final, despite the prospect of performing on stage at the Kaleidoscope Festival, despite this being her dream scenario, Petrina was proud and incredibly stubborn.

'I'll have to do it alone,' I said. 'We've already pre-recorded Petrina's part so I can just play along without her.'

I was nervous beyond belief and it didn't help that everyone I knew would be in the audience. At least five hundred people were expected to watch Camel Toe compete against Perkitits and the local press were there, as were two local TV news channels, plus a number of critics from well-respected music magazines. NO PRESSURE THEN!!!

Bob arrived with brand new band T-shirts for us. Not only do I have the Ludlow Loos logo on the back, but it seems that Matthew had persuaded Paulette the Ruthless Entrepreneurial Monster to invest in Camel Toe too.

Ludlow's Luxury Loos & Dempseylove.com

Bomb the porcelain sea in comfort and find true love.

Much as I hate to say it, I think that online dating while on the toilet is pure genius. If your partner-to-be sees you at your very worst on your first date, then surely the only way is up after that?

Perkitits were on stage first and Walter and I watched from the wings with Felix and Toby, who had produced all of the tracks that they were singing. Somehow, I managed to congratulate the annoyingly talented producers on doing a first-class job without uttering something embarrassing.

The audience went crazy, wolf-whistling and cheering their approval as the slangers gyrated and writhed out on stage wearing black spandex body-stockings covered in shiny pearl buttons that spelt out the word 'VIXEN' on Fiona's back and 'SHE-DEVIL' on Lucy's (I can't help feeling that 'DOG-BREATH' and 'DUH-BRAIN' would have been more appropriate). They looked like a couple of cockney prostitutes with a bad case of worms, but their voices were irritatingly good and their onstage energy was infectious. They were slick before, but somehow the professional lighting and general vibe of the venue had made them seem more glamorous and charismatic. In front of the stage on the left were the judges, all on their feet (or on the table in Josh's case) and dancing with the upmost approval. Seeing Margo Tittledown waving her arms about and proudly singing her heart out, I knew that Camel Toe didn't stand a chance (especially now that Camel Toe was a solo act). This was Fiona's contest, bought and paid for by Mummykins. Yes, the slangers probably did deserve to be in the final, but they'd won the competition before any of the other fifteen bands taking part had even played a single note.

'Beat that, Bumface,' sneered a hot and sweaty Fiona after Perkitits had come off stage to rapturous applause. Their entire set had been awesome, complete with pyrotechnics (we hadn't even thought of that), dancers (we hadn't even thought of that) and a hydraulic giant hand that lifted the slangers high above the audience (WE'D THOUGHT OF THAT!).

'Where's your corpse bride?' asked Lucy, looking around for Petrina.

Walter ignored her. 'I'd better get into position,' he mumbled before heading off to take his place at the front of the stage.

Lucy wasn't going to give up. 'So has Poohead really chickened out?'

'No . . . she's . . . err . . .' I was struggling to find an excuse.

Fiona couldn't hide her delight at Petrina's absence. 'Oh well, you better throw in the towel right now then,' she said with a smirk. 'You really don't have the charisma to be a solo act.'

'Yeah,' agreed Lucy with a laugh. 'Why don't you just admit defeat? Put yourself out of your misery.'

Maybe they've got a point. This could be utterly humiliating. But I've come this far . . .

'Think about it,' Fiona reasoned. 'You've lost anyway.'

'I, erm . . .' I was getting flustered.

'Give it up, Bumface.' Fiona's sweaty face was inches away from mine.

She's right. I probably should. The band is over.

'Camel Toe are . . .' I began.

Fiona folded her arms. 'Camel Toe are what?'

'Camel Toe are going to win,' said the defiant voice next to me.

PETRINA!

'You might use deceit and lies to achieve your goals, but we'll always be victorious when it comes to artistic integrity.'

Wow. When she makes powerful statements like that, it's clear that Petrina could easily be the next prime minister. Or work as a team leader in a call centre.

Petrina and I stood together in the wings, waiting to be introduced on stage.

'He's gay, you know?' she said quietly.

'Who?'

'Leon.'

Oh.

Petrina looked me directly in the eyes for the first time in weeks. It was only because her mega thick lenses acted as a microscope that I noticed the tears she rapidly blinked away. That's twice I've broken her emotional dam in a week.

'But even so,' she continued. 'I wouldn't have cheated on Walter. I couldn't. He's my soul mate.'

I felt dreadful. How could I ever have doubted her? What kind of terrible friend was I?

'I'm so sorry,' I whispered. 'I'm a massive quimboid.'

'Yes, you are,' she said bumping her shoulder briefly against mine. Knowing that Petrina keeps all physical contact down to an absolute minimum, this gesture was all the reassurance I needed to realise that I had been forgiven.

'OK, ladies and gentlemen,' came Margo Tittledown's

screeching voice over the speakers. 'It's time for the second finalist. Please welcome to the stage . . . Camel Toe.'

'Let's do it,' said Petrina.

I felt calm, composed and content – as close to a Zen state of mind as I was ever going to be – that is if it weren't for my burning (but beautifully decorated) lady parts, which had begun to itch like MAD.

Whatever you do, don't scratch. Put your hands behind your back and think of something non-itchy. Like stainless steel. Or broccoli. Or pork. Mmmm. Tasty pork.

I struck a G chord on Cassiopeia, who Bob had already tuned for me.

PORK SCRATCHING! Arrrrgggghhhhhhh.

I stag-leaped on to the stage – the only way I could think of to get a bit of relief from the unbearable prickling that was going on my underwear. I managed another two leaps to get me to the mic stand, where I was able to use Cassiopeia as a shield to have a quick (blissful) and discreet scratch. Scanning the vast crowd I saw Walter giving us the thumbs up from his agreed position in the mosh pit; Mum and Dad (dressed in his Morris dancing gear) at the back; Breeze and Andreas (who still had a red glow after his fiancée forced him to try the Spicy Thai Vegetable Soup last night); Mei and Kirsty (standing separately on opposite sides of the venue); Leon (lingering alongside Josh Raven, who was waving from the judges' table) and Paulette Dempsey drinking Coke at the front of the stage. With nothing to lose (apart from the competition which, let's face it, we'd already lost before we even entered) we were going to give this show everything we'd got.

The stage descended into darkness and the loudly buzzing crowd hushed into an expectant murmur. Then a single bright spotlight was switched on that shone directly down on me.

'Good evening, Honey Dome!' I said into the mic. 'We're Camel Toe.'

And as we launched into the energetic 'Nork-Grabbing Quimboid', a million stage lights flooded the room with an angry red glow. I looked at Petrina and grinned. This wasn't just a gig, this was a rock CONCERT!

We ploughed through our high energy set: 'Lutraphobia, 'The Man With An Eggy Beard', 'Touch Me Anywhere And Everywhere (But Don't Touch Me There)' – which was a particularly relevant song given the raging fire burning on my lady parts – and ended with our crowd favourite, 'Poncerama'. Just before I played the opening chords, I double-checked that Walter was ready and waiting. One public stage dive catastrophe was humiliating. If I hit the floor twice I would not only risk a gummy mouth and a trip to A&E, but I'd also NEVER live it down. I could hear the taunts already.

'Here comes Bumface, Braceface, Fall-on-fat-swollen-gummy-face.'

As Camel Toe approached the second verse, I made my way confidently to the front of the stage, pulling my best 'bass face' to show that I meant business.

I am standing on the golden diving board that juts out over the heads of the excited gig-goers. I am NOT wearing a bikini or a revealing swimsuit even though I am vajazzled right up to my navel. Instead I am dressed in a leather wetsuit that does not make me look like a kinky gimp pervert in any way. The crowd below me are waiting, their arms reaching up, ready to receive my body. Tonight, I will attempt the classic rock 'n' roll swan dive. I stretch out my arms and . . . DIVE.

I am floating . . . floating . . . into Walter's arms.

Once again (as expected), the crowd parted when they realised I was about to jump. To my absolute horror, just as my feet left the stage, I noticed a fracas at the back of the venue. Walter was desperately trying to free himself from the sharp-nailed claws of Fiona and Lucy. They must have caught him off guard and dragged him away at the very last second.

So if there's no Walter to catch me then I'm going to . . .

I braced myself as I dropped, ready for the impact of my body crashing on to the concrete floor.

Suddenly I felt a pair of sturdy hands grab me firmly across my ribcage.

And then I was being lifted. Up, up, up. Another pair of hands took hold of my shoulders. Another pair of hands were on my thighs. And then another pair of hands

Whoa . . . those hands are on my bottom!

Somehow, against all the odds, I was crowd-surfing, hundreds of hands passing me above the heads of the chanting audience.

'Poncerama oooh, Poncerama oooh,
It's no wonder that nobody loves you.'

I looked towards the front of the stage. It hadn't been Walter's hands that had saved me from certain indignity, so whose hands were they? In amongst the sea of bouncing, sweating spectators, my eyes were drawn to a pair of feet, suspended motionless for a moment, at head height. One second they were there, the next they'd disappeared. And then they were back. And then they were gone again. Some reckless quimboid with a death wish had decided that the front of the mosh pit was the perfect place to do a caterpillar breakdance move. But the crowd were LOVING it. They stepped aside to make room as his body rippled smoothly amongst them, their appreciation clear from the smiles and cheers spurring him on. It wasn't until I caught a glimpse of his strawberry blonde hair that the identity of the mystery break-dancer dawned on me.

The lesbian transsexual in the gay nightclub, the helicopter pilot, the cigar-eating band manager, the Scottish warrior and the breakdancing wrestler. Of course . . .

MATTHEW LUDLOW!!

Exhausted, but pumped full of adrenaline, Petrina and I slumped into the chairs back stage in the dressing room to await the verdict of the judges. We knew we wouldn't win, but we didn't care – after tonight, we were more determined than ever to take Camel Toe to the next level. The band was our future, our dreams – our EVERYTHING.

Suddenly our peaceful afterglow was rudely interrupted by the slangers, who came barging into the dressing room.

'How does it feel to know that failure is only minutes away?' Fiona jeered.

'I think we'll survive,' Petrina said firmly. 'Shame your attempt to sabotage Blossom's stage dive was in vain.'

Lucy shrugged. 'We have no idea what you are talking about.'

The sudden sight of Fiona had made my lady parts feel itchy again. I shuffled uncomfortably in my seat.

'Have you got crabs or something?' she asked. 'You were scratching on stage as if your knickers were made from horse hair.'

'No,' I explained. 'I've had a glamorous bikini wax.'

For some reason, this made the slangers LITERALLY double up with laughter. I felt myself getting angry.

'Yeah . . . well what about you and your Hitler muff?'

Fiona glared at me.

HA! That shut her up.

'You've got a Hitler?' asked Lucy looking shocked.

Fiona shuffled around uneasily.

'I am so offended,' Lucy continued with her hands on her hips. 'My family is Jewish and there's you with a hateful fanny? I thought you were my supposed to be my best friend.'

'I AM your best friend,' whimpered Fiona. 'And my fanny's not hateful. Anyway, it's more like a Charlie Chaplin than a Hitler. So it's actually a very funny fanny.'

The four of us stood together on stage – a bittersweet triumph for the feminist movement. Here we were, a glorious, all-female final, but any sense of camaraderie that might have been, had been destroyed by the underlying animosity between us. We were two pairs of young women – united by our gender yet divided by our school social status. Weirdos vs. Winners. If Emmeline Pankhurst had been alive today she would have burned her bloomers in disgust.

Joining us on stage were the three judges, with Josh Raven sending every girl (apart from Kirsty Mackerby and Paulette 'my only true love is money' Dempsey) and Leon (whose eyes had been firmly fixed on him all night) into a screaming frenzy as he waved to his adoring disciples. Even the usually cool Mei Miyagi became momentarily hysterical until she remembered that she was supposed to be a lesbian. In his tight black T-shirt and uber hot skinny black jeans, Josh looked like a massive, sexy black pudding, which I found incredibly erotic (I will never look at a full English Breakfast in the same way again). The evening's 'compère' (which in this case is code for 'cheat', 'fraudster' and 'all round spineless weasel') Margo Tittledown, attempted to quieten the raucous, overexcited crowd, but even though she was speaking into a microphone, her screechy voice still couldn't be heard over the din.

Pete Hartley watched her for a moment, almost as if he was enjoying seeing her efforts fail. Then he roughly snatched the mic from her. 'OI!' he yelled at the crowd. 'SHUT IT.'

The noise lowered to a hum. I wasn't entirely sure if it was Pete's slightly menacing tone that had made everyone take notice or simply the sight of a middle-aged man wearing a fluorescent pink Hawaiian shirt open to the waist and a pair of white shorts that were so small they might as well have just been Y-fronts.

Whichever the case, now that he had the full attention of the venue, Pete passed the mic back to Margo Tittledown, who began to explain (in really drawn-out, boring detail) how difficult the judges' decision had been. Throughout Margo's long, laboured waffle, I couldn't help but notice that Josh, who was usually so perky and animated, seemed subdued, staring down at his feet and chewing the inside of his cheek.

'And so,' said Margo proudly. 'It's time to reveal the winner of this year's Battle of the Bands, sponsored by Ludlow's Luxury Loos, Cak Energy Drinks, Dungelbert's Burgers and not forgetting the Brambledown Sports and Leisure Group, who are committed to developing the best facilities for a fitter and more fun United Kingdom. And that winner is . . . '

Josh's fists were clenched and his brow furrowed. He shook his head and clenched his jaw in way that made my stomach flip.

He is SO intense. I wonder if there is an ounce of homohetrual in him?

Fiona and Lucy (who were holding hands) had already broken into their celebratory grins, but Pete was blatantly uncomfortable, as if he'd rather be anywhere else than here, which was odd because he'd been coming to the Honey Dome regularly for decades – it was his second home.

Petrina gently bumped her shoulder against mine and winked at me. I smiled back. We knew the outcome. We'd accepted our fate. It was cool, we might not have won, but this was an awesome platform and we were going to use it to springboard Camel Toe to the next level. We waited patiently for Perkitits to be announced as winners, but on stage the sense of tension and expectation had given way to something else. Something waspish and distinctly angry that buzzed aggressively amongst two of the judges.

Wowzoids! This is the longest dramatic pause in history.

'PERKITITS!!!' a delighted Margo finally shrieked into the mic.

The slangers shrieked and embraced each other. The audience cheered and applauded. Margo Tittledown looked at her daughter and her best friend proudly. But Petrina and I just felt weird. It was an anti-climax – no disappointment or tears of envy, just a muted recognition of the inevitable.

Yet beside me, the unease that had been building in Josh was becoming ever more apparent. His knuckles had turned white and his forehead was glistening with sweat.

Oh no. I have an overpowering urge to bottle his sweat and wear it as perfume. I have SO reached a new low.

Then Josh walked right up to Margo and snatched the mic angrily away from her.

'This is WRONG,' he snarled in an uncharacteristically butch voice. The excited audience simmered down. Margo made a feeble attempt to grab the microphone back, but one forbidding look from Pete and she timidly stepped away.

'This was never a showcase for new music,' continued Josh. 'This has all been about money.'

The slangers had turned a sickly pale colour.

'Perkitits put on a brilliant performance tonight.' Josh

turned to Fiona and Lucy. 'All credit to you girls,' he said kindly. 'But the judges weren't allowed to deliver the verdict that they wanted.'

Margo's expression was horribly familiar to me. She was hoping for the ground to swallow her up or wishing a massive meteorite would crash through the star painted ceiling and land on her, killing her instantly (I know this feeling SO well that I *almost* felt a pang of sympathy).

'Music is about talent and creativity, not all this corporate guff.'

The crowd gasped. The panic rising in the eyes of the slangers was visible for all to see.

'And so,' stated Josh in an authoritative voice that made him sound even more like the next prime minister than Petrina. 'I have to do what's honest and right.'

Margo Tittledown made a desperate last-ditch attempt to lunge for the mic, but Josh pulled it away, leaving Fiona's mum to crumple on the floor.

'The judges disagreed with the decision that had been made for us,' continued Josh. Petrina and I were dumbstruck as he turned to face us, his face beaming with pride. 'The rightful winner of The Battle of the Bands is . . . Camel Toe.'

WOWZOIDS!!!!.

In amongst the following hubbub of family and friends wanting to congratulate us, I noticed Walter edging ever closer towards Petrina. Sensing him next to her, she turned and looked directly at him. They stood like this for a few moments – the calm in the eye of the storm until Petrina broke the stillness by gently moving Walter's fringe to one side for the briefest of moments so that she could see his eyes.

She whispered something into his ear and he smiled before whispering something back. They looked at each other in a way that only true soul mates can, so I left them to it and nipped through the fire exit for a breath of fresh air.

Leaning against the cool brick wall (which I had sniffed carefully to ensure that nobody had used it as a drunken urinal), I closed my eyes to take in the enormity of what had just occurred. Not only had Camel Toe beaten Perkitits to win the Battle of the Bands, but we'd also now be performing at the MASSIVE Kaleidoscope Festival, alongside some of the biggest bands and artists in the world. As I contemplated my future and dreams, the fire exit door opened and Matthew poked his head out.

'Hey,' he said with a big grin on his face.

Moonlight is obviously very flattering. Matthew looks quite handsome in the silvery glow. I can't even see any of his spots.

'Hey,' I replied.

He came and leaned against the wall next to me, his spicy chocolate scent mingling with the warm night air.

'You were pretty awesome tonight,' he said.

'We couldn't have done it without our awesome manager.'

Matthew looked down at the ground bashfully and gently kicked a stone towards my purple vegan DM boot. I playfully kicked it back to him.

'How's your mum doing?' I asked in as careful a voice as I could manage.

Matthew kicked the stone with conviction across the path. It bumped loudly into the wooden fence.

'I'm not being nosey,' I said apologetically. 'I just . . . wondered if you were OK.'

'She's still away,' he said, his eyes fixed on the path. 'It's been almost seven months this time.'

I wasn't sure what to say. There didn't seem to be the right words to fill the hopeless silence that hung between us, so instead I reached out and took Matthew's hand with my own. Together we stood with our backs against the wall, listening to the sounds of passing traffic and people on the street and the rhythmic, muted bass thud from inside the Honey Dome.

'Blossom?' Matthew was facing me. He was still holding my hand. His fingers noticeably softer than I recalled Vince's to be. His blue eyes were pale in the moonlight and it dawned on me that I'd never really noticed them properly before – perhaps because Matthew isn't really one for eye contact or perhaps I just hadn't bothered to look until now. It occurred to me that there were a number of points that I needed to add to the 'Matthew Ludlow Pros List'

PROS

1. *He is funny*
2. *He is kind*
3. *He is quite nice-looking*
4. *He is a great kisser*

5. He smells lovely (a bit like a baby covered in spicy hot chocolate)
6. He has good dress sense
7. He has nice strawberry-blonde hair
8. He has good legs
9. He likes me
10. He can burp the entire alphabet in one breath
11. He is loyal
12. He has a nice Adam's apple
13. He is super generous
14. He is thoughtful and considerate
15. He has a mild nut allergy (so I won't have to share my Ferrero Rochers)
16. He can beatbox
17. He is supportive.
18. He has lovely eyes.

Hmmm, so the pros outweigh the cons eighteen to ten. Who'd have thought it?

Matthew swallowed hard and I was reminded of how his Adam's apple bobbed so enticingly when he had once demonstrated his beatboxing skills.

'I wanted to tell you . . .' he began in an unsteady voice. But his sentence was rudely cut short when the fire exit door was flung open.

'All right?' said Felix, who was looking proper real time HOT in his bum-hugging blue jeans. 'Just thought I'd say you know . . . nice one for winning, yeah?'

He raised his brown eyebrows cheekily and my stomach fluttered as I realised I knew the colour of his downstairs fur ball. I tugged discreetly at my fringe to make sure I wasn't showing too much of my own pubic eyebrows.

'Thanks. I hope Fiona isn't too upset,' I lied.

'I wouldn't know,' he said callously. 'She's nothing to do with me anymore. Hey, do you get free tickets to the Kaleidoscope Festival then?'

'I suppose so.'

Matthew, who I'd forgotten was still beside me, let go of my hand and took a step back into the shadows.

'Cool. Umm . . . do you wanna go see a film next week, or maybe grab a milkshake?' asked Felix.

OH. MY. GOD. He's asking me on a DATE! Ha ha ha ha ha!!! Is he joking? Act cool Blossom. Play it really cool.

I'm not certain if it was because he'd caught me off guard or because the adrenaline from performing was still running through my veins, but my reply to the question that I never thought I'd hear Felix ask was to scream as loudly as my lungs would allow right into his clearly terrified face.

Yeah, not quite as cool as I'd hoped.

Rubbing the inside of his ear with his finger, Felix smiled. 'Great. Don't forget to get those festival tickets for me, yeah?'

I nodded a little over-enthusiastically. Felix winked at me and disappeared back inside the Honey Dome. I turned back to Matthew, but he wasn't there. It's a well-known scientific fact that alcoholics feel the cold more than the rest of us, so he must have got a bit chilly and gone in for some warmth.

From: Noodlebrain12
To: RavenGirl007
Sent: August 24th 22:46:43

Hey!
So turns out that I was being an idiot after all. That girl I told you about isn't interested in me. I can't really blame her – she's out of my league. I hope this doesn't sound cheeky, but I'd like to take you up on that offer of meeting up sometime. It's not a rebound thing – I just thought we could cheer each other up.

Cheers
Noodlebrain12

From: RavenGirl007
To: Noodlebrain12
Sent: August 24th 22:47:35

Hi!
Well if you ask me, that girl doesn't know what she's missing. You're probably too good for her anyway!! But I'm afraid I'm going to have to turn down your offer as I've just been asked out on a date!!!!

RavenGirl007
P.S. You're not drunk are you?

No. I'm not drunk.

Cheers
Noodlebrain12

When I arrived home the full Corn Moon was high in the sky. Looking out into our garden from the kitchen, I could see Mum and Dad performing their naked monthly ritual in the centre of Polystyrene Stonehenge. I made a cup of tea and went straight up to my bedroom. Camel Toe have been allocated a thirty-minute set on the Kaleidoscope 'Carousel Stage' at 3PM on Friday. Petrina has calculated that we should be able to squeeze in seven tracks, so we're going to work hard to make sure we select the ultimate set-list. Although my parents will be coming along too, Petrina and I have chosen to travel with Walter, Matthew and Bob, who has kindly agreed to be our roadie for the weekend. Things are looking pretty good for me right now – I'm in a top band, playing at the second biggest music festival in the country and I've got the absolute, most brilliant friends in the world. All I need now is to get some decent exam grades (I get my results in the morning) and maybe find myself a new boyfriend (although who knows – maybe I've met that perfect someone already!!!!!!!).

THE END

THE SCALE OF SHAME BASED ON MY OWN EXPERIENCES

LEVEL 1: THE BURDEN OF AN EMBARRASSING NAME

e.g. B.U.M., P.O.O., W.E.E. or my dad's poor friend Phil Ness (Mr P Ness!!! His school life must have been verging on impossible).

LEVEL 2: MINOR FACIAL BLEMISHES e.g. Getting a large spot on my lip that I mistook for a sexually transmitted cold sore after having a drunken snog with Matthew Ludlow.

LEVEL 3: EMBARRASSING PARENTS e.g. When the YouTube video of my blue-dreadlocked, naked, horse-riding mother went viral worldwide.

LEVEL 4: BOWEL ISSUES e.g. When I yawned and accidentally let out a ginormous fart in my English Lit exam.

LEVEL 5: AWKWARD PHYSICAL CONTACT

e.g. Accidentally brushing against a naked Paulette Dempsey in the showers after our swimming lesson while she vigorously washed herself ALL OVER. (N.B. There should be some kind of law that forces everyone to keep their swimming costumes on in the communal showers. BLEURRGGHH.)

LEVEL 6: MAJOR PHYSICAL DEFECT e.g. When school SEX GOD Felix Winters pointed out that I had a long piece of dental floss caught in my brace (WHICH WAS MORTIFYING).

LEVEL 7: UNKNOWINGLY REVEALING UNDERWEAR e.g. The moment my old brown Scooby Doo knickers fell out of the leg of my trousers in the middle of a conversation with Felix Winters and Fiona Tittledown OR when I ended up riding round on a motorbike with two pieces of processed ham Sellotaped to my bra.

LEVEL 8: FREUDIAN SLIPS/MISINTERPRETATIONS OF WORDS e.g. When I thought 'Camel Toe' was a euphemism for a nork cleavage and told everyone that I wished mine was as wide as the Grand Canyon.

LEVEL 9: PERIOD ISSUES/ NUDITY e.g. When my sister caught me dancing naked in my bedroom or when Mum suggested that I should be in a band called Vulva (at least 'Camel Toe' is funny).

LEVEL 10: WATCHING A SEX SCENE ON TV WITH YOUR PARENTS OR ACTUALLY CATCHING THEM AT IT e.g. Getting trapped in between my parents on the sofa during a documentary about people who have sex with ghosts and then having to listen to Mum recount her own supernatural sex experience. GROSS.

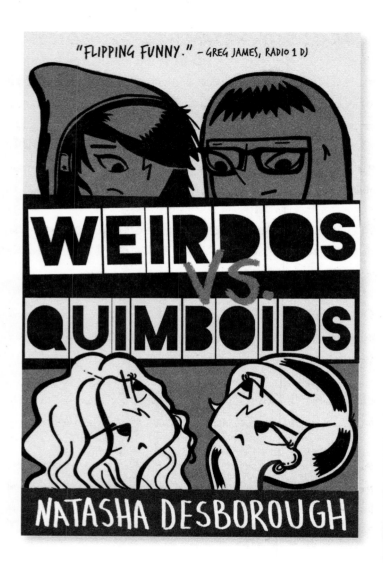

"FLIPPING FUNNY." – GREG JAMES, RADIO 1 DJ

WEIRDOS vs. QUIMBOIDS

NATASHA DESBOROUGH

ISBN 9781846471711 - PB - £6.99

PRAISE FOR WEIRDOS VS. QUIMBOIDS:

'This is the third most important publication in the world after The Beano and Steve Brookstein - My Struggle. It's also flipping funny. In fact, it should come with a free pair of socks because you'll laugh off your current ones.' Greg James, Radio 1 DJ

'A graphic and hilarious insight into what it's like to grow up to be a woman. It made me grateful that I'm a man.' Jon Holmes, comedian and Xfm DJ

'People should read more books in general, and they should all start with this one. Only when they have finished Weirdos vs. Quimboids should they progress on to other literature e.g., Dickens, Shakespeare.' Chris Smith, Radio 1 Newsbeat

'I LOVE it! I'm hooked . . . think Georgia Nicolson meets Adrian Mole. B.U.M. is my new literary heroine – sort of – a bloomin' delightful read!' Nemone Metaxas, BBC 6 Music DJ

'This is a definite must read, laugh out loud book. If you're feeling low and a little weird in a Quimboid-filled society then read this book.' Geek and Book Nerd Site

'Full of awkward dates, embarrassing parents, and frequent naked moon dances, there's definitely something in there to make everyone laugh and I would most definitely recommend it if you're looking for something light and funny to read to relax. When can I read the next one?!' Cheezyfeet Books

'This is completely and utterly hilarious. Desborough captures the dialogue of her teen characters superbly.' YA Contemporary

ABOUT THE AUTHOR

Natasha was born on the summer solstice and shares a birthday with Prince William, which makes her part hippie and part royalty in equal doses (and that is an actual scientific fact). After school, she skipped university to try her luck as a runner on feature films and pop videos before a programme controller lured her into the magical world of radio. She spent the next twelve years having THE BEST FUN EVER hosting shows on Xfm and BBC Radio 6 Music.

Natasha has appeared on TV shows such as Richard and Judy, presented radio shows with comedians such as Jimmy Carr, interviewed loads of international celebrities, including Dave Grohl from Foo Fighters and Chris Martin from Coldplay but none of them liked her enough to want to be her friend – possibly because she's just as weird as the characters she writes about . . .

Natasha now lives in Croydon with her husband Jim, sons Oscar and Wilfie and two Glastonbury cats, Derek and Mavis, and Enid, her chocolate Labrador rescue dog.

User Name	Tagline
QUITE_IMMATURE_FOR_MY_AGE1	*I love the softness of a furry bum. . .*

THE BASICS
AGE: *perfect midlife crisis-aged.*
SEX: *Female*
HEIGHT: *5ft 8*
BUILD: *slim and with large bum and thick ankles*
HAIR: *reddish brown*
LOOKS: *square jaw, pointy nose. I look a bit like a butch witch (but less green).*

PROFILE
I love the softness of a furry bumblebee sitting in the palm of my hand. I also like to hold toads, frogs, worms and all things slimy that can be found in my garden.

IDEAL MATCH
Someone who loves dogs, alternative music, plays guitar and likes to go on long country walks. I'm thinking maybe Chris Packham from Spring/Autumn/Winterwatch or Dave Grohl from the Foo Fighters. I like to imagine the three of us singing songs by The Smiths as we skip through the woods together holding hands.

You can find out more about Natasha at:
www.natashadesborough.co.uk
@tashdesborough

To find out more about *Weirdos vs. Bumskulls*
as well as discover other exciting books, visit:

www.catnippublishing.co.uk

KIRSTY EAGAR

RAW BLUE

LIVE IN THE PRESENT TO FORGET THE PAST

Carly might be living but it's not much of a life, working
the late shifts in a kitchen, renting alone and trying to get by
without being noticed. The only time she feels alive is when
she's out in the ocean, when life is only about the swell of the
sea and your feet on the board. Out on the waves she can
forget about everything – forget her own dark secret –
and enjoy the moment.

But Carly can't surf forever.

ISBN 9781846471551 - PB - £6.99

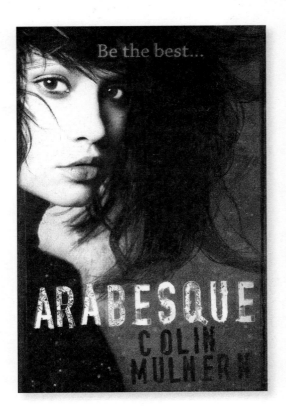

How do you know you're the best until you're tested?
Until you're pushed to the limit?

A botched kidnapping drags Amy and her best friend into the
depths of a criminal underworld, a world where the players
think with bullets and blackmail. A world where they will
stop at nothing to get what they want.

And what they want, only Amy May can provide.

ISBN 9781846471483 - PB - £6.99